JACOB'S
PAPERS

JACOB'S PAPERS

A Novel

Tom Foran Clark

The Bungalow Shop Press
Menifee, California

Published in cooperation with XLibris by
The Bungalow Shop Press, P.O. Box 214, Menifee, California 92586

Print information available on the last page.

Advance Reading copy
Rev. date: 03/10/2016

To order additional copies of this book, contact:
Xlibris
1-888-795-4274
www.Xlibris.com
Orders@Xlibris.com
737191

For David Bourbeau

"'What have I earned for all that work,' I said,
'For all that I have done at my own charge?
The daily spite of this unmannerly town,
Where who has served the most is most defamed,
The reputation of his lifetime lost
Between the night and morning...
Yet never have I, now nor any time,
Complained of the people.'"

William Butler Yeats
From *The People*

"When I was a child
I caught a fleeting glimpse
Out of the corner of my eye.
I turned to look but it was gone."

Roger Waters, David ~~Gilmore~~ *Gilmour*
From *Comfortably Numb*

CHAPTER ONE

He lived in the mountains in the end. He loved mountains. But, more than mountains, more than anything, he loved paper. Paper, paper, paper. Mountains of paper. He couldn't get enough of it. He wrote on it – he wrote and wrote and wrote. He traveled some – he wrote about that. He walked a lot – he wrote about that. He worked in bookstores, and wrote about that. He worked in museums, and wrote about that. With ballpoint pens or 2H pencils on almost endless legal size lined white and yellow paper tablets he wrote and wrote and wrote.

I speak of my father, Jacob Friedman Wright, most of whose life was lived in a time when computers were still a novelty and there was not yet the Internet.

In the annals of our family lore, much of it preserved to this day on his lined white and yellow paper tablets, was the story of his being raised in California by newspaper hoarding nomads. I'm a kind of a vagabond now myself, Jillian Rose Wright, presently a screenwriter living in Hollywood among trillions gadzillions of screenwriters, all of us at our cell phones and laptops 24/7 at the coffee shops, all enmeshed in the world wide web, seriously oblivious to our surroundings. As much as I like to travel, coming from a family of travelers, still I have two closets and a laundry room at my current home-base, in my apartment, all stuffed to brimful with my father's tons of papers. The rest of the place is relatively empty. Seriously. I'm so not like him.

As for his parents, my grandparents, their only possession, at least that stayed with my father in his writing or in the telling to his children, was a red briefcase or valise carrying the book *The Spiritual Interpretation of Nature* and newspaper clippings and magazines filled with tons of articles about Chinese immigrants building America's railroads, nomads in the Sahara, Aztecs bowing before Quetzalcoatl, Jews and Gypsies saved in the Holocaust, the lens grinder Spinoza, the traveler Ibn Battuta, the sage Giordano Bruno, Saint Francis of Assisi. Nowadays you would just Google everything, but then they navigated the world with these papers in their trunk, all their favorite magazine articles and newspaper clippings. These always accompanied my father's family, travel where they would.

The two big family lore footnotes to the above story were tales of Jake Wright's two main heroes – I have tons of articles about them – Eiler Larsen, the Laguna Greeter, and George Whitman, who ran the Shakespeare and Company bookshop in Paris, both legendary oddballs my father often called his mentors, two famous jolly old eccentric wild-haired beatnik nut cases, neither of which my elegant father particularly resembled at any point in his lifetime at all so far as I could see.

You see, my otherwise quiet father loved to open up and regale us – my older brother Mark and me – with stories of the sandaled, bearded, grinning Greeter welcoming visitors (primarily him, Jake at age seven) to his "childhood home away from home," Laguna Beach (not too far from Hollywood, where I am now), and episodes from his adventures walking and hitchhiking, taking a triangular trek, at age 26 (my age now), from Rotterdam to Amsterdam then southwest to Paris (there discovering, across the Seine from Notre Dame, George Whitman's Shakespeare and Company bookstore), then east to Vienna (I know it was to make a pilgrimage to see Pieter Bruegel's painting *Hunters in the Snow*), north to Aarhus (birthplace of Eiler Larsen, the Laguna Greeter), next hoofing it back to Paris again to work at, and live in, the Paris bookstore, where he met our mother, Minna (née Wilhelmina Annagret Ziege). He was working at the front desk. She bought a book from him: Hemingway's *A Moveable Feast*. Seriously. As they say, "Their eyes met" – the rest is history.

Jake said he was seventeen when he and his parents had first landed in Massachusetts, not on the Mayflower but in a car, ha ha. Very funny, Pops. They bought a three-room 1912 Craftsman bungalow in Framingham, where his stoical former-soldier father famously became a full-time cemetery groundskeeper and part-time barber; his famously soft-spoken mother got office work in the state court system. Jake, while attending Framingham High, famously worked afternoons at the Framingham Public Library, where he discovered art, architecture, and the Arts & Crafts movement and learned that the bungalow he lived in was representative of the American Arts & Crafts era, which had really been thriving, all across the country, apparently most famously in the year 1912.

Once upon a time when I was still an infant, my brother Mark took me aside one fine day, whispering, "The grown-ups are certainly very odd. Doesn't it feel like we're growing up in a *museum*?" Do birds fly? Do fish swim? Seriously, our father was *all about* museums – he had studied to be a *curator*. Yes, it did feel like we were growing up in a museum, but I think it was more like we were growing up in a tribute to, or emulation of, legendary high-bouncing George Whitman's brilliant ragged Paris bookstore where my parents had met.

Our old man was a *collector*. The house was filled with *stuff* – flea market finds – thrift shop junk. He would pick things up off the street. Seriously. My mother hated that. He collected "artifacts," as he called them. And books. Books about the Arts & Crafts movement, mainly, along with every sort of miscellaneous book about life on earth, philosophy, planets, and physics. If the book was published in the year 1912, or the author had been born or had died in the year 1912, so much the better.

You talk about 1912. Jake had been named not only for John Jacob Astor 1V, who'd died aboard the Titanic in 1912 – so we had all these books all about the Titanic – but also partially for the nuclear physicist J. Robert Oppenheimer's brother, particle physicist Frank

Friedman Oppenheimer, born in New York City in 1912, inventor of the first interactive museum in America dedicated to art, science, and perception – so we had all these books all about that, as well.

Frank Oppenheimer had earned his Ph.D. at the California Institute of Technology and, after working on uranium isotope separation, had joined his brother on the Manhattan Project at Los Alamos. After the bombings of Nagasaki and Hiroshima, he'd been a physics professor at the University of Minnesota. In 1949, after harassment from the House Un-American Activities Committee during the McCarthy era, he'd worked ten years in Colorado as a cattle rancher before becoming a high school science teacher, taking his students to used parts dumps to teach them the principles of mechanics, heat, and electricity. After the University of Colorado offered him a higher post in 1959, he received, in 1965, a Guggenheim fellowship, enabling him to pursue a different project. After prowling through the best of Europe's museums, he'd returned to America to propose his so-called "Exploratorium," opened in 1969 inside the then empty San Francisco Palace of Fine Arts. So of course we had all these books all about Colorado and California, too.

Mark and I would hear from the old man all through our childhood about how the Palace of Fine Arts had been built from drawings made by Bernard Maybeck, an eccentric architect who obviously, so far as I could see, looked an *awful* lot like the Laguna Greeter and George Whitman – so of course my father couldn't get enough of Bernard Maybeck. The lunatic had designed the thing after failing, in 1912, to win a commission for San Francisco's City Hall. The carefree Bohemian's pleasure in classical antiquity and German and English medieval motifs had made him one of the most colorful influences on the Arts and Crafts movement in America. As it turned out, the most popular building at San Francisco's 1915 Panama-Pacific International Exposition was Maybeck's Palace of Fine Arts and, though abandoned prior to Frank Oppenheimer's opening his "Exploratorium" inside it, the Palace was the most enduring. It was the last Exposition building standing.

To get back to Framingham, Jake liked to tell us how he'd been assigned, as a teenager, the job of painting a huge sign out front of the Framingham Public Library. He'd been marking out the letter-forms in chalk, daydreaming probably about Bernard Maybeck, Giordano Bruno, the Laguna Greeter, or Saint Francis of Assisi this one fine sign-painting day when, suddenly, he was knocked down by a passing pedestrian who'd been flung into the air from a nearby sidewalk after being struck by the inebriated driver of a silver BMW convertible. He insisted this was exactly what happened, more or less. Though painter, passerby, and driver all emerged without injury, this highly unlikely collision famously got Jake to pondering his mortality and not only the true nature of things themselves but of the things behind things.

Seriously. It was a fateful time. Four days after being hit by the car-struck flying walker, the generally sleepwalking daydreaming Jake, on his toes now, happened to catch a library book just then falling from a shelf as he was passing by, an elegant little blue tome titled "Treasures of Lucretius: Selected Passages from *De Rerum Natura*" published in London: by Watts & Company in 1912, of course, by a solitary vegetarian pacifist Englishman named Henry Salt who inspired Jake, nineteen, to feel he might himself like to lead a hermit's life. My father famously packed a rucksack and departed Massachusetts.

He apparently spent two months hiking and exploring in the wilderness around the village of West Yellowstone, earning some income doing odd jobs at the Madison Hotel there, then enrolled at Utah State University in Logan, taking up the study of astronomy while working evenings in the school library. He found a place to stay – a cabin (a garden shed, actually) – in the backyard of one Professor John K. Sheen, then a teacher of philosophy at the university. My father said it was Professor Sheen who told him his education would not come to him through the University but via the school of hard knocks. Sheen would have a heart attack at sixty-four, dying two years after Jake left Logan, Utah with a Bachelor's degree in Astronomy with a minor in Art History.

Apparently, he then hit the road again – that is, he roamed – i.e., he walked a little and hitchhiked a lot – now all over the great Southwest, no small territory, north from Yellowstone down to Moab and Arches, clear down to St. George and Zion. He said he was gathering and clarifying certain ideas he had about someday opening up a stargazing-camping store, bookshop, or toy store somewhere out there in that territory – or a combination stargazing-camping store / toy store / book store.

But my father famously next instead headed *east* on a seeming whim (courting fate, he claimed) and somehow or other got himself an assembly line job at the Whirlwind Toy Company in Batteryville, Vermont, of all places. His boss, of all people, one Saul Mortenstein, thought it was from God that an astronomer should be seeking work in *his* toy factory. A squat round man with silver hair and a waxed moustache, Mortenstein loved to speak of the old times when, in *his* youth, in the 1950s, he'd lived in Manhattan and worked at the New York City Public Library where he'd fetched books from closed stacks on roller skates. Seeing how the piles of books acquired by Jake day after day were rising higher in the staff room – Mortenstein pulled some strings, set up an interview, and the next thing Jake knew he was working at the Batteryville Town Library.

Jake went to work in the library's local history archives, organizing thousands of wildly strewn papers in dozens of scrunched boxes piled ten-high. He moonlighted two evenings a week as an astronomy teacher at the Arts and Science Center next to the library. Occasionally he got together with his former boss, Mortenstein, who, over beers, regaled Jake with stories of the New York Public Library and a year he'd lived abroad in Rome. It wasn't long before Jake was itching, like his namesakes John Jacob Astor and Frank Friedman Oppenheimer before him, to board a ship and make his own pilgrimage to see the wonders and the treasures in the museums of Europe.

My father took a boat from Baltimore to Rotterdam then famously hitchhiked and walked from there to Amsterdam and on to Paris, next turning east to Vienna, then north to Aarhus and back to Paris again, where he encountered our enchanting German mother. But the legend of his being some kind of big Wright family nomad world traveler was rendered small by my mother's larger claim. In the annals of our family lore was the story of her insistence on her being a reincarnation of the Greek goddess of the fall harvest, Demeter, making me, in her mind, once I did finally come into the world, a reincarnation of the Greek goddess of the underworld, Persephone. As my mother has often pointed out to me, I was perversely never in any particular hurry to come down from heaven to be born into this interesting family, but my brother was always in the meantime, she said, *impatient* to get in. Seriously.

Jake had got work in an advertising agency in Munich, moonlighting evenings as an English teacher. Before the year was out he and Minna were married and living in a tiny one-bedroom apartment. It wasn't long before my *impatient* brother was born – Mark Lloyd Wright, aka (according to Minna) "Iacchus." Within two weeks of that birth, around the time Thanksgiving was being celebrated all across America, the father of Iacchus famously came down with a hopeless case of homesickness for his homeland. Jake sold all the books and artifacts and things he'd wasted all his money on while working in the ad agency. In mid-December, the three famously crossed the Atlantic on a boat bound for Boston, found a tiny two-bedroom apartment, and celebrated their first Christmas as a family.

I was there too, my mother insisted, in the sky over them, not yet born – "amused by everything." She wasn't kidding. Persephone pondered at her leisure whether or not to come into this world – into this family.

CHAPTER TWO

It wasn't very long before the Wright's Boston apartment, directly across the park from the new Museum of the New Physics, was already bulging with books, pictures, and things. My father famously got work at the museum as an unpaid Intern, organizing the archives of one Judson Bethel, who had written on the Austrian Erwin Schrödinger's quantum theories (and about his famously ambiguous cat), on the Dutchman Baruch Spinoza's concepts of *Natura naturata*, "Nature natured" or "Nature already created", and *Natura naturans*, meaning "Nature naturing", or "nature doing what nature does", and on the Frenchman Jean-François Champollion, the Professor of Egyptology who had translated the Rosetta Stone. Jake also wrote papers on these subjects during his time in the Graduate School of Museum Studies at nearby Wordsward College.

At the end of his second year at the Museum and at the school, he got his Master's degree from Wordsward. Saddled with student debt and short on funds, Jake shaved off his Laguna Greeter beard and went job hunting. He saw, pinned to a bulletin board in the neighborhood laundromat, a note about paid employment in the Archives of The New Physics Museum. He applied, got the job, and started growing his beard back. He was now being paid for doing exactly what he'd been doing previously for free. He was more than content with that. My beautiful mother loved to tell of how beautiful it was to see him cheerful like that all the time.

My father loved to tell of how his boss there, one Ruth Templeton, took him aside one afternoon and explained to Jake that in the Museum of the New Physics staff members should not be over-jolly, but rather show due dignity and solemnity. She insisted Jake refrain from being so merry. She said his *joie-de-vivre* free-reign ramblings in the institution, coupled with his whistling and humming, was bringing her – not to mention *all* the Museum's regular employees – to a boil.

Ruth Templeton of disgusted aloofness and sour face, ritually arrived late and left early, my father said – except on Tuesdays, when she stayed until 9:00 p.m. In the second week of March, around 8:30 p.m., Ruth Templeton went after Betsy Barris, her assistant, blaming her for leaving unfinished some project for which Ruth Templeton was responsible. A deadline had passed. Jake heard Ruth Templeton shrieking at trembling Betsy, admitting she was on the verge of hitting Betsy in the head. Jake, who'd been working in an adjoining room, stepped forth just *after* Ruth Templeton knocked Betsy down. Jake stepped into the room and quickly steered Betsy to safety. He could see she was red faced and shaken. She was shaking, in fact.

Ruth Templeton, immediately after her assault on Betsy, in Jake's company, wrote out "A Verbal Warning" on a piece of paper and asked Betsy to sign it. Jake was incensed. He insisted Betsy not sign anything. But the timid, shaking girl proceeded with it. Templeton was punctual the next morning, arriving at work on time for the first time, hand-delivering a copy of her "Verbal Warning" to Betsy to the Personnel Department with a letter releasing Betsy from employment at the Museum.

Soon, lawyers got famously involved in it – in the harassment case brought forth by Betsy against Ruth. As it turned out, because Jake hadn't actually *seen* the assault, Ruth Templeton's attorneys reasoned there had been no witnesses. Betsy begged Jake to lie, to say he had seen with his two good eyes what had happened, to assert that he *had* witnessed Ruth Templeton's having smacked Betsy in the face. But my reticent, tight-lipped, upstanding, conscientious, moral mummy of a father couldn't do it. He said he had no problem with saying he'd *heard*

Ruth Templeton hit Betsy, nor that he'd heard her yelling like some jungle banshee prior to smacking Betsy in the face. He said he would tell anyone everything he'd *heard* with his two good ears.

Suffering Jake visited his adviser at the school who recommended he just *shut up* about it. "Let grass grow over it," he said. For Jake to tell his saga of Ruth Templeton's unprofessional behavior, indecency, dishonesty, cunning, wickedness, black heart, and so forth would *not* topple her from her high place. It would serve only to link *her* name and *his*. Was this something Jake wanted? The museum and library community of New England was a small, close-knit one, Jake was warned, and if Jake persisted in his folly, Ruth Templeton's name and his would be joined inextricably all his days. "Let it go," Jake's adviser advised. "If you fight her, Jake, your name will be entwined with hers. It's a stink of a name to be linked up with, to go down with in people's memories."

Me being impulsive, I would have probably pulled this Ruth Templeton's ears and told her to shut her face, but my father was not like that. He yielded half-heartedly, taking his advisor's tepid advice. Betsy Barris was forced to depart. She went home to Kansas City. She told Jake she'd be glad of being back amid the gentle winds and splendid sweeps of golden grain prevailing under sunny skies across the vast miles and miles of open fields out in the Great Midwest. *Good for her*, Jake thought. He wrote this all down: "At the Museum of the New Physics, dark clouds were sweeping in. Heads would roll."

Shortly after that, after Betsy Barris went back to Kansas, there came a big morning meeting for all staff in the Museum's Spinoza Auditorium. The session was set to begin with the arrival of the Chairman of the Board of Museum Trustees, who had not yet arrived from his home on the elite North Shore. When he finally showed, he bumped his nose on the microphone, then spilled his water when he began speaking. He began by admitting to the assembled that he'd been having a hard day.

According to my father, the Chairman of the Board of Museum Trustees said, "Bad things happen in threes. First, I burned the toast. Then the train broke down. The third thing —"

This led to a long explanation of the Museum's financial crisis, the Museum Board calling on the administration to trim about $2 million from a projected $5 million deficit for the fiscal year that had just begun on July 1st. Layoffs, of course, were just part of the "package." Sixty employees would be let go. The number of projected exhibitions would be cut from twenty to just twelve.

"The insurance costs for things on loan to us are going right through the ceiling," the Chairman of the Board mourned.

Next, the round, bald, red-faced, trembling Museum Director stepped up to the microphone, my father explained. "The Board of Curators has the ultimate authority for all decisions," the man declared. "They make the policy. That is what our charter and our bylaws say." He compared his job to that of a ranch foreman who kept his cowboys fed and clothed, emphasizing that the ranch was not his to do with as he pleased. *He* was not responsible for decision making.

News of the deteriorating situation appeared in papers throughout New England. "Roping in the Cowboys at the Museum of the New Physics" was headline news. Reporters derided "a hyperactive rumor mill" at the "world class" museum. "Intrigue is spiraling out of control. Staff morale is sinking below sea level."

Even as, I'm sure, the humble Wright family kitchen table was getting buried under fresh paper piles – news clippings. My father saved *everything*.

Disgruntled museum employees were complaining not only of the Museum of the New Physics' curator keeping *his* job, but also of his keeping his *home* – a house provided him by the Museum's Board of Curators. It was said by the blushing curator that this was common practice – big city museum curators were *usually* provided with a residence. Public relations officials at museums in New York, Philadelphia, Chicago, San Francisco, and Dallas quickly jumped in, saying *their* curators weren't.

The curator of the Museum of the New Physics kept his job a while longer. Ruth Templeton kept her job a lot longer. Within two months of Templeton's attack on her assistant, Jake was let go. Strangely, Ruth

Templeton did not just boot him out on his last day there, but let him wander freely through the institution's labyrinthical sacred chambers, letting him whistle and hum to his heart's content. Throughout the building former staffers, variously screaming or mumbling bitter accusations, packed their things. In my father's shoes I expect I would have told that old bat a thing or two, but not my father. He kept quiet – except for the humming and whistling, his lips were sealed.

The next day, my taciturn father famously got a call from a member of the Board of Curators of a small village arts and science museum in Camperdene, Massachusetts. As it happened, Jake was invited to interview for the job of curator of a museum that was all about everything having anything to do with the year 1912 – ha ha, what a coincidence! – which seemed apparently to be exactly the kind of quiet work in exactly the kind of innocuous and charming place that my mother was hoping he would find.

Wishful thinking, as it turned out.

CHAPTER THREE

The trustees of the so-called Museum of the Year 1912 had been looking for a new curator for their institution for a while now. A few members of the board had apparently cautiously approached the Dean of Wordsward College, one Roger Preston, to point out to them a few graduating candidates they might invite in to interview for the post. My father was on their short list, he knew, because – as my father liked to joke – "Dean Preston told me so." But Dean Preston had also wisely counseled Jake to do his homework before applying for the job, handing him a copy of *"A Study of The Museum of the Year 1912,"* prepared by one Hollie Greenspan, the institution's most recent curator, who had moved to Canada the previous spring.

"Camperdene, population 22,326, is a stable, well-tended Massachusetts town enjoying good economic circumstances," Hollie Greenspan's study began. "Formerly an important manufacturing center for the paper, granite, and shoe industries, the hum of Camperdene's quarries and factories has died down. Its downtown blocks hold empty storefronts among the occasional shop or restaurant. Cinemas and malls have, by and large, replaced the factories.

"Camperdenians come in all colors, shapes, and sizes and enjoy an array of diverse cultural activities, from numerous ballparks to a local symphony orchestra, which townspeople are willing to support financially. Camperdene is reputed to have a quality newspaper though only a so-so radio station (it is improving). There is a good school system in, overall, soundly constructed buildings.

"The town has no public library of its own but enjoys shared borrowing privileges with the Public Library of neighboring Beckham, which services Beckham, Marbridge, Dunham, and Camperdene. Camperdenians are obviously pleased, in the absence of a public library, to have the Museum of the Year 1912 and the Association that has made it possible, as the museum is so quaint and does not rely solely on the public's tax dollars. There would be greater use and enjoyment of the museum's collections and programs," Hollie Greenspan observed wryly, "if the acquisitions budget and staff salaries were more adequate."

The objectives of the museum were listed: "(1) To educate and to enrich life, (2) to provide an opportunity for life-long edification, (3) to provide career inspiration, and (4) to help fulfill the obligations and meet the needs of the constantly expanding vistas of active minds. The museum can no longer be a mere storehouse," the curator declared. "It should be a dynamic institution having a responsibility to tell its story to the people who support it."

Hollie Greenspan had appointed Julia Seymour-Stanton to be the Children's Collections Coordinator. "A cheerful, dedicated helper," Camperdene Daily Journal reporter Alice Armour Armstrong had written of her in a brief front page piece about Hollie Greenspan's sudden departure from the museum, "who will go to any length to attract children and their parents."

The Museum Association had made Julia Acting Curator of the museum (Hollie Greenspan, it was noted, had recently been called to Nova Scotia). A lifelong Camperdene resident, Julia was a charter member of the Camperdene Historical Society. She had worked there part-time when attending Camperdene High School. Two other full-time, permanent staffers made up the museum crew: Audrey Morris and Mary Tuchlein, both of whom had been working in the museum since the 1940s. The Museum of the Year 1912 Association had appointed rotund, red-cheeked Hayden Brown custodian, paying his salary from the interest on certain trust funds available to them.

When, that summer, the Association Curator Search Committee arranged to meet with Jake, they sent the committee chairwoman, blonde, talkative Carlena Lagorio, to fetch him. She arrived in flowing red silk in a black Cadillac at the Wright's brownstone apartment around the corner from the Boston Museum of the New Physics and personally chauffeured him west to the beautiful brick and sandstone edifice, The Museum of the Year 1912, for his interview.

Lagorio handed him a copy of the job description to read in the car on the way: "Responsible for routine to complex curatorial, administrative, supervisory, and professional work in planning, organizing, and supervising the overall operation of the museum. Responsible for the operating expenses, the development of resources, and physical maintenance of the facilities. Responsible for assisting the Association in developing long-range objectives, policies, and plans for the future direction and development of the museum as a community resource and information center. Responsible for associating with the general public and important community leaders."

Jake was handed the Association's Bylaws: "The Museum of the Year 1912 is owned and operated by The Museum of the Year 1912 Association of Camperdene, Massachusetts, a non-profit tax-exempt Corporation, chartered under the laws of the Commonwealth of Massachusetts in 1913, and so recognized under the Internal Revenue Service Code 501 (c) (3). The Association is composed of Corporators, all residents of Camperdene. The Corporators elect a Board of Directors. An Executive Committee is elected annually by the Board of Directors. The Executive Committee appoints committees to oversee the various facets of the museum, and to make recommendations for action as needed.

Next, he was given a copy of the Association's 1913 Act of Incorporation: "Robert Lagorio and his children Simon and Louisa Lagorio and their associates and successors are hereby made a Corporation by the name of the Museum of the Year 1912 Association, with all the powers and privileges, and subject to all the duties and liabilities set forth in all general laws which now are or hereafter may be in force and applicable to such Corporations. Said Corporation shall have authority to hold real and personal estate to the amount permitted by general law. The management and control of the property of said Corporation shall be vested in a Board of Directors, consisting of not less than five in number, to be elected by said Corporation. The Directors shall be citizens of Camperdene; the Board of Directors shall have power to adopt all necessary by-laws and regulations for the management of the same, subject to the approval of the Corporation. So long as said Corporation shall allow the inhabitants of the town of Camperdene access to the museum at reasonable hours, for the purposes of using the same on the premises, said town may appropriate money for the purpose of defraying the expenses of maintaining said museum.

In 1986, the By-Laws had been amended: "Any adult resident of Camperdene may be elected a Corporator of the Corporation after consideration by the Executive Committee and by a vote of two-thirds of the Corporators present at any annual or special meeting of the Corporators. The annual meeting of the Corporators shall be held on Monday following the annual business meeting of the Town of Camperdene to hear and act on the report of the Directors, to elect a Clerk of the Corporation, to fix the number of Directors, and to elect a Board of Directors to serve for the ensuing year, and to transact any other business that might properly comer before the meeting. Special meetings of the Corporators may be called by the President, a Vice President, or by any five Corporators by giving at least seven days' notice in writing to each Corporator. The President, or in his absence a Vice President, shall preside at all meetings of the Corporators. A Board of Directors consisting of not less than five, and not more than twenty-five, shall be vested with the control and management of the Corporation. The principal staff of The Museum of the Year 1912 shall be appointed or reappointed to their on an annual basis by the Board of Directors. Full-time staff include a museum curator, children's collections curator, and two clerical staff assistants. Part-time staff are appointed by the Association on an as-needed basis."

Carlena Lagorio pulled up before The Museum of the Year 1912. Jake followed her through the big glass front doors into a large room full of elegant long tables and dozens of luxurious available chairs – a perfect place for an interview, Jake thought – and down a long hallway past almost whimsically madcap arrays of display cases to a small room where nine unsmiling faces met his. No one stood nor offered a hand to shake nor any comment. Carlena offered Jake a flimsy folding chair, and took a seat herself.

A scrawny ashen silver-bearded little man who at first, my father like to say, at first had reminded him of his California childhood hero Eiler Larsen, the Laguna Greeter, politely asked Jake if he knew why he was there.

Jake had gone right into his *spiel*, saying he felt this obviously would be a *great* place to work. Boldly he declared he'd *always* felt he'd *love* to work in just such a cultural center in a town, state, or country – a place not only where there were housed interesting things to see, but a place where things could *happen*.

"*Interesting* things to see, indeed!" the old man blurted out. "*Extraordinary* things to see! Do you know *anything* at all about anything that *happened* in the year *1912*?"

"As it *happens*," my father played his hand, "I do know a thing or two. I know that American Arts & Crafts era was at its peak in America in the year 1912. He mentioned his partial namesake John Jacob Astor IV, who'd died in 1912 aboard the Titanic, and J. Robert Oppenheimer and his brother Frank Friedman Oppenheimer, inventor of the first interactive museum in America dedicated to art, science, and perception, had been born in New York City in 1912. How Bernard Maybeck had, after failing in 1912 to win a commission for San Francisco's City Hall, went on that same year to build San Francisco's Palace of Fine Art. How the British physicist Ernest Rutherford had been joined at the University of Manchester by the Danish physicist Neils Bohr in 1912. How Einstein had left the German University of Prague to be a professor at the Swiss Technical College in Zurich. He also mentioned that Carl Jung and Sigmund Freud had enjoyed a good relationship until 1912, when Jung had published a book that was at odds with Freud's ideas, "The Psychology of the Unconscious." And on and on.

My father wrote this all down after the fact. He wrote, "The withered disgruntled little man asking the questions was one of twelve on the search committee – Richard Cunningham; looking somewhat like the Laguna Greeter, he should have been friendly but instead revealed an egotistical fat-headed mean streak." Jake would soon learn the nickname of the volatile man: "Powderkeg." The other eleven were Roland Henselmeier, Barney Parker, Solomon Cramer, Peter Henderson, Stan Jameson, Carlena Lagorio, Cindy Service, Jennifer Soriff, Dotty Carter, Barbara Dennis, and Jean Garrison – "in all, six stone-faced scowling men and six stone-faced pouting women."

Carlena Lagorio escorted Jake out of the room. The twelve voted. Jake was then led back into the room and was handed an index card on which was written: "The Search Committee of The Museum of the Year 1912 Association is pleased to offer Mr. Jacob Friedman Wright the position of Museum Curator, subject to the approval of the Executive Committee of the Museum Association."

After the interview, in the back room behind the fireplace – the curator's office – Carlena Lagorio, in her red satin dress on this hot summer day, introduced Jake to the distinguished, silver haired president of the Association's Board of Directors, Wallace Barrow – him in a black three-piece suit. Madame Lagorio sang Jake's praises, insisting she just couldn't say *enough* about "Mister Wright." My father loved to tell of how Barrow had raised his hand to silence her, then had moved in closer to him, had placed a long arm around his shoulder, and had famously whispered – ominously – "Don't get this *wrong*, Jacob *Wright*. You're the dog. Don't let the tail wag you."

Chapter Four

Now my father had abundant fresh paper scraps to collect, he himself being in the news.

"The Museum of the Year 1912 Gets a New Curator" read the September 26th headline of The Camperdene Daily Journal. Reporter Alice Armour Armstrong noted, "The Museum of the Year 1912 Association has named Jacob Friedman Wright to be its new curator. Wright and his wife Minna have one son, Mark, two years old. Though appointed by the private Museum Corporation, Wright will be a town employee, paid from public funds."

Mark remembers well that the season of his father's walking now ended and his season of commuting began, Jake driving his red Volkswagen sedan between Boston and Camperdene. On his first day at the museum, in mid-September, he rose early and left the apartment on a cool, foggy morning. Mark remembers his father saying it was always smooth sailing straight west from Boston to Camperdene. He apparently arrived at 9:00 sharp that first morning of his new job, even as his new colleagues Audrey Morris, Mary Tuchlein, and Julia Seymour-Stanton strolled up the cobblestone walkway to the edifice. Jake later recalled, "It was picture-perfect. They may as well have approached hand-in-hand, singing." Bald, hard-of-hearing Hayden Brown, the red-cheeked, red-suspendered custodian, was polishing the brass plates on the front doors. He let the four in. My father said that was the regular morning ritual, the same duty performed every morning, Hayden's letting them in.

"Good morning, Hayden!"

"What?"

"Good morning!"

"Fine. How are you?"

Jake said he entered and made salutations and gestures of exuberant greeting all around, feeling humility under the grandiose, arched, high vaulted ceilings. There were old books and artifacts galore crowding the shelves, cabinets, and display cases all over the place. I'm sure my father felt at home.

Audrey explained in some detail how the place had looked before recent renovations. At every turn, she stated disappointment and enthusiasm together. The situation at present was both good and bad. She would tell Jake months later that she'd been intimidated by his combined youthfulness and authority. She'd admit she'd been afraid of saying the wrong thing, and so had covered her ground, saying "whatever came to mind that seemed to have a nice ring to it."

Quiet, diligent Mary Tuchlein had gone straight to her work counter in the back room, repairing or polishing damaged or dulled artifacts. Julia Seymour-Stanton went straight downstairs to start her work day. When Jake went down to have a look at her territory, she was busy helping two mothers with homework assignments given their seven year olds. She was pleasant, matter-of-fact, informed, informative.

Two of the Search Committee members, Captain Powderkeg Cunningham – local character, chairman of the Historical Commission, organizer of the museum's historical records – and Carlena Lagorio – chatty, concerned, adamant, always out and about running errands in her red Cadillac, which carried her like a ladybug in a galleon – but never very far from the museum – were busy in coming and going – doing just what of import Jake couldn't make out – throughout the day.

Things went on like this, Jake driving, writing, and apartment hunting when not at either The Museum of the Year 1912 or The Boston Museum of the New Physics, all mixed up with eating, shaving, showering, eating, procreating, sleeping, dreaming.

My mother says he wore himself down, writing and driving, running between school and jobs, listening to stories, answering inquiries, finding answers. He sought out all the fresh information he could find about the year 1912, familiarizing myself with all the new institutional rigamarole of this place, getting to know staff members' better – their assorted quirks and bents. He learned the ropes.

In Jake's office, in the room behind the stately front fireplace, he studied the files left by his predecessors: he figured out how bills were paid, he read job descriptions, he learned about former and present volunteers, he did his homework – he got the hang of things. Audrey was eager, each day, to tell him more – and ever more – about the place: how it once had been, what it had become, and about all the patrons, the people who frequented the museum, how things had run through the years.

At staff meetings, Audrey, Mary, Julia, Hayden joined him in cooking up ideas for activities, learning, fun. They brought in local storytellers, artists, folksingers. On October 20, the Camperdene Daily Journal told of a curator "planning to bring the historic Museum of the year 1912 into the 21st century while maintaining its commitment to serving the people in the community. Jake Wright wants to get more community involvement; he wants to draw more people in."

On October 27th, the Camperdene Daily Journal announced, a "Get Acquainted" reception: "The members of the Search Committee of The Museum of the Year 1912 invite the public to meet Jake Friedman Wright, the new director, and his family, on Sunday from 3 to 5 p.m. Refreshments will be served."

Early the next morning the chair of the Association's defunct Search Committee, Carlena Lagorio, telephoned the offices of the Journal and railed at them, demanding a correction. The correction appeared the next day: "A gathering Sunday for Jacob Friedman Wright, the new *curator* of the Museum of the Year 1912, *is by invitation only.*"

The reception was an elegant affair, the opulence and smooth functioning of which was not disrupted except by the presence of Eddie Johnson, who was said to be a bookie, a bum who used a bench at the museum as a meeting place, there closing his deals. Eddie showed up uninvited, mixed and mingled, and left, but not without first filling his blue windbreaker pockets and blue baseball cap with snacks. The other new fellow in town, Jack Morrison, the Lutheran minister, dipped heavily into the punch, spiced by the vodka he'd brought with him in a flask, had sat with Eddie all afternoon, smiling and raising his cup to the distinguished guests passing silently by on their high horses, as it were.

That afternoon he came up with the bright idea that, until Jake got an apartment in town, he should come live with him in "the German neighborhood," in the Lutheran Parish House. Minna agreed to it, noting this arrangement was going to be *very* temporary. So Jake moved to Camperdene, paving the way for being joined there by his wife and child. His host, the Congregational Minister, Reverend Morrison, drank vodka morning, noon, and night. There was beer enough for legions, armies, entire countries, in the fridge. The television was left on at all hours – noise. The house was in total disarray.

"*Mi Casa is su Casa*," he assured Jake. Some *Casa*! In Jack was an inner disarray similar to the disarray of the house the Church had provided him, in which, he said, he did not feel at home. The congregation had brought him in, he said, and then left him to sort things out. He only seemed to see people when he preached at the Church on Sunday. No one came to visit or help him the other days of the week, and he felt this was totally hypocritical.

Jake shared his thoughts with Jack. He said he thought the expectation was that Jack should venture out and visit others, ministering to them. He said he *would*, in time – so soon as he could get his bearings.

On Halloween evening Jack scared the daylights out of the kids that dared approach the Parish House porch. He dressed up as Count Dracula in a three piece suit with fingernails that looked like railroad spikes and assured the kiddies, ominously, as he put black and crimson jelly beans in their bags, "Don't worry sweet children, I won't kill you."

Jack was talkative. He told Jake all about himself, his youth, his attendance at a divinity school in the mid-west, his internship in Kansas, the differences between the many and assorted protestant religions and the reasons why the Lutheran religion is the one true religion, the religion for which his love flows over. He refilled his cup of vodka three or four times and began losing track of the days of his youth, then reeled off, around midnight, each night, to bed.

This idyllic season in the house that Jack had on loan to him was cut short when Captain Cunningham came up with a lead on an apartment he thought Jake would like. It was new, not expensive, and within walking distance to and from the museum.

Minna and Mark drove out to look at it. The two Buchans signed the lease that same afternoon. Minister Morrison, Eddie the Bookie, and The Captain and two of his daughters, Gabbie and Lizzie – motley crew! – helped them unload the U-Haul truck.

At their first Camperdene Thanksgiving, Jake's nomad parents, Mark's grandparents – eventually *my* grandparents, too – showed up. Mark's grandma had brought him a nice new shirt to wear. He tried it on and found it not to his liking. Wrinkled. His grandpa famously suggested he ask his grandma if she'd *iron* it. "What is *that*?" Mark asked. "*Iron* it?"

"Oh," Mark's grandpa said. "That means to *press* it – to get an iron and get it good and hot and flatten out clothes."

Mark went off in search of his grandma. "Grandma," he famously requested, "*can you make my shirt flat?*"

Jake's car overheated on the way to the airport, so they took a taxi, leaving the Volkswagen on the Expressway, which enlivened his father tremendously, but didn't sit well with his son, who insisted *you don't leave a car parked on the parkway.* "Lighten up," advised the grandfather, tickling his stern, fuming grandson, Mark.

The Volkswagen was tossed into a junkyard. My parents bought a used navy blue Dodge Caravan. Minna, Jake, and Mark lived off the leftovers from his mother's superb Thanksgiving feast for weeks and weeks afterwards – breakfast, lunch, and dinner.

Santa Claus showed up on skis for the museum's Christmas celebration. Mark remembers pitching in, helping to string popcorn, cranberries, clove apples, and paper chains from the museum's Christmas tree. Wallace Barrow, in a three-piece suit and a red carnation, thanked everyone for coming, and introduced Camperdene's Superintendent of Schools, Michael Bonaventura, who read from the poem "A visit from St. Nicholas." The High School choir sang selections from Handel's Messiah.

My father insisted there was no visible ill-will anywhere that day.

The new year brought a resolution. Jake assured Wallace Barrow he'd see to it that the Association's many and various committees – Artifacts and Collections Development, Computer Services, Building and Grounds, Preservation – would all meet, and would be meeting regularly through the coming year.

The Artifacts and Collections Development Committee met in mid-March, and began facing important decisions concerning the museum: What policies should exist concerning the management of it? How should its collections best be displayed? What should be the curator's working relationship with other heads of institutions holding similar and/or related collections?

At the end of March, the well-regarded colorful local character, salt-and-pepper-bearded unofficial town historian and Museum Association Vice-President Captain Powderkeg Cunningham, took it upon himself to announce to the press, from out of the blue, that he had begun the "breathtakingly laborious task" of cataloguing the museum's collections, book holdings, and archives. He searched diligently through drawers, cabinets, storage cases and shoe boxes in search of any lists of holdings compiled by his predecessors (or anyone else) and, through photocopying (in conjunction with scissors and glue), Captain Cunningham made ready to meet the reporters.

CHAPTER FIVE

Captain Cunningham gleefully held his surprise news conference, answering questions about the museum's efforts to organize, preserve, and make more accessible *all* of its collections, peppering his explanations with charming anecdotes about the history of Camperdene and assorted historic buildings in the town. When a librarian from the Boston Public Library came to Camperdene to peruse "hands-on" a dozen "priceless" titles supposed safe and secure in the museum library's stacks, Captain Cunningham arranged to have a Camperdene Daily Journal photographer come in to photograph him in the act of showing off the titles. To his embarrassment, only four of the twelve books sought could in fact be found.

It was at the Captain's bidding that the defunct Museum Curator Search Committee should now be merged with the defunct former New Directions Committee. Association President Wallace "Wheel" Barrow appointed Carlena Lagorio to be chairwoman of this new Committe, the Planning Committee. The first meeting of the Planning Committee went poorly, with some of those present miffed because certain other people present had also showed up. Carlena Lagorio gave an ultimatum: certain members of this committee simply would not be staying in the committee if certain other members of the committee also remained.

Upon reading a statement concerning the committee that Jake had written ("One of the priorities of the planning Committee will be to consider not only short-range plans for making the best of the existing museum, but also to imagine and to formulate guidelines and long-range plans, as the population of Camperdene continues growing and as the populace becomes more diverse, toward expanding the museum"), an incensed Carlena Lagorio announced, nostrils flaring, "This is ludicrous." Lagorio told the committee it was *not* to give any consideration to expanding the present museum facility.

A substantial portion of the committee's original membership did not show up at the second committee meeting. The fate of the "Museum Renovations Funding & Publicity Team" (Ben Mulvane, Julia Seymour-Stanton, and Veronica Pillsbury) was similar: dissolved at the outset ("Committees can be formed only by the authority of the Executive Committee, and we don't want this").

In the meantime, Nicholas Wentworth of The Friends of the Museum, in cahoots with Julia Seymour-Stanton, with the financial assistance of the Camperdene Arts Lottery Council, had organized what would turn out to be one of the Museum's most successful programs: "Movies based on 1912 Events." The six-part program would include viewings, readings, and discussions of both books and films. The first gathering, eager to discuss the theme "Men Aboard the Titanic Who, Dressed in Women's Garb, Jumped Into Lifeboats," came at the tail end of a cold, hazardous, stormy, snowy day.

That same evening, the first House Committee (or "Buildings and Grounds Committee") met. A "special guest" at this initial meeting – by virtue of Jake's having invited him to be at it – was the eagle-eyed, kindly old former curator of the Holyoke, Massachusetts Arts and Science Center, Herbert Sherman. Early on in the evening, Carlena Lagorio took Jake aside and communicated to him in no uncertain terms that she was miffed by "Old Sherbert's" presence. Mid-way through the meeting, Carlena asked Veronica Pillsbury, "Isn't there anything you'd like to *tell* the committee, Veronica?" She graciously bowed out: silence. Steely, persistent Carlena Lagorio: "Come on, Veronica, tell them. Tell them what you told me." Ms Lagorio plowed ahead, "She told me she did not understanding what a Planning Committee was expected to do. Mr. Wright, will you inform us as to what a Planning Committee is supposed to do?"

Jake explained that the Planning Process was a process through which museums identified and recorded short-range and long-range goals, and attempted to determine specific situations and problems that demanded attention, and then set objectives and a time-line for implementing goals and remedying problems.

"In order to help museums from floundering in this, Planning Process models have been created to help museums guide themselves through the process," Jake said. "We can use one of the existing models, adapt an existing model to our own needs, or create an altogether new plan."

Upon that, Carlena Lagorio informed her colleagues, "This Committee is not to be concerned with long-range plans at all, but rather with practical matters – where the photocopy machine should go, and what to do about handicapped access."

At the end of the meeting, Carlena Lagorio took Jake aside. She gave him her dire warning: if the old man was going to be on the Planning Committee, Jake could be sure that she, Carlena Lagorio, and Veronica Pillsbury, would *not*. "He's just an old fusspot who goes around in circles and can't get anything done."

The next day, Jake got a phone call from Carlena Lagorio. She had donated some random *objects d'art* a few days before and had, in turn, received a thank you note from museum staffer Audrey Morris.

"I would expect to get a nice letter – from the *curator*," she declared.

"Sorry," Jake murmered.

"You're not *sorry*," she scolded him. "You have no *idea* what *sorry* is. You don't have a *clue*! You have no *clue* who you are *dealing* with here, Mister Jacob *Wrong*! I will *damage* you! I will bring *harm* to you! I will – I will... I will damage you *bad*!"

I'm quite sure that if I'd been my father, I would have told that old buzzer what to do with her harm and damages. But not my father. He just took his ear away from the phone.

"Well?" Carlena Lagorio asked impatiently. I can just see her stamping her foot or wrapping the telephone cord around her wrist. (This was in a time in which there were still telephone cords.) If I had been there, I'm sure I would have wrapped the cord around her neck.

"I don't know how I should respond," Jake said calmly. "I *said* I'm sorry."

"I will *injure* you!" she screamed, and hung up.

Carlena Lagorio refused to speak with Jake when next she saw him. She spoke to him only to say that another member of the committee had been dismissed. The committee's two remaining members – Carlena Lagorio and Captain Cunningham – drafted the final version of the Mission Statement: "The Museum of the Year 1912 will primarily illuminate, through the display of appropriate artifacts and art objects, the highlights of the year 1912 while secondarily functioning to supply informational and entertainment offerings to the community."

"There's nothing I hate more," Jake overheard Carlena Lagorio tell the Captain that night, "than group editing."

The next day, Wheel Barrow crossed the street from his home and place of business, the Barrow Family Funeral Home, to the museum, and he took Jake aside.

"You know," he said, "I am concerned with matters of consequence. I am a man who is naturally interested in matters of consequence. I've got a lot of *troubles*. The last thing I need, Mr. Wright, is more *troubles*. The last thing I need is troubles *at the museum*. You know, I have to deal with a lot of women. In my profession, I'm not dealing with men, I'm usually dealing with the wives, I'm dealing with the daughters. In any case, I always deal with the *women*. You have to know *how to deal with women*. You have to learn *how to get along*. I know how to take care of women! It's something *you* have to *learn*."

When the House Committee – that is, Captain Cunningham and Wallace Barrow's Neanderthal look-alike son Reggie – met, focusing on possible renovations, Reggie, before leaving, confided, "Don'cha tell no one about no renovations. We may not get to that this year. You *understand?*"

Jake understood – but he'd already told Daily Journal reporter Alice Armour Armstrong of the fund drive. Three days later, here was the headline: "Well-traveled curator settles in Camperdene." Under the photograph of an uncomfortable, officious- looking Jake squinting in raw winter sunlight out front of The Museum of the Year 1912 ran the story:

"It was a long road that took Museum Curator Jake Wright to Europe and eventually back again. 'New England is the middle – Ralph Waldo Emerson called it "The Hub of the Universe" – and that's where I like to be,' said Wright as he sat in his office at The Museum of the Year 1912, which stands like a stone fortress in the town of Camperdene."

The article detailed Jake's assorted museum-related experiences, his travels in Europe, his meeting Minna, their winding up a while in Boston, his having started work in September, and Minna's having begun working part-time in December as a waitress downtown at the Mill Wheel restaurant.

"The museum plans for the year," the article closed, "include starting a fund raising drive to create more interactive children's exhibits and activities."

In the article, there was no mention of several special exhibits underway: a series concerning "The Art of the Book from the Year 1912 to the Present Day" – papers and papermaking, printing, printmaking, bookbinding, and calligraphy. Camperdene's own preeminent bookbinder and leader of The Friends of The Museum of the Year 1912, Nick Wentworth, was putting some of his best work on display, also making an appearance one evening to talk about his work. Other notable printers and bookbinders in town would soon follow suit, helping to coordinate a year-long series of displays and discussions and presentations at the museum. None of which was mentioned by reporter Alice Armour Armstrong in the Camperdene Daily Journal that day.

Later in the day of the publication of the Daily Journal article about Jake the "well-traveled curator, "he was invited over to Wallace Barrow's Funeral Home. Captain Cunningham was there. Wallace intoned half cheerfully, half ominously, "I like that article, Jake. Gave us a lot of leeway. 'Starting a fund raising drive to create more interactive children's exhibits and activities.' Yea, that gives us *a lot of leeway*. You think I'm kidding. No, it's just *great*. Really good. Gives us a lot of *leeway*."

It was dark and hushed in the mortician's back room. Wheel drew in closer and laid his cards on the table: "Jake, we *seriously* need to know, and your answer must give us pause: who do you feel *closer* to, Jake – the Association, or... [dramatic pause] ...The Friends of the Museum, or ... [dramatic pause] ...your staff?"

This struck Jake immediately as being the least good question ever put to him. He kept his mouth shut. Captain Powderkeg also kept his silence.

Wallace, though clearly infuriated, spoke in whispers. He softly said he *needed* to know this information, of Jake's *allegiance* or *non-allegiance* to the Museum Association, so that he would know what to do henceforth – for example, would know whether or not to include Jake for the duration of each Executive Committee meeting, or whether Jake ought better simply to report to the committee at the beginning of each meeting and then be dismissed.

In my father's shoes I think I would have told old Wallace Barrow to take his Executive Committee and his *allegiance* or *non-allegiance* and jump into an empty effing cask and close the lid behind him, but that was not my father, who responded awkwardly, saying weakly that the conversation they were having seemed *strange* to him – it felt like extortion – it was weirdly secretive – *Masonic*.

"I *am* a Mason," Barrow whispered ominously.

The next day Jake politely wrote Barrow a letter, asking who the conductor of a symphony orchestra should feel closer to when conducting – to the Philharmonic Orchestra Association, to the musicians, or to the audience? Jake insisted this was, at root, *a bad question*. He said he felt strongly he ought to feel closer to *the music*, and ought to play for *the people* – those who had come to *hear* the music. Jake said he ought to feel a responsibility and commitment to doing a good job of *conducting*, to getting the *music* right, thus serving everyone appropriately, in particular those who had come to *listen* and to *enjoy*.

When next Jake saw Wallace Barrow, the mortician pierced him with a look. "You puzzle me, Wright," he said. "I *still* can't figure out what the hell your *conducting an orchestra* has to do with *anything* we're doing *here*. You listen to me: you *conduct your goddam orchestra on your own time*."

CHAPTER SIX

It was in the springtime. The Corporators of The Museum of the Year 1912 Association began having assorted private Corporation dinners and testimonials, to which the curator and his staff were not invited. Via the radio and the Camperdene Daily Journal, Museum Corporators told of how, in 1908, wealthy manufacturing heir Simon Lagorio had married Louisa Burton, then the official historian of the town of Camperdene. Louisa had, in that capacity, already traveled widely throughout Massachusetts, examining libraries and private holdings and collections, writing on the Arts and Crafts Movement in America. The Arts and Crafts Movement had come to America from England – from Thomas Carlyle, John Ruskin, and William Morris – though it had itself been influenced by Americans – Ralph Waldo Emerson, Henry Thoreau, and Walt Whitman. In his "Craftsman" magazine, Gustav Stickley advanced the ideas of the Arts and Crafts Movement – rusticity and an appreciation of beautiful handmade things. People loved crafts – woodworking, metalwork, pottery, textiles, leatherwork, and bookbinding.

In 1910, a Campardene institution arose: Louisa Burton's School for Instruction in the Practical Arts. Crafts instruction was mandatory part of the curriculum. In 1911, Louisa priavetley published "Come Again," a volume of poetry. By 1912, Louisa's School for Instruction in the Practical Arts had developed into the Camperdene Craftsman Guild. The Craftsman Guild was not so much an organized movement as it was a shared lifestyle. While the school lasted, its crafts training program gave focus and direction to the community of Camperdene.

It was at the end of that year, in December 1912, that Simon and Louisa Lagorio had proposed their museum, The Museum of the Year 1912. Simon and Louisa went west to gather arifacts from the then emerging pre-planned city of Torrance, California. They traveled and collected stuff through all of California, from Berkeley to San Diego, gathering their first museum specimens. Back in Camperden in 1913, the Lagorios got the good news that the Massachusetts State Legislature granted the city of Camperdene $9,000 to build a Craftsman-style building which would be their proposed Museum of the Year 1912. They could "Bungalowize" it to their heart's content.

At a meeting of the Camperdene Historical Society, the original Corporators of The Museum of the Year 1912 Association were named. Eight members of the Association were elected to the Corporation board. Monthly meetings were arranged. Camperdene city officials granted Simon and Louisa a "life lease" on the museum buiilding, donating water, electricity, and fire/police protection in perpetuity.

The museum contractors were Wattleston, Richmond, and Smith. Modeled after traditional homes in India and popularized in California, the original museum edifice emphasized horizontal lines, overhanging roofs, expansive porches, and huge windows. The elaborate exterior included an octagonal center lantern-style rotunda with weathervane, multiple dormer and bay windows, a tile roof flanked by an ornate brick chimney, and half-timbered gables. Natural building materials like cedar shingles, stone fireplaces, and slate or tile roofs reinforced a rustic look. The 1913 Camperdene Town Report would state, "The beauty and convenience of the new museum has been greatly admired, not only by residents, but by visitors from abroad."

In keeping with the Arts and Crafts Movement aesthetic, the museum's rooms were decorated with mission oak furnishings – pottery and mica lamps and art glass lanterns set on davenports, settees, buffets, desks, bookcases, tables, chairs, bedsteads, and dressers from the L. & J.G. Stickley Company, sturdily made of solid, quarter-sawed oak. There were throw pillows on the expansive window seats of the many six-over-one windows having original rippled glass, providing all the rooms with ample light. In the central chamber was a stone fireplace and a stately 1912 oak billiard table.

From 1913 through the early 1920s, the museum was the scene of many private parties and receptions. The general public had then understood the museum was committed solely to the town's elite. What the Corporators did not mention was that in 1912, Simon and Louisa Lagorio had been initiated into an esoteric branch of Freemasonry cult called the *Ordo Templi Anodopetalum*, the O.T.A., where they'd together begun partaking in "The Greater Mysteries."

Nick Wentworth of the Friends of the Museum put into Jake's hands a pristine copy of a 1912 magazine, "The Orifice, illuminating the cult the museum's founders had joined, this O.T.A., which had grown out of the esoteric traditions of Knights Templars, Gnostics, Voodoo, and the occult ("Our order possesses the KEY which opens up all Masonic and Hermetic secrets, namely, the teaching of sexual magic, and this teaching explains, without exception, all the secrets of Nature, all the symbolism of Freemasonry and all systems of religion").

The *Ordo Templi Anodopetalum* had been founded in the 1877 in upper state New York by assorted Spiritualists, Qabalists, Freemasons, and Rosicrucians. Anodopetalumy claimed to offer an alternative to material science. Anodopetalumists believed in esoteric wisdom-teaching, archaic secret traditions which world advance humanity's spirituality in the modern world.

The Arts & Crafts Movement had arrived in America in 1876, at the Centennial Exposition in Philadelphia. There, visitors marveled at Oriental pottery and French barbotine with glistening ornamental underglaze. Gustav Stickley's "Craftsman" magazine was introduced in 1901. There, Stickley paid homage to William Morris and John Ruskin. In upper state New York,

Elbert Hubbard's crafts community, the Roycrofters, had meanwhile started making beautiful books a la Morris, and had started manufacturing a line of furniture in his Arts and Crafts style. Though he was not a designer, Hubbard used his business acumen to create a huge appetite in Ameria for his books, furniture, and small metalwork.

Albert Valentien, the first professional designer for Rookwood Pottery, first visited San Diego in 1903, where he pursued his interest in painting wildflowers. He and his wife Anna, who had also worked for Rookwood for over twenty years, left the company in 1905 to move to California.

At the close of 1904, in Berlin, Germany, Rudolf Steiner had lectured on the history of Freemasonry, regaling his audience with tales of "snoozing forces" needing "to be woken up again." It was Steiner's duty, he felt, to awaken people to the Eleusinian Mysteries – the Terrestrial and Celestial, the Visible and the Invisible – the *Mysteria Mystica Aeterna*.

In 1906, in Camperdene, Louisa Lagorio, had become an associate editor at "Awaken Now" magazine, advocating adherence to the principles of Steiner, then rising up from being a Goethe specialist and an archivist into a full-blown occult teacher. Steiner now granted Simon and Louisa, across the waters, "apostolic succession," giving them authority to spread his ideas of karma, reincarnation, occultism, Christianity, and the writings of Goethe in America.

The archives of The Museum of the Year 1912 held not only every issue of "The Orifice," the journal of the *Ordo Templi Anodopetalum*, but also numerous papers handwritten by Rudolf Steiner in that year, talking up Northern European esoteric knowledge generally – Masonry, mysticism, the occult – and, in particular, Steiner's clairvoyant daily communications with "archangels" and others descended on the "astral plane" from the people of the lost continent of Atlantis – some Japanese, some Mongolians, and some Eskimos. Steiner had claimed to have access to the "Akasha Chronicle," a supernatural scripture containing knowledge of higher realms of existence as well as of the distant past and future.

Almost equal to the mass and maze of papers generated by Rudolf Steiner in Germany in 1912 were papers generated by The Progressive Party in America that year, most of these illuminating how quickly

Progressive Party organizations had, after the Republican convention of 1912, aligned the Party with then-dominant Southern racial mores – racism. Southern Progressives had demanded Roosevelt deny the legitimacy of blacks attempting to participate in the 1912 elections. Official reports had noted, in 1911, that sixty black Americans had been lynched that year. In the year 1912, sixty-one black Americans were lynched.

After the Progressives and the Republicans lost the 1912 election to the Democrats – Woodrow Wilson was elected – America faced the prospect of enetering World War I. In 1915, Elbert Hubbard died aboard the Lusitania. Gustav Stickley went bankrupt in 1916. Rudolf Steiner claimed, in 1916, to be in contact with the spirit of the dead former chief of staff of the German high command, General Helmuth von Moltke, who told him The Great War was the result of an international conspiracy against Germany's national spiritual life. But the revolutionaries of the 1919 Munich Council Republic denounced Steiner as just another witch doctor on the side of decaying capitalism – causing industrialists to see Steiner's notions in a new light. After the defeat of a revolutionary uprising of the German working class, Steiner was invited by the director of the Waldorf-Astoria tobacco factory in Stuttgart to establish a company school. This provided the foundation for what would become the Waldorf education movement. Steiner's Waldorf schools were to be staffed only "by teachers with a knowledge of man originating in a spiritual world." Steiner would emphasize repetition and rote learning, insisting the teacher should be the center of the classroom and that a student's role was not to judge or even discuss the teacher's pronouncements.

After World War I, Simon and Louisa Lagorio began an extensive tour of the world, looking for more stuff to house in their Museum of the Year 1912. They traveled coast to coast across the U.S., then took a ship to England (Morris; Walker; Kelmscot, Doves press, Gill); Vienna (Wiener Werkstatte; Klimt; Schiele); and on and on – collecting ashtrays, beer bottles, beer mugs, bells, belt buckles, bottle stoppers, cloaks, daggers, swords, letter openers, silver ingots, shot glasses, cutlery, decanters, straight razors, thermometers, magnets, sundials, thimbles, clasps, pipes, tumblers, clocks, wall hangings, bookends, bookmarks, bowties, buttons, flasks, gavels, goblets, hat pins, jewelry, keyrings, pocket knives, postage stamps, postcards, candles, canes, cigarette cases, combs, cufflinks, door knockers, doorknobs, drawer pulls, earrings, tokens, figurines, statuettes, graven images, flags, potholders, radiator caps, rubber stamps, lapel pins, leather belts, suspenders, wallets, lamps, medallions, miniature replicas of the ark of the covenant, money clips, paperweights, pillboxes, watch fobs.

In 1925, in January, Simon and Louisa attended President Calvin Coolidge's inauguration.

In 1927, in February, Louisa gave birth to a daughter, Carlena. In March, 1927, Simon, Louisa, and Carlena moved into the so-called "Mausoleum" – what would later be Wallace Barrow's funeral home, located directly across from the Museum of the Year 1912.

CHAPTER SEVEN

In the 1930s, the Lagorio's primary concern, beyond the raising of their daughter, was obtaining adequate funding for the museum. On March 18, 1931, Simon and Louisa hosted a fund-raising dinner for more restoration work (they raked in over $7,000). After 1932, The Museum of the Year 1912 was open only sporadically, due to Louisa's failing health. In 1933, new museum construction started west of the original museum. Construction advanced, but by April the federal CWA had disbanded, replaced by the Federal Emergency Relief Association, and work began to be sporadic, at best. President Franklin Delano Roosevelt, a Thirty-Third Degree Mason, a member of The Ancient Arabic Order Nobles of the Mystic Shrine, was very kind to the Lagorios, assuring them in November, 1935 that work on the new building should resume under the auspices of the Federal Works Progress Administration (WPA). Construction progressed. A 1912 Craftsman bungalow was torn down and reassembled as a wing on the northwest corner of the museum, and a further outbuilding was constructed. In November, 1936, the WPA declared the museum project complete.

In January, 1937, the renovated and enlarged museum was dedicated. Between 1937 and 1942, Simon and Louisa wrote frequently for the Camperdene newspaper – primarily about Museum exhibits, local history, and historic figures. By the time World War II had erupted, Adolf Hitler had dissolved the ten Grand Lodges of Germany. Prominent dignitaries and members were sent to concentration camps. When

Austria was captured by the Nazis, the persecution was continued. Masters of Vienna lodges were confined in concentration camps, including Dachau in Bavaria. The same was repeated when Hitler took over Czechoslovakia, Poland. Holland, Belgium, Norway, and on and on. The Gestapo seized membership lists and looted libraries and collections of Masonic objects. Much of this loot – after being exhibited in Joseph Goebbels' Anti-Masonic Exposition in 1937 in Munich – would eventually find its way to The Museum of the Year 1912.

The Lagorios saw a direct connection between this material and their hero, Rudolf Steiner, who'd initially set up shop in 1912. Steiner elaborated a systematic racial classification system for human beings. He taught that, to be properly understood, races needed to be arranged hierarchically, with the Nordic-Germanic race, the Aryan race, being the most advanced group. Steiner believed only enlightened Nordic-Germans would evolve; their spiritually inferior neighbors would degenerate and die out. Steiner taught that the lower, "darker" races of humans were closer to animals than to the Nordic-German higher races. He denounced the immigration of dark-skinned people to Europe, decrying its effects on "blood and race." Of course Steiner's notions dovetailed neatly into the ideology of the Nazis.

In 1942, with their daughter Carlena away in Boston attending a Waldorf school, Simon and Louisa Lagorio had resumed traveling. At this time, they had turned over the administrative duties of their Museum to Henry Barrow, Wheel Barrow's father. The first actual curator of The Museum of 1912, hired in 1943, was one Susanna Seymour.

"The keynote of the museum is advertising," Miss Seymour proclaimed. "Museums, like business houses, have adopted the plan of going out into the byways and hedges and making themselves known and felt. Pictures of the museum have been framed with printing below telling the hours of opening, setting forth some of the advantages therein, welcoming all and sundry to come in. One of these framed pictures has been hung in each mill in the town, and one in the train station."

At the end of that year, 1943, Louisa Lagorio entered the Camperdene Home for the Elderly. On April 2, 1944, she was hospitalized. Following a heart attack, she died on April 9. The funeral was held out front of the Museum. The then Masssachusetts Governor (a Democrat) delivered the eulogy.

On May 28, Simon Lagorio reopened the Museum to the public. On August 22, Simon re-filed the articles of incorporation. A Boston consulting firm was hired to examine all state agencies recommending that funding of the musuem be discontinued because it was a private organization. The city of Camperdene ignored the recommendation, appropriating $2,000 annually to the museum for Fiscal Years 1945-1946.

From 1945 to 1947, Simon Lagorio and Henry Barrow directed museum activities as chairman and secretary. In 1947, a federal consultant met with them to introduce organizational and conservation techniques for the museum's library and archives. Museum committees were formed for Budget, Property, Custodian, Finance, and Insurance. The museum's buildings were insured. The board strengthened its policy concerning donated articles. In August, Henry Barrow was elected board president. In October, Association membership dues were introduced (set at one dollar per year).

By 1948, the museum's staff had grown to three full-time employees – two custodians and a curator responsible for collections maintenance and visitor supervision. Museum facilities were used by the Camperdene Garden Club and other organizations for meetings. The Garden Club began the Louisa Lagorio Memorial Rose Garden. In 1949, the Museum archives became available by appointment. In September, 1950, museum curator Susanna Seymour departed suddenly. Carlena Lagorio came aboard.

In the 1950 Town Report, the acting curator, Carlena Lagorio, made no mention of the resignation of Susanna Seymour. There was, however, much mention of "extensive damage to the building accomplished in just three months." Happily, there had aslo come "iimprovements," including "more room and light. Lowering of the floor of the museum, enlarging of windows, opening the roof to three attic windows, building shelves under museum wall cases, doing over the walls, adding new radiators, furniture and lights – all have resulted in attractive exhibition space." The 1954 report noted an "especially gratifying" installation: "New battleship linoleum."

In the 1958 Town report the curator called for expansion: "There is no adequate work space. A curator's office is needed. These are problems that present opportunities to our Trustees." In 1960 she wrote, "On March 19th excavaton was begun on the lawn preparatory to putting in basement windows. Five months later work was completed, providing in the basement public toilets and a new heating plant with oil burner. New plumbing went in. Extra storage space was made.

In the mid-1980s, Carlena Lagorio stepped down as acting curator. The Museum Corporation recruited Hollie Greenspan to be curator. Then had come Jake's time.

One day in February Veronica Pillsbury came in to see him, to say that she was very seriously thinking of not being on the Planning Committee anymore. She said that she and Carlena Lagorio had had a "falling out." Jake said he could not imagine – he'd thought she and Carlena were *such* good friends. "I had thought so, too," Veronica said resignedly. "But Carlena recently decided otherwise. That's just how she is," Veronica said, making a sour face. "For now, she has made it clear to me that we *are not friends.*"

Jake held his tongue. Then he asked Veronica if she thought she would become reconciled to Carlena. "You never know with Carlena," Veronica said.

That same day, Madame Lagorio came in with a letter Jake was told he needed to duplicate, sign, and send out with this message: "The museum's Planning Committee has appointed Carlena Lagorio chairwoman. She has graciously accepted. The committee requires committed participants. If you feel, for whatever reasons, that you can't assist the committee in its work, please inform Carlena Lagorio. Thank you, Jake Wright (signed)."

At the end of the month, Jake and Captain Cunningham were at a meeting of the Town Finance Committee held in the Camperdene Middle School's Faculty Lounge. To make ends meet, it was proposed that Camperdene have a volunteer fire department and that The Museum of the Year 1912 should receive no further town assistance.

The next day, Mark broke his arm. Minna had left him with a neighbor for an hour – with her kids Donny and Bergundy. Mark had fallen out of a trash barrell. He'd landed on his left wrist, cried, and then fallen asleep – still in the barrel. That evening the Wrights went to the hospital. An x-ray revealed Mark's radius and ulna were both broken near the wrist. His arm was put in a cast. Mark cried himself to sleep.

That same evening, the New Acquisitions Committee held a meeting. Jake followed up on Captain Cunningham's suggestion that the Committee be run a little differently, so that not only Carlena Lagorio would be involved, chattering away," as the Captain said. People took turns, going clockwise around the table. Veronica Pillsbury was last to speak. She set in, aggressively thrusting fistfuls of pictures cut from assorted antiques and collectibles magazines at the committee. Jake made a grave mistake: he reminded the committee of its obligation, which wasn't to flood the museum with only one sort of item but to represent a broad range of potential acquisitions relevant to the year 1912 and hopefully of interest to the community of Camperdene. Veronica took that hard. She was livid, she was flabbergasted – she was furious. "*This* is what the community wants!" she cried out, holding up her ads. She informed Jake she was *through*. She resigned from the New Acquisitions Committee. Carlena Lagorio grinned ear to ear.

I probably would have told Veronica Pillsbury to go drown herself in a sewer, the bitch, but not my father. No, after the meeting, he simply took Veronica aside and tried to calm her down, to smooth her ruffled feathers. Jake apologized – he did so sincerely – for anything he may have said that hurt her – *maligned her*, as she put it, *in front of the others*.

The next day, Ben Mulvane came in and told Jake he'd handled himself like a gentleman at the New Acquisitions Committee meeting. Jake mentioned his having apologized to Veronica. He said, "What *for*?

She owes *you* an apology. Things sure are screwed up around here." (I think I would have liked to have met Ben Mulvane.)

At the end of March, the Friends of the Museum held a "Dip into the Friends" party. Jake brought the dip and reported to the Friends – to the two who showed up, and their daughters. He waxed eloquent concerning program successes. He said he hoped to see more programs like the "Movies from 1912 Events and Books," for example, programs with combined viewings, readings, and discussions of short stories from 1912 and notable films made from short stories from 1912; a program with combined viewings, readings, and discussions of immortal comic works from 1912 and related early classic comic/slapstick films; and so on. He suggested the Friends ought to find a "lever" or "mechanism" – public relations – by which the Friends might obtain more Friends. He suggested they concentrate on that. There was plenty of leftover dip to take home.

When next the Planning Process Committee (Carlena Lagorio, Captain Cunningham, and Ben Mulvane) met, Julia Seymour-Stanton was also present. At the previous meeting, House Committee member Reggie Barrow had asked the committee to formulate a statement detailing goals, objectives, and general orientation of The Museum of the Year 1912. Jake had thought Julia's presence would be useful to the Committee in its discussion. When persevering Julia showed up, Carlena Lagorio scowled, saying to her sourly, "You are *not* to be present at this meeting." Julia graciously deposited with Carlena her prepared notes (activities/objectives) and departed without a word.

Jake reminded Carlena that he had asked Julia to be at the meeting – as he'd thought her presence would be useful to the Committee in its discussions. Carlena to Jake: "She is not a member of the committee. She has no business being here. She has no right or reason to be present here. You should feel honored that you are still here."

My ass. I would have wrung Carlena Lagorio's neck on the spot. But not my father, Gentleman Jacob. He took it in his stride.

Ben Mulvane then blurted out that he just did not understand at all what a Planning Process Committee was expected to do. Jake now tried to help clarify things for Ben, along these lines:

Through the planning process, museums identify and record short-range and long-range goals, and determine specific situations and problems that demand attention, and then to set objectives and a time-line (deadline) for implementing goals and remedying problems. When faced with such a task, most museums flounder. In order to help museums from floundering, "Planning Process" models have been created to help museums guide themselves through the process. The Museum of the Year 1912 Association can either use one of the existing models, adapt an existing model to its own needs, or create an altogether new one. The Committee is simply obliged to create a set of objectives, A-Z, and to create a timeline for implementing them, A-Z, and to see that they are implemented, A-Z."

Outcome:

Carlena ultimately told the committee that it is not to be concerned with "long-range plans" at all, but rather with "practical matters" like "where the photocopy machine should go," and handicapped access: "The Executive Committee has been talking forever about handicapped access, but nothing's been done about it. We should be telling them to get to it, and to get it done."

Jake sincerely liked that.

Two Drafts for Collection Guidelines:

"Two important goals of the Museum of the Year 1912 Association are: (1) to ensure that the Association's collection reflects the needs and interests of the community it serves, and (2) to assure community access to these resources and to all programs and services of the museum.

"The collection development goal is to build a collection geared toward entertaining and enlightening most visitors most of the time. The museum will not develop a strong scholarly research collection, as it is located amid many and fine University and other school museums and arts and science centers, with little community demand for a scholarly research collection of any kind.

"A good, up-to-date, appropriate museum collection of museum reference books will be developed and maintained. An effort will be made to develop a small collection of books printed in the Arts & Crafts style by local printers. Some of the museum's most valuable but cover-damaged rare books will be re-bound by local binders. The Association's collections will reflect the informational and entertainment needs and interests of the community."

Carlena moved that, with the approval of the Committee, she and the Director would edit the final versions of the "Mission Statement" and "Collection Development" Guidelines.

Carlena's motion was approved. She set the date of the next Planning Committee meeting: "Is Tuesday, April 4th, at 7:00 p.m. all right with everyone?" Jake looked in his datebook and quickly informed her, "Nope. Not good. Carlena, that's the same evening as the next Preservation Committee meeting. There's a conflict there for me."

"Well, we'll just have *our* meeting *anyway*," Carlena Lagorio snapped at him, "and you can simply come to *ours* when you are done at *theirs*."

The next day, Wheel Barrow and Captain Cunningham were in to see Jake. Barrow said, "You know, I've got a lot of *troubles*.... The *last* thing I need are more *troubles*. Wheel again recited his liturgy of how, as a mortician, he has to deal with a lot of *women*. "The women usually outlive the men, you know, and if I'm not dealing with wives, then I'm dealing with the daughters. In any case, I always deal with the *women*. You have to know *how* to take women. You have to learn *how to get along with women*. I know you think I'm a macho, that I don't treat women like I ought to. But *I know how to take care of women*. It's something you have to learn."

When Jake reminded Wheel that he'd been around, and that he'd been *around women*, and that, in fact, he was *married* to a *woman*, Barrow told him of his marriage to Candyce, a Scandinavian: "The first years were glorious. She hardly spoke a word of English. Now she's zipping away, talks American like all the other women. Nothing's the same." Barrow now got to the point: "We want you to – and this will test your metal, see what stuff you're made of – we want you to call up Veronica Pillsbury and offer her an apology."

Jake informed Wallace Barrow that he'd already done that – twice. *Alles klar, Herr Kommissar*. Okay. It was fine with him, not a problem. He'd try again. It's what he wanted anyway – to set this right and have things running smooth.

Peaceable Jake called Veronica late that afternoon. She asked him to call back again – the Monday after Easter.

On Easter Sunday, my brother Mark was up early. The Easter bunny had come in the night and had eaten part of the carrot my father had left for him, and had drank most of the milk my father had left for him. Easter day turned out to be "a brisk and sunny springtime day – dazzlingly clear" – as my father diligently recorded.

On Monday morning, Jake Called Veronica Pillsbury and arranged to meet with her at 1:00, at her house. Out on her back porch, the two talked Veronica assured him that she had only been interested in getting things for the museum that reflected the community's interests, and not her own. "I know you were," Jake assured her calmly, "I know you were."

The air was cleared. She was adamant and loud. She was full of indignation. She was proud of Camperdene. She wished messy people like her young neighbors across the road would just go away. Jake remained at Veronica's through his lunch hour. She gave him a quick tour of the house. He was shown Veronica's book collection. She was especially proud of her many cookbooks. Before Jake left, he asked Veronica about whether she would be returning to the Planning Committtee. She said she would. Jake promised her he would be bringing by a document he was working on, something that would help provide the Planning Committee with direction.

"It needs that," Veronica said squarely.

A few evenings later, Jake returned to work from his dinner and found the Planning Committee assembled in his office – Carlena Lagorio, Ben Mulvane, Connie Pederson, Roger Peters, and Captain Cunningham. Carlena Lagorio said, "Jake, will you please stay out just a while longer? We'll call you when we need you."

Roger Peters left the meeting early, shaking his head and rolling his eyes up as he departed, indicating his dismay. He went over to the circulation desk to say goodnight to my father. "Though they've got every reason to be clear about what they ought to be doing," he said, "they don't seem able to do it. It's the strangest thing. They seem *intent* on remaining *confused*."

Shortly after 8:30, Carlena Lagorio called over to Jake, "You can come in now." He took the seat vacated by Roger Peters. Carlena turned to Ben Mulvane: "Benjamin has something he wants to say to you, Jake. Ben?"

Ben explained the committee did not feel it existed in order to create a "Master Plan." They had already created their Mission Statement and a statement concerning guidelines for Future Artifacts Selection. Captain Cunningham, Jake was told, would be composing further "abstract guidelines." Then their job, Ben said, would be done.

Then everyone began to speak at once. Jake finally was able to say, "That's fine with me, Ben. That could be 'Phase One.' This committee could be re-labeled the 'Guidelines' Committee. You could then follow through with just the 'Service and Management' guidelines and be done quickly. A new committee, a Planning Committee, could then be organized at a later date."

Carlena Lagorio pointed out that the committee had no intention of doing any further work on service or management goals – or anything like them. She deferred to Ben Mulvane: "Benjamin, isn't there something else you wanted to say?"

Ben: "Well Jake, when I was growing up the museum was quite different from what it is today. It's all different now." Ben said. "I don't think we need to be modifying any further the original articles of The Act of Incorporation of The Museum of the Year 1912. And we won't be needing additional staff. What makes you think, considering the town's financial situation, that you're going to get another full-time employee?"

Jake: "I don't *think* it. I have been advised, by an Executive Committee member, that we ought to try to get in a Special Article for the Town Meeting in the spring, aiming to get another full-time employee in here, which we sorely need."

"Who says we need another full-time employee here? This committee doesn't say so. And, what's this? 'Provide a welcoming, professional atmosphere in the museum. Send staff members to appropriate occasional workshops.' What are these *workshops?*"

Jake explained. He told them of his having sent Mary Tuchlein to a workshop, for example. She'd gone, had taken notes, and had then reported to the others at a staff meeting. "It is good, from time to time, to have these discussions with others in one's own professional situation. I myself have gone to a few such workshops," Jake told them. "They're on Tuesday or Thursday mornings, and so I've gone on my own time, at no cost to you." (To the town, he meant, which paid his salary; no great matter: it was widely known that he put in 40 to 50 hours a week and was only paid for 35).

Carlena Lagorio: "I don't think there's any call for staff members to be going to any workshops."

Jake: "You're entitled to your opinion."

Carlena: "I am."

Jake: "You are."

Meeting adjourned.

Three days passed. Mary told Jake with distraught and warning terribly apparent in her voice: "You have a call – Carlena Lagorio."

Jake picked up the phone. "This is Jake."

"I want to add an artifact to the Artifacts Committee's Wish List."

"Shoot."

"*Art Nouveau* style hair brushes.

"Okay. We'll look for some."

"It's too bad you were so upset at the Planning Committee meeting the other night."

"Was I?"

"Well, I think so."

"I don't recall having been upset." *I'm not going to fall for this,* he resolved. Hold your tongue. Wait for Carlena's next devious maneuver or denunciation, or whatever else is up her sleeve.

"Don't you have anything to say?" she instigated. Jake could hear the trembling in her voice. *Ecstasy?*

"No, I don't," Jake said.

"You will regret this," Lagorio said. "I can do damage to you. You'll see."

"That would be too bad."

"Yes it would be. Good-bye."

"Goodbye."

It was all he could do to keep from blurting out, "Sticks and stones can break my bones but words can never hurt me."

That night, in bed, his darling son Mark wanted, for a goodnight story, "The Three Little Pigs."

"Who's afraid of the Big Bad Wolf?" the father asked.

Mark famously answered, "*I* am not afraid."

CHAPTER EIGHT

On Mark's fourth birthday, brave Jake went in to work early and took the afternoon off. Minna had organized a party, but she was not feeling well that day. When Jake arrived, the kids had just finished eating pizza. Out back of the house, Minna had been trying to get them to play "Musical Chairs," but whichever kid wound up without a chair had set in bawling. Now the kids were just running around and standing and sitting as they saw fit. Jake came onto this scene and headed straight to the kitchen to grab the last remaining pizza slice. Minna sensed his presence and called out in despair, "Jake, get down here and *sing* something! Make them *sit down*!" He did. Then he famously got all the kids up again, doing calisthenics – jumping jacks. He wore them down. He wore them *out*. The party ended quietly. Seriously.

In the morning, the Wrights went to the church of Minna, the Lutheran Church. Pastor Osgood delivered a sermon on expectations and arrogance and how these get in the way of belief and faith and hope and love. At one point the congregation recited, "We are ready to pray and think and rejoice. We are burdened by excess baggage as we travel the roads you send us down. Too often we wish to be served rather than to serve. After the service, Wallace Barrow seemed genuinely lighthearted, taking Jake aside to whisper in his ear, "Carlena Lagorio called my wife. I know what's going on. People are of all kinds. I tried to warn you. That Planning Committee was all your idea." His wife Candyce walked up, holding snooty Carlena Lagorio's hand. "Good morning," Jake said politely, even as he waved to the approaching town postmaster, James Copperstown, smiling huge as a full moon.

On Monday, Jake took a break from work to go over to one of Camperdene's old folks' homes for a gathering of the Camperdene Historical Society. Ben Mulvane spoke about his old neighborhoods and his father and his brother Joe who were so close that when his brother was diagnosed with a brain tumor his father died, followed by his brother a month later.

On Tuesday, the Planning Committee met again. Ben Mulvane read his minutes for the previous meeting, prefacing his report with thanks to Reggie Barrow, Chairman of the House Committee and to his father Wallace Barrow, Chairman of the Executive Committee.

"The Planning Process Committee has met four times. There was discussion, and questions were raised regarding the Master Plan submitted by the museum curator. The results of these meetings are being submitted herewith for action. The understanding of our responsibilities is that we were to consider the needs and the direction for growth for both the adult and youth departments. However the specifics for their implementation were then to be carried out by the appropriate committees. With the presentation of Mission Statements, Collection Development Guidelines, and Suggestions for Action that have been attached and have been approved by this committee, we feel we have completed the task for which this committee was established."

Mid-way through this meeting, Carlena Lagorio telephoned the Barrow household. Reginald couldn't make it, but the father would be right over. Wallace Barrow, just back from his Rotary Club meeting, showed up in a flannel shirt so rich in its royal blue blueness it looked like it would light up in darkness. "Just back from the Rotary," he informed the committee merrily. "Just changed my shirt."

Carlena, speaking for the Committee, asked Wallace if, having submitted its report, this committee had not now discharged its duties.

"Carlena," Wallace said. "You're asking me what I can't tell you. The Executive Committee will be meeting Thursday. I'll ask the committee if this committee ought to be disbanded or not. Each of you will receive a letter, saying whether or not this committee will be disbanded or kept intact. I can't tell you. You'll be getting a letter."

That night, back home after the meeting, Jake went quietly over to Minna, horizontal on the couch reading Herman Hesse's *Unterm Rad*. Laying himself down on the floor parallel to her, he asked if he could interrupt her reading long enough to ask how she was doing these days. My father says she said, "I'm pregnant," and that was all. That was it. Just that. "I'm pregnant."

She was pregnant, of course, with me. She'd tell me in future time of how I'd previously been in heaven, devising to be born. "And, when once you'd decided to whom and under what circumstances you'd like to be born, and when you were finally good and ready to join our family, you were born."

Jake announced the news to Mark the next morning, him still lighthearted in the aftermath of having had his cast removed a few days before. "You're going to have a little sister or brother."

Mark responded at once, smiling: "Sister."

"What will be her name?" Minna asked.

"Jillian," Mark said.

Now it would be my turn to be. Temperamental me. I was the next big story.

My father recorded there was glorious, sunny springtime weather. My mother had planted a splendid array of flowers out front of the apartment. The first buds of April were coming up green and beautiful. Minna told Jake she had not been feeling very well. She told him, dispassionately, that it really wasn't so much that she had morning sickness as it is that she had morning-afternoon-evening sickness. Minna said she'd been feeling sick generally. She was, she said – homesick. "Jake," she announced, "I'm going to go to Germany – for a month."

Though he said nothing, my reticent father wrote down that this did not sit well with him.

That same night of my mother's shocking new news, the museum's House Committee met. Reggie Barrow and Captain Cunningham discussed the eventual installation of "energy-savers" – new lighting and the disposal of the old, oversized basement water heater, replacing it with a new and smaller one. They may as well have said the museum was to be torn down, paved over, and a parking lot put in. But Jake wasn't actually paying much attention.

At the next meeting of the Executive Committee of the Museum Association, procrastination on these issues – the new lighting in the adult area, the disposal of the old, oversized basement water heater, and the replacement of it with a new and smaller one – was unanimously approved. Then the strangest thing happened. The Committee approved a request *my father* had made, which had been set on a back burner – way back. Now they were knocking him out of his chair with news of their approving a Special Collection at the museum, "The Art of the Book in Camperdene."

That same evening, the Friends of the Museum held their Annual Meeting downstairs. Jake ran in and announced to local bookbinder Nick Wentworth, the president of the Friends group, that the special collection, The Art of the Book in Camperdene, was going forward. He promptly closed out the meeting while Jake closed the museum, then the two went together to Greene's Corner Grocery and got some potato salad and ale and walked to Borden Street, to his shop, Cock's Crow Bindery, to celebrate.

They repeated the celebration the following evening as well, and Jake got a good night's sleep and woke up at 10:00 on Saturday and showered and shaved and went to the Lutheran Church for their "White Elephant Sale and Luncheon" where he chatted with Rudy, a colorful local character who'd also lived in Montana and Switzerland. He'd already met Jake's wife and son. He knew all there was to know about the Association's antiquarian holdings. He wondered what had become of stuff no one was now able to account for anymore. He'd seen the stuff before it had been missing, before he'd up and gone west to Montana.

Later that afternoon, Jake headed over to the museum. He took the phone book in hand. As had already happened once before, he again managed to dial up Walter Barrow in error, intending to call Captain

Cuningham. So he ended up explaining to Wallace Barrow the idea he'd intended to share with the Captain.

Says Barrow: "Listen here, young man. Get your mind off of the museum. You've got too much energy. You have to learn to just kick around, waste time, you know, just go out shopping with the wife – go to a mall and shop around and forget the rest and be with your family."

Jake knew Barrow was right on that count, and he told him so. He reached the Captain later in the day, asking if he, as head of the Historical Commission, would speak at the museum, talking about the history of Camperdene, some historic town buildings, the Museum Association's current efforts to organize, preserve, and make accessible its collections, and to introduce the new special collection, The Art of the Book in Camperdene. The Captain okay'd this. He said, by the way, that his wife was going to be out that evening, and he'd probably be spending his evening at the Museum.

That afternoon, Jake drove his wife and son to Springfield, where they got on a bus going to Boston, to Logan Airport, to board their plane going to Germany.

On Monday and Tuesday, Jake attended an arts and sciences museums conference, then went to the Regional Council Meeting of the Massachusetts Museums Association, then a Camperdene Chamber of Commerce Luncheon, followed by an Executive Meeting of The Museum of the Year 1912 Board of Curators, followed by his and their attending together the Council on Aging Special Forum "Elder Concerns," then the Friends of the Museum Book Sale, the Garden Club's annual Plant, Food, and Tag Sale on the museum's front lawn, and then the Veteran's Day Parade, in which he joined, wearing a red shirt and suspenders, waving a straw hat to the cheering crowd, shaking hands, telling jokes, kissing babies.

It was, as my father ambiguously recorded it, "a glorious springtime." It wasn't really clear in his writing if it was glorious despite our absence or because of it. He said the trees filled in explosively, obscuring the view to the pond out back of the house. From Germany, my mother sent an ultrasound printout made at the time of her amniocentesis test.

She'd seen me on the ultrasound scanner screen. The doctor had got his amniotic fluid samples. Jake got an ultrasound snapshot of me growing in her.

She and Mark were staying at my Oma's – Minna's mother's – house. She had not been well. Alzheimer's, apparently. She seemed healthy, still strong, but she believed Prince Charles had moved in with her, and so forth. Having been a somber, sullen person most her life, she was now, in her old age, jolly and silly and fun. Minna reported Mark was enjoying his jolly old Oma very much.

Now Jake revealed that his heart ached whenever he looked at the pictures of Mark and Minna that lay all around the empty house. He was currently filing them chronologically in a shoebox, he dutifully reported.

At work Jake kept busy organizing, among other things, a temporary watercolor exhibit with three accompanying workshops and organized a "Disaster Preparedness" workshop, "The Fine Art of Dealing With Disaster" (The Camperdene Daily Journal touted it thus: "Thirty area museum workers watched grinning, some grimacing, yesterday afternoon as Camperdene's Museum of the Year 1912 Curator Jake Wright focused a stream of water on a heap of photographs, furniture, fine art, and books. Before the hosedown, some cardboard was set on fire and the folks practiced using fire extinguishers and setting up pumps. A crew and truck from the Camperdene Fire Department came by and shot some water around. The idea was to impress everyone with just how much water one hose can deliver in a short time. Then there was an object removal drill. Human chains were formed and the groups saw how quickly they could get art works and books out of the building. Jake displayed two milk crates full of frosty books, and showed how to wrap them in freezer-paper so they wouldn't all congeal. A de-briefing centered on two key issues: The importance of having one person in charge and also of having a good working relationship with the fire department. Once the fire department arrives on the scene, the group was reminded, they own the building. 'Over my dead body,' joked

Museum of 1912 Association President Wallace Barrow of the Barrow Funeral Home, directly across the street from the museum.")

Susan Seymour-Stanton organized "A Salute to Museum-going Children." Within two days, Carlena Lagorio was calling again furious: "I want to know why I did not receive an invitation."

"To?" Jake asked.

"Don't give me that!" she barked. "The reception."

"Reception?"

"Who sent out the invitations?"

"Invitations?"

"Don't give me that. I didn't receive an invitation and I think I should have got an invitation. You are in trouble. I will see to that."

Veronica Pillsbury had just come in prior to Lagorio's call. Now she saw Jake holding the phone away from his ear, and she heard the caller squawking.

"Carlena," Jake asked, would you like to speak with Veronica Pillsbury?"

"No," Lagorio said. Then she changed her mind. "Yes. Put her on."

Jake looked pleadingly at Veronica Pillsbury who, with obvious reservations, took the phone. She told Jake, after she got off the phone, that Carlena was *furious* with her – and Jake – for not inviting her to the "Salute to Museum-going Children."

Now had it been me, I would have told Carlena Lagorio to go jump in a lake. But not my father. Before heading home, Jake phoned Wallace Barrow to ask for five minutes of his time. He went over to the mortuary. Barrow met him at the office door with beads of sweat on his forehead and an oriental fan in his hand. He led Jake down a hall to the cool, dark funeral parlor. "I hope you don't mind a dead body in the room," he says, gesturing Jake toward a chair. A white-haired old lady was laid to rest, encircled by flowers, on a broad-topped oak bureau. Jake sat.

Barrow asked him, would he care to know something helpful to know as concerned Carlena Lagorio? Jake thought on it. Barrow barged right on, whispering. "She tips 'em in."

Jake was looking over at the body at the bier.

"Did you hear me?" Barrow whispered. "I said, she *tips 'em in*." He was gesturing, with his right hand, the gusty downing of a tall drink. "She is known to take in a little from time to time."

As Jake departed the funeral home, Wheel was again telling him, for the umpteenth time, "You are going to have to learn how to deal with *women*."

CHAPTER NINE

"Summer arrived," my father wrote, "and the days began to melt together." Jake had a rough season of dealing with record-breaking heat, a broken air conditioner, and volunteers on a prison work-release program – courtesy of Camperdene District Court Judge Abraham Niemand, who had assigned sixteen year old Billy Sideauli to the museum. A new air-conditioner unit was being installed even as Jake welcomed Billy and set in with him, re-allocating shelving space in assorted display units. Billy hated the hard work, insisting museum work was for sissies solely. One day he just didn't show up. That was that.

Wallace Barrow walked over to the museum to make photocopies. Jake introduced him to Billy Sideauli. "No ball and chain?" Barrow guffawed. He admired the air-conditioner. Jake opened a file folder he was carrying, holding all the information about the unit's special features. Barrow ran his finger down the list, speaking out loud the most important considerations regarding the machine's proper use. He then opened the folder he'd brought with him, and made his photocopies. Jake asked him if he had a small saw he could loan to the museum. Billy would be needing it for the shelf re-allocation project. "Just make sure that jailbird doesn't saw through any window bars!" Barrow guffawed loudly, going out. "Call my boy, Reggie at the monument shop," he called back to Jake. "Reggie will have a saw."

Jake now noticed that his file folder with the information about the air-conditioner was gone and, in its place, was Wheel's folder. While waiting for Wheel to come back for his folder, Jake thought to have just a little peek inside.

The next morning Jake called Wallace Barrow to ask him if he'd taken home the air-conditioner file folder the day before, leaving behind his own manila folder by accident.

"Just a moment," Wheel said. "Damn! It's true. I'll be right over."

Wheel brought back the air-conditioner papers and retrieved his own papers and the copies he'd made of them. "Did you switch these?" he asked accusingly. "It's just not *like* me to do something like that."

"Wallace, you took the wrong folder with you when you left here yesterday."

"No, I surely did not."

"Wallace..." Jake started. But then, as he later recorded it, he decided just to let it go.

CHAPTER TEN

Now Jake had plenty to think about, him perusing a second set of photocopies made – these Jake had made – from the papers Wheel had unwittingly – wittingly? – left overnight at the museum.

When, in the middle of August, Reggie Barrow married Association Treasurer Angela Perry's daughter, Joan, the Barrow family had a big Barbecue party afterwards. This gave Jake plenty of opportunity to pick people's brains, to check up on some of the new information Jake now had about the museum. He took Captain Cunningham aside, and asked him how it had happened that, in 1950, museum curator Susanna Seymour had departed so suddenly.

"She didn't have anything to say about it, really" the Captain said plainly. In 1947, the Chairman of the Board, Carlena Lagorio's father Simon, had discussed a controversial idea with the Board Secretary, Wheel Barrow's father Henry. Henry adamantly blocked Simon's intent to bring his daughter Carlena on board as a museum staff member. By 1950, with Henry in bad health, approaching death, one of the last things he did was to oust the sitting curator replace her with his daughter. In 1950, when Simon died, Henry Barrow was made Chairman – contingent on Carlena's becoming acting curator.

"Simon was buried next to Louisa?" Jake asked.

"No one knows."

"No one knows where Simon was buried?"

"Nobody knows where *either one of them* was buried," Cunningham said, shrugging his shoulders. "It's a mystery."

"Carlena Lagorio became acting curator in 1950?"

"In September."

"Susanna Seymour disappeared?"

"It's a mystery."

"Did Carlena do a good job?

"I'd say yes," the Captain said. "By 1953, the number of summer visitors reached 2,000 people a month. The museum building was enlarged with a north addition. The $9,400 cost was funded partly by the State and partly by a local doctor, Walter Morton. The addition was given for the purpose of housing Morton's collection of Arts & Crafts pottery and Indian artifacts. Carlena put a five-year plan to beautify the Museum's grounds into place. The stockade fence around the museum was removed. New outbuildings were erected and old ones relocated. A sprinkler system was installed and 120 rosebushes planted. By 1958, summer visitation averaged more than 4,000 people per month. The staff was increased to four – Carlena, a curatorial assistant, a custodian, and a part-time gardener."

"And this was all funded how?"

"Mainly through the museum's own endowment fund, enhanced by private contributions and some annual allocations from the town and state. The town budget for Fiscal Year 1960 included $8,800 in capital improvements. A membership drive increased the total Association membership to around 800. In December, 1961, an archivist was hired and microfilming of archival papers began. The Queen Anne style carriage house was built by the Rotary Club at about that same time. Outside lighting was installed on the grounds. Carlena requested $17,000 from the town of Camperdene for Fiscal Year 1962-1963. A small gift shop began operating in the carriage house."

"It all ran quite smoothly?"

"Until 1965. The 1964-1965 city budget for the museum was set at $20,800. in 1965, Association President Henry Barrow pressed the Association to hire a professional curator – one having a Master's degree – for the Museum. That meant Carlena would have been out. She didn't like that. My understanding is, she went to some people she knew in the Hermetic Order of the Golden Dawn – friends of her parents – and, through the good offices of the Qabalistic Alchemist Arcanum, had a curse put on the man."

"Excuse me? "I said.

"Oh yeah," the Captain said. "She had some *connections*, let me tell you."

"The Cabbalist Alchemy Archivy?"

"The Qabalistic Alchemist Arcanum."

"They put a *curse* on Henry Barrow?"

"In fact."

This jelled *exactly* with what was in Wheel Barrow's file. "So?" I asked. "Did something awful happen to him?"

Jake

"Well for *one* thing," the Captain whispered in Jake's ear, "he *died*. That summer, visitation to the Museum exceeded 37,000 monthly. In the spring of 1965, the Museum Association voted Carlena Museum Curator, though she did not have the now mandatory Master's degree. That year, 1965, the museum got its first volunteer help. Carlena introduced "Annual Museum Day" that year. It drew in over 500 people. To Carlena's chagrin, Wheel Barrow was made Chairman of the Board in 1967. He met with state legislative committees and got the state budget for the museum *reduced*. He singlehandedly restructured the museum board and its committees, giving himself increased power in the running of the museum."

"Did he abuse his power?"

"What? Were you born yesterday?" Cunningham now shouted. "Of *course* he abused his power! Does the name *Clarence Richeson* mean anything to you?"

Jake scratched his head and shrugged his shoulders, pretending he'd never seen or heard the name.

"The Reverend Clarence Richeson. In the year 1912, the good Reverend Richeson, who'd murdered his former fince, Avis Linnell, was electrocuted."

"The electric chair in the Museum – that's the chair he was electrocuted in?"

"That's *right*," the Captain confirmed. "The thing is," he continued, "all the papers, documents, magazine articles – everything about the case – letters and diaries written by both Richeson and Avis Linnell – all are gone."

"Stolen?"

"It's supposed. Also correspondence between the Reverend Richeson and his lawyers which the writer Theodore Dreiser had gathered, along with Dreiser's notes toward a first draft of an abandoned novel he'd been writing about the case. The papers disappeared in 1967, the year Wheel came on Board as Association Chairman. He accused Carlena Lagorio of 'borrowing' the papers and things – and never returning them. He claimed Carlena had put them in a bank vault in Switzerland – all except certain of the papers which she'd kept for herself to sell at auction."

"Did she?"

"How would *I* know?" the Captain said, now shrugging *his* shoulders. "I only know that the next thing we knew, Carlena had resigned, and fled the country with an older man named Grady McBreeze, a friend of Carlena's father. She returned to Camperdene three months later, and was made Association Secretary. Frederick McCallom, having a Master's degree and ten years of museum experience under his belt, was hired to be Museum Curator. He was very professional. Everybody *hated* this guy. He clarified the relationship between the Museum Association and the town of Camperdene, recommending that the operations of the two should be wholly separate. The Association didn't agree, and took the town's money again that year – the Town appropriation for Fiscal Year 1970-1971 was $76,400. In June, the Bungalow wing was expanded on its west side for more research room. Final arrangements were made for the purchase of property east of the museum. Visitors that summer reached 37,400 monthly. Association membership rose to 164. Six hundred researchers used the Museum Archives. When I joined the Association, I just stayed in the background at first – I just kept my eyes and ears open."

"Waiting for something peculiar or unusual to happen?"

"Well, not so much *that* as just learn the ropes, get to know people, make my *own* power plays – know what I mean? In 1972, yet another 1912 Craftsman bungalow was purchased by the Association, and plans were formalized for relocating it to the museum grounds. Town funding for the museum was set at $72,300. A separate state appropriation of $29,100 was provided for relocation/restoration/renovation purposes. In September, the new wing arrived on the museum grounds. Renovation efforts flopped. In November, Board members agreed on the need to hire another – a *new* – curator."

"Whooosh, like *that*, McCallom was gone."

"That's right. In 1973. McCallom was courting the affection of the Massachusetts Department of Finance, which was attempting to claim title to the Museum's collections, citing a State Attorney General's opinion that the holdings of The Museum of the Year 1912 in fact should have reverted to the Massachusetts Historical Society after the death of Simon Lagorio. The museum board refused to send the State a list of museum holdings. The Massachusetts Historical Society made several attempts, through various state agencies, to assume control of The Museum of the Year 1912. State Senator Iris Holland, a Republican from Longmeadow, rebuffed their efforts. In 1974, Republican 33rd degree Mason President Gerald Ford appointed Republican 33rd degree Mason George Bush head of the the CIA. In 1974, The Museum fell into complete disarray, occasioning public criticism. No Annual Museum Day was held, due, as Wheel Barrow put it, asI recall, to a perceived 'general antipathy of the community toward the museum at this time.' Under considerable pressure, Frederick McCallom resigned. On May 1, Hollie Greenspan was selected from 55 applicants to become Museum Curator."

"My predecessor. Now in Nova Scotia."

"Your predecessor," Cunningham said. "She came aboard. Wheel, as Board Chairman, set up a volunteer auxiliary, which grew rapidly. In June, 1973, the first Folk Arts Fair, on the Museum grounds, attracted more than 5,500 visitors. In September, Sam Barnaby, a Camperdene developer, offered to donate the historic J. Marsden Bungalow to the Museum if it was removed from his recently purchased property. The Museum Board set a goal of raising $35,000 for the relocation. A community-wide fund-raising campaign began. Wheel directed the fund-raising committee; I managed publicity for the campaign. The Marsden Bungalow was moved, intact, six blocks, to the museum grounds. Hundreds lined Osborne Street to watch. The successful move got media attention across the state. The town appropriation for Fiscal Year 1974-1975 included funding for a second full-time maintenance worker. The Museum's staff now included five full-time and five part-time employees. Nearly 40,000 people visited the Museum. Over 500 researchers consulted the Archives."

"How do you keep all this inside your head?" Jake marveled bluntly.

"*Idiot Savant*," the Captain said. "I can read the Camperdene telephone book backwards, close it, then tell you everyone and their middle initial, if it's given, who lives on Juniper or Prentice Streets. It's just one peculiar gift, like any another. Sometimes I wish I could change it, trade it in so that I had greater virtue, moral power, more nobility, dignity, higher consciousness, and so on."

"You seem like a pretty decent guy," Jake volunteered.

"Don't get me wrong," he said. "I have my qualities. But I – well, there are things that matter which I will never tell you of, which you should know about. Well, anyway, Wheel Barrow was offered a million dollars for his property immediately opposite the Museum, but he refused to sell it. Back in the mid-70s, the Folk Arts Fair drew 4,000 visitors. A fellow named Willy Bishop was hired to coordinate the Museum's educational programs, for which the state legislation had just approved $65,000, and the volunteer auxiliary. Outreach programs included traveling artifact kits. The Camperdene Artists Guild secured a five-year lease on the west wing for a combination workshop/gallery. In the late 70s, the volunteer force increased to fifty. Artifact and archival holdings grew apace. During the winter, four new employees were hired under a federal program that funded the jobs for periods varying from six to eighteen months. In early 1980, the 1912-style windmill was constructed on the grounds. Cuts in Federal spending led to the loss of six employees in the spring of 1981.

"Extensive work on Museum properties began as workers removed rental properties adjacent to the museum. A major renovation of the museum began, including restoration of the stone fireplace. A new exhibit, 'Opening the Family Trunk,' displayed clothing – outfits, fashions – people had worn in 1912. A reduction of state agency budgets by ten percent prompted the Museum to increase fund-raising efforts and raise Association membership dues. In the mid-80s, the gazebo was constructed on the west lawn. Funds for the professional education of museum staff increased to $4,000. New shelves were installed in the museum library to hold 8,000 volumes. The cumulative total of items cataloged reached 19,400. Museum visitation totaled 75,000.

"The first computer, acquired for use in the Archives, was obtained, at which time the state reduced the Museum's budget by nearly half. Still, new programs were introduced, expanding the Museum's role in public education, including high school and college level scholarships. A grant from the Institute of Museum Services funded expansion planning. Further property was purchased west of the Museum but a freeze on state spending restricted further development. The Memorial Rose Garden was completely rebuilt. A water garden and a goldfish pond were installed near the windmill. Visitation increased to 90,000, and volunteers donate a total of 22,000 hours in the late 80s. The Archives acquired its largest single collection, the George P. Farrow collection, which includes over 1,700 maps.

"The Museum began a closer association with the Massachusetts Archaeological Society and we gained accreditation from the American Association of Museums. Out of 6,500 museums nationwide, only 700 had received this designation. Plans were under way for expansion on the western end of the museum with a 30,000-square-foot building – half exhibit space, half storage. Forward planning also includes expanded book publishing and publications efforts. In the mid-90s the Amphitheater and the northwest parking lot were completed. A new entrance was cut into the west side of the museum, providing improved handicapped access. Rob Czjesch was hired as graphic artist and exhibit designer. The Board voted to remove Hollie Greenspan as curator. Our reason? We didn't feel obliged to give one. Julia Seymour-Stanton was made acting curator a short while. Then you were interviewed – and hired. This may come as a surprise to you Jake, but Carlena Lagorio assumed, from your name – Jacob Friedman Wright – that you were Jewish, perhaps descended from such Friedmans as had certainly once hobnobbed with the leading Jewish families in the good old days – the Wertheimers, Oppenheimers, Schusters, Sterns, and Rothschilds, etcetera. She insisted that was your best selling point. Wheel said you looked like some dumb goof who couldn't tie his own shoelaces in the sunlight, but this time Carlena prevailed. Excuse me," the Captain now said abruptly, lurching away very briskly. "Barrow beckons."

Wheel Barrow, in a blood-red apron and a high white chef's hat, had just stepped away from a hot barbecue and, with both hands in multicolored cooking mittens, was waving Cunningham over very vigorously.

Along about 3:00 that afternoon a big truck pulled up, filled with "energy efficient lighting." After months of scheming and calculating – and what with a rebate offered by the Electric Company on this "energy efficient lighting" – Wheel Barrow and Captain Cunningham had bought these lights for the Museum. Their understanding was, the Electric Company was going to also install them. They were told, this was not at all the case. The two decided on the spot, while eating their spare ribs at the wedding feast, to return the whole batch until such time as the Electric Company could have their installers present and ready to install the lights.

About a month passed. A second truckload arrived, but – again – no installers. The Captain called the firm to set up an appointment for him, the truck driver, and the installers all to be at the museum at the same time on the same day. The Electric Company's representative informed Captain Cunningham that they had never intended to install any lights. They only sold the lights. And so the lights again went back to the warehouse – forever perhaps.

CHAPTER ELEVEN

Things continued to roll out much that way. When the September Fall Festival weekend came along, it rained all day on the Saturday, which was good in that it brought the people in to the great hall at the High School to see the exhibit booths. The Friends joined the museum staff at the festival. My father was all smiles, joking around with everyone, shaking everybody's hands. Audrey said she had to hand it to Jake, for his having got sullen Mary Tuchlein to participate.

On Monday, a blue, dazzling, chilly early autumn morning, Mary complained bitterly of the cold. She said she couldn't work under such circumstances. She told Jake she'd be going home for lunch when Audrey came in, *and she wouldn't be coming back.* Jake looked her straight in the eyes and said, "Mary, I believe it."

Reggie Barrow dropped in. "You got a minute?"

Jake took him over to the 1912 Olympics display case at the end of one of two long reading tables. Barrow Junior said, "I got a problem. It's probably a misunderstanding. Don't get me wrong. I know you'll take this well. You know these displays of local bookbinders you're having?" he began.

"Yes."

"Well, did you work it out with the Artifacts Committee? Carlena Lagorio says you didn't, and that you just went and put an article in the paper about all these upcoming displays, and she says she don't know nothing about it."

Reggie said he didn't know what to do, but he would try to figure *something* out, and he'd be getting back to Jake on it.

Jake wished him luck, then got back to reality again.

Jake called Captain Cunningham and asked that the Temporary Displays Committee meet in order to discuss these and other matters. The Captain said Jake had taken certain display cases out of the hands of the Temporary Displays Committee, had not asked their permission to use them, and that he had showed he was not willing to work with them. Jake suggested to the Captain that he and Carlena should actually hold Temporary Displays Committee meetings occasionally, that they should communicate with him, the museum director, and with each other, and that the museum should have thematic, informational, interesting, enlightening temporary displays.

The Captain suggested local factories ought to show off *their* wares in the display cases. Jake told him this was *fine* – if they could just see to it that these would be *interesting* displays.

Jake left Camperdene just before 11:00 and arrived at Springfield's Sheraton hotel shortly after noon – just as notoriously eloquent Wordsward College Library School Dean Preston – bald, dome-waxed, and wearing a silvery satin three-piece suit – was finishing his Keynote Speech at the New England Library Association Fall Conference. He'd been illuminating the intricacies of conflict interpretation, grievances, and other problems that result from collective bargaining contracts. At half past noon he finished, asking, "any questions?"

A hand went up. The woman began: "I met you last year at a conference and asked you a question and you gave me a beautiful response which changed my life." Dean Preston interrupted quickly, quipping, "Just don't tell my wife," and left the room.

Afterwards, Jake joined Dean Preston at the hotel bar for beers. Old Preston apparently talked on and on about the death of God, rampant tumultuous stupidity and evil, and imminent apocalypse, then the two went down under the Sheraton to the parking lot to Jake's car, so he could drive Preston over to his parking spot. At the car, Jake couldn't find his parking stub.

"No matter," Jake said.

"It matters," Preston countered. "They'll charge you for *the whole fucking day*, and that's *no small change* at the *Sheraton*." Preston suggested Jake may have left the stub at the registration desk upstairs. But he hadn't. And it wasn't at the Hotel's front desk, either. Jake went all over the place, looking for it. Ultimately, he found it in his front shirt pocket. Embarrassed, he went back to Preston, standing patiently by Jake's clunker of a car, his spinach green Jeep. He began to explain. Preston interrupted, saying, "It doesn't matter." The two then went to where Preston had parked his spinach green *Jaguar*. Now at its wheel, departing, having rolled down the side window, Preston sang out to Jake, "You can't always get what you want, but if you try sometimes you just might find God works in mysterious ways!"

CHAPTER TWELVE

Back in Camperdene, Jake set to work with renewed energy, promoting the "Art of the Book" artisans – bookbinders, printers, calligraphers. The initial guest exhibitor was Camperdene bookbinder and Camperdene Museum Friends president Nicholas Wentworth, who gave an introductory presentation illuminating Elbert Hubbard and the Roycrofters movement in East Aurora, New York in the early 1900s, focusing on the book "The Myth in Marriage" written by Hubbard's wife Alice and bound in stamped leather by the papermaker and designer Dard Hunter.

In the middle of this presentation, Jake got a call from Veronica Pillsbury, recently separated from her husband, Rolf who, up to his ears with *troubles*, had moved out. Veronica's Tequila-drinking sister Ginny had moved in. Veronica's brother, an apparently good-natured ski bum, Bernard, had moved in, too.

Bernard and Ginny had taken Veronica's new car and gone shopping at a mall. Veronica was now calling to say that Bernard and Ginny had called to say Ginny had lost the car keys. Veronica would have to go and get them. Could she borrow Jake's car? After Nick Wentworth finished his lecture and everybody emptied out of the museum, Jake closed it up and went out in search of Bernard and Ginny. They'd be at the so-and-so mall, at the so-and-so fast food restaurant there. They were very grateful when Jake got there. It would be weeks before he'd hear about what became of the car: new keys were obtained, the car ultimately broke down and, still under warranty, was returned to the dealer.

It was at this time that problems with the computers flared up. Audrey flatly refused to have anything to do with the Internet. Mary Tuchlein warmed up to it, however. Audrey was furious, what with Mary networking away. Mary had always insisted that she'd never have anything to do with computers and now, there she was, typing away. Audrey was livid. By 5:00, Jake could see that Audrey was turning purple at the circulation desk. Upon leaving for dinner, she blurted at Jake, "I've never been so furious in all my life."

"Because of the computer?"

"Not the computer," Audrey said. "She – *at* the computer. *She was against it, too.* I'm *honest.* I tell you what I *think*! Some people *aren't* so honest."

Audrey stormed out. Jake called after her, "I think we should assume we're *all* honest people here."

"Not everyone!" Audrey called back at him and, tears flowing, she was *out.*

Wallace Barrow came in with a dull, military-display-propagating pal. This time they had Polish woodwork – a box, an eagle, an old man carved from a gnarled branch, etc.– contributed to the museum by Mr. and Mrs. H. Kamininski. As they installed their exhibit, Jake said courteously, "If you need any props or signs or anything, just let me know. Nice pieces. What a lot of work. Well, they're going to look good in there," he lied. "Great display."

News from Minna, swelling as her pregnancy neared the final month. Minna was making arrangements to return to Massachusetts. She was in touch with a midwife in New Hampshire, Jean, who would deliver me.

Amid all the regular flurry of projects, basic workload, taking care of the daily details and all of that in those swiftly passing late autumn days, Jake took a day off to go to Boston to pick up Minna and Mark at Logan Airport. This went well. Jake cried when he saw them.

Then it was Halloween. Jake took Mark out Trick-or-Treating in warm, eerie, rainy weather. Mark (Superman) was dragging his paper bag as he went along. He was just going up the steps to the tenth or twelfth house when Jake noticed his sagging bag bottom had broken open. He looked, and began to cry. As it happened, the bag had *just* broke. In the headlights of a passing car, they could see the straight line of Mark's candy stretching across a lawn and the street to where they stood. Jake quickly assured Mark that all was well, and went and stuffed his coat pockets with the candy. A neighbor saw their plight and volunteered a new plastic bag and they continued Trick-or-Treating.

Thanksgiving came and went. Still no baby. Then, at the end of the month, in their home, a midwife, Jean, amid great confusion, strife, and bounty, delivered me, Jillian Rose Wright. A time of joy and love and fun followed despite (as my mother said later) my not letting them get any sleep.

CHAPTER THIRTEEN

Captain Cunningham had invited Jake, just prior to my birth, to get away – to join him in hiking in Vermont's now snow white Green Mountains. The Captain, besides being the custodian of the Lutheran Church and Vice President of The Museum of the Year 1912, was also the head of the Camperdene Historic Commission and of the Conservation Commission. He and a bunch of his Conservation Commission cronies were leaving Camperdene that Friday evening, returning Sunday night. Jake phoned The Captain to announce my birth and to say he wouldn't be joining in the hike. He'd be spending time with his family, getting birth announcements out, and...

"In other words," Cunningham interrupted, "*No?*"

"Yes."

"*Don't* spend the weekend at the *museum*. Promise?"

"I promise."

He stayed away, in fact. Then, on Monday morning, another miracle happened. A man bearing a gift appeared at the museum. Herman Glucklischsman came in and handed Jake a check for a substantial chunk of money, given in memory of his father, Herbert Glucklischsman, "a patron and staunch supporter of The Museum of the Year 1912 in his time." Herman stipulated that, as his father had been "a printer and a designer and a maker of books," his contribution would be earmarked solely for use in developing the special collection, 'The Art of the Book in Camperdene."

My father's growing plans for the collection included having, beyond representative bindings, also samples of handmade papers, marbled papers, works of calligraphy, and so on. He'd already begun to gather, in file folders, information about Camperdene's book people, as he liked to call them – including papers donated to ~~me~~ *him* by each of them. He supplemented this with purchases of books illuminating calligraphy, typography, printing, and bookbinding. Camperdene's book artisans were beginning to be more eager in contributing to the Collection. Jake was working on having each boookbinder re-bind one or more of our most valuable but cover-damaged books – each as he or she saw fit.

The whole project had begun in Jake's head – just an idle scheme, really. A big concern of the book people was that their works would not be cared for in the unknown future – in the absence of a curator or anybody else who might give a hoot about keeping the collection intact. But Jake was thrilled and just went forward with this scheme. He got it through – or past – the Executive Committee of the Board of Curators of the Association, and now Herman Glucklischsman had appeared from out of nowhere, a generous donor securing the collection's existence and to sustain its growth.

There was much to celebrate. Beyond his enjoyment of loving, and of the pleasure he had in the progeny that had come of their loving, my father had also made many friends – decent colleagues and associates living in this community otherwise densely peppered with unhappy people – wretched, cranky, angry, mean, vile, misguided people. But not everything that happened was ridiculous or insane. All in all, I know he felt quite blessed. He went along, lighthearted mainly.

The Camperdene Garden Club decked the museum's rooms beautifully. The Annual Holiday Celebration drew more than a hundred children and nearly forty adults. There was singing and there were stories, and then St. Nicholas arrived – silver-bearded Friends' President and bookbinder Nick Wentworth seated by the fireplace in gold-trimmed purple velvet robe with shining satin sash, delivering a buoyant, cheering reading of Dylan Thomas' *A Child's Christmas in Wales*. My brother Mark would still be singing *Jingle Bells* and

Rudolph the Red Nosed Reindeer come April and May, so strong were the impressions made that day.

On Christmas morning, while snow fell, my family merrily cooed and sang, lighting candles and sparklers we'd placed in our tree. Then we opened our presents. Mark got his prayed-for red wooden wagon. I got about a dozen pairs of Winnie the Pooh pajamas from well-wishers all around the globe. There was nothing sweeter to my father than hugging and tumbling around with us two kids in our flannel pajamas that Christmas morning. A few local people had sent Christmas cards. Oddly, Carlena Lagorio had telephoned with Minna on Christmas Eve, meanly wishing our entire family our just desserts and so forth, putting a damper on any festive mood Minna might have been in prior to the call.

Jake sent out *Happy New Year* greetings to all Museum Association committee members, setting dates for first-of-the year meetings. He was eager to get the ball rolling. He would raise the dead, if need be, he said. He was up for it – anything – bring it on.

CHAPTER FOURTEEN

At the outset of the new year, Wheel Barrow was front page news: "Wallace Barrow Oversees Change at The Museum of the Year 1912."

"Wallace Barrow, known as 'Wheel' to his closest associates, a lifelong Camperdene resident, once visited the museum as a child, never thinking he'd eventually be running it as President of the Museum Association," wrote Alice Armour Armstrong. "The Association is a private Corporation composed of twenty-five trustees and Corporators who meet once a year to elect officers, and an executive committee to oversee museum operations. The Association runs the museum, which serves the town of Camperdene but is not owned by it.

"'The four winds blow —east, west, south, and north – and still the Association has not changed much,' said Barrow, who lives next door to the museum in the Barrow Company Funeral Home, a firm founded by his grandfather. 'By God!' Barrow exclaimed, 'I've been around. I've traveled. Wherever I travel – and I include Europe – I never forget the Museum. I've been to Europe seven times. My Swedish wife speaks Swedish. The two of us go all over, going into buildings and looking things over, you know,' Barrow was quoted as saying.

Three days later, Jake delivered a speech before the Camperdene Rotary Club, talking of the importance of the elastics and suspenders industries in the early history of Camperdene. He spoke of Simon and Louisa Lagorio and how Simon had become a suspenders manufacturer and philanthropist, with a focus on religious and educational institutions and causes. Jake spoke of how Simon's wife Louisa had almost single-handedly brought the Museum of the Year 1912 into being in the year 1913.

Rotary Club member Wheel Barrow was not present at the Rotary Club meeting when Jake spoke. He did show up for the first meeting that year of the museum, proposing to have the museum be closed every Thursday, all day, between February and September. He proposed hiring temporary "Designated Help" for filling the places of staff members out sick or on vacation. The Designated Helpers were named: (1) Wallace Barrow's wife Candyce; (2) Captain Cunnigham; and (3) Carlena Lagorio." The proposals were approved unanimously. Jake proposed developing a new Museum of the Year 1912 logo. He had brought in a sketch he'd made with the help of Friends' President Nick Wentworth. Carlena Lagorio requested an alternate design. A Museum Logo Design Committee was proposed, and adopted, with Carlena Lagorio at its head. Within the space of six days, the committee would meet, reject *all* of the logo ideas, and then disband.

At the same meeting, Barrow formally acknowledged a recent Christmas gifts to the museum, a television donated by the Camperdene Media Cable Company. He said he had a friend, a past president of the Rotary Club, Roland Henselmeier, who'd told Barrow he'd donate a stand from the Arts & Crafts era, "probably from 1912," to put the TV on.

The next day, the Camperdene Daily Journal carried an article about community service organizations – the Lions Club, the Rotary Club, and so on. It focused its attention on the Rotary Club, quoting one Roland Henselmeier at great length. "The results of their contributions are visible all over town. Henselmeier, past president of the Rotary Club, said that in the past year the Club built a new pavilion at the Town Park, awarded scholarships to Camperdene High School Students and donated a coffee table dating either from the year 1911 or the year 1912 to the Museum of the Year 1912."

Jake wrote to Roland Henselmeier immediately, informing him the museum hadn't actually received any table from the Rotary Club, asking for help in determining what kind of table the Rotary Club believed it had contributed. Henselmeier told Jake it had been a nightstand, but he in fact had no idea when that might have happened or where it had been put, if anywhere.

At a special emergency meeting of the Rotary Club, Roland Henselmeier stood up amid his fellow Rotarians and denounced the Museum of the AYear 1912 – especially Jake's "provocative" letter. Corporation president Wallace Barrow, present at the session, was not pleased. He departed the meeting in a huff. He phoned Association Vice President Captain Cunningham and arranged to meet with him prior to the closing of the museum that night. The two entered ominously. They announced to Jake they needed to speak with him. He closed the museum and sat down with them at one of the long tables in the periodicals room. He was instructed, plain and simple, to write an apology to Roland Henselmeier – post haste.

I would have told Cunningham and Barrow to go hang themselves, but not my father. Oh no, not him. "Mr. Barrow," my unflappable, sanguine father responded calmly. "Mr. Cunningham. I did nothing out of line. Mr. Henselmeier has no right or reason to speak poorly of this institution." But Barrow again *demanded* Jake apologize to Roland Henselmeier, to set the matter right. And my father complied.

As Jake could not reach Roland Henselmeier by phone. he wrote out longhand a polite, brief note: "I intended a courteous inquiry, but I see now that I as much took you by surprise as I myself had been taken by surprise. Now we're both stuck with a misunderstanding, and I apologize. This matter pains me very much. I am sorry things took the turn they did."

Roland Henselmeier responded, "I appreciate very much your letter and look forward to continued efforts in support of the Museum of the Year 1912. Sometimes things go astray, but most often, as in this instance, can be put back on track to the advantage of our interests. I accept your comments and look forward to future contacts as well as correcting the oversight that gave rise to our communication."

In the meantime, a new Corporation member was assigned by Wallace Barrow to the newly formed Artifacts Committee: Mr. Roland Henselmeier. In one of the Museum display cases Henselmeier boldly installed materials he had collected in his travels in Alaska in the 1950s along with his wife's 1920s umbrella collection and several of her most prized antique kitchen utensils.

To my father's surprise, my mother turned out to be a huge fan of the display of Mrs. Roland Henselmeier's collections of umbrella's and kitchen gear and Mr. Henselmeier's collection of Alaskan souvenirs. Though that irked Jake, he also felt deepening tranquility arising from their mystical bond – the peculiar struggle and aggravation of their marriage, their sharing through thick and thin, their surviving. But that wouldn't sustain them. I think my mother felt no pain at all from things that just about *crushed* my father, whose avocation seemed avid, dogged recognition of wrongs, him ever dedicated to discerning what was evil from what was good. In my mother's way of thinking, there were many more worlds and lifetimes of train wrecks and accidents and opportunities for fixing everything. Why get bogged down? And what was the hurry? It made him crazy.

Henselmeier next installed a "Salute to America" exhibit of "popular culture artifacts" – a plastic hot dog, a baseball glove with a tennis ball, an American flag, patriotic medallions, cross-country maps, a three-cornered Revolutionary War soldier's cap, a Coca Cola bottle, and Chinese firecrackers.

Now Captain Cunningham was headline news: "Powderkeg Cunningham – Preserving the Past."

"Dick 'Powderkeg' Cunningham is sitting in an alcove of the Museum of the Year 1912," wrote Alice Armour Armstrong for the Camperdene Daily Journal, "recounting why it took him so long to make his mark in Camperdene. 'I distrust these pretentious clowns who move to town and immediately start meddling,' he says carefully. He tells of his moving to town twenty years ago, when his six children were toddlers. 'Now they're all grown,' he chuckles wryly. Bearded, with a pipe poking out from one of the front pockets of his plaid flannel shirt, Powderkeg's salt-and-pepper eyebrows bob up and down over his bifocals as he talks. As a Town Meeting member, clerk of the Conservation Commission, Vice President of the Museum Association, chair of the town's historical commission, and as an active member of the Camperdene Historical Society, he says he's quietly gone about becoming 'unofficial guardian of the town's heritage.' Powderkeg, who also sweeps and vacuums at the Unitarian church, says he's lucky to have a wife with a good assembly line job at the elastic company, enabling him to dedicate himself to his 'higher calling'."

CHAPTER FIFTEEN

Wallace Barrow completely forgot the January meeting of the Corporation's Executive Committee. Corporators called him and he crossed the street. Jake joined them after closing the museum at eight o'clock. There was considerable discussion going on, concerning a pen sketch of the museum that one of Carlena Lagorio's nephews had made, which she proposed as a new logo for Museum Association business cards and stationery. Jake kept his mouth shut.

Barrow introduced a new plan concerning the purchase of ~~books~~. *artifacts.* Veronica Pillsbury had told him that people were asking her when would the museum ever be getting any new *stuff*? This, despite Jake's buying several fine items in recent months.

Barrow said, "From now on, only Artifacts Committee Chairwoman Carlena Lagorio can sign the "Authorization of Payment" form. Only the Artifacts Committe will order any acquisitions, and the Artifacts Committee will pay for them." And that was that. The curator was now out of the picture.

At the next Artifacts Committee meeting, Carlena Lagorio brought in a pile of clippings from New York City antiques store catalogs. These were discusssed. Each and all of the items went on the *to be ordered* list. Veronica Pillsbury and Jake had brought in other items to discuss. But by then Lagorio had got the others off and chatting about entirely other things.

At the end of January, the Captain came in, poking around while Jake was out. He left a note for Jake, refusing to sign the "Authorization of Payment" form: "Carlena Lagorio is the only one who will sign for new acquisitions – after Artifacts Committee approval. You'll have to differentiate other expenses and list them separately. Also – no Board of Museum Coalition Incentive Grant monies are left for buying items so I don't know what account they possibly could to be paid from."

Association treasurer Angela Perry came in, and Jake simply had her sign the Authorization for Payment form. He wrote a note for Captain Cunningham: "All acquisitions received that had been ordered by the Artifacts Committee prior to the Executive Committee decision to make Carlena Lagorio sole acquisitions purchaser are being paid for herewith. Please note that no new acquisitions have been ordered since that decision was made."

In early February, Town Department Heads met, Camperdene Mayor Barton Driscoll presiding. Afterwards, he took Jake aside to tell him, "I want you to hear it from me. The museum is going to be eliminated."

"Eliminated? I don't think so. Now begins the 'Save the Museum' campaign."

"We'll burn that bridge when we get to it," the mayor said, shaking his head in disappointment as he turned and walked away.

Jake went back to the museum. He called Wallace Barrow. He left a message to have him call Jake at his earliest opportunity. He reached Captain Cunningham later in the afternoon. He said he had some time to come over. He and Jake went out for a short walk. Jake told him what Mayor Driscoll had said.

"*Eliminated?*" Cunningham asked coyly. "He said the Museum is going to be *eliminated?*"

"That's what he said," serene all-bearing Jake reiterated.

"I'd like to eliminate *him*," the Captain blurted out. "We could strap him in the electric chair in the museum – the chair Reverend Richeson was electrocuted in. No one would need to know. You know, I've done some sleuthing. Do you remember my telling you I'd discovered

Carlena Lagorio had *borrowed* the Richeson/Avis Linnell papers gathered together by Theodore Dreiser – an archive estimated to be worth around two million dollars? I'm sure now that most of these are sitting in a bank vault somewhere in Switzerland – except for those papers Carlena long since sold at auction. She *stole* them, Jake. I can't prove anything, but I know I'm right. Gads, we sure could use such money *now*. But no. Carlena Lagorio is rolling in dough, and the Museum is struggling. Only Carlena can sign the Authorization of Payment form for new acquisitions – after Artifacts Committee approval. There's no Board of Museum Coalition Incentive Grant monies left. And the mayor wants to eliminate the museum. What are you going to do?"

"*Do?* I'm going to initiate a very active and highly visible campaign to keep the museum open."

"Do you know how Reverend Richeson got caught?"

"Pardon?" Jake said.

"*No*, he certainly didn't get *pardoned*," Cunningham scoffed. "He didn't get caught red-handed, but he was, as you put it, 'highly visible.' He could have done things differently." The Captain took from his inner coat pocket a photocopy of a newspaper account of the Reverend's confession: "January 12, 1912" (The Hansboro Pioneer, North Dakota): "Prominent Boston Pastor Confesses" – "Rev. C.V.T. Richeson, former pastor of Immanuel Baptist Church of Cambridge, Massachusetts, today made a written confession to the effect that he poisoned his former sweetheart, Miss Avis Linnell. The statement was given into the hands of his counsel who made the confession public at 1 o'clock on Saturday. Just before noon the judges of the superior court and district attorney went into conference at the court house and about an hour later representatives of the press were called to the office of William A. Morse, leading counsel of the accused clergyman and given the confession, which was dated three days previous. Counsel refused to comment on it. It is said the only hope of saving Richeson from death in the electric chair after his confession, is by having him adjudged insane or by commutation of his sentence by the governor and the executive council. The death penalty is the only sentence that can be inflicted by the state upon a verdict of guilty of murder in the first degree. District Attorney Pelletier admitted Richeson might possibly be brought into court before the day set for the trial, but that such action depended upon the attitude of his counsel. This is regarded as an indication that the district attorney and court might find a legal way to accept a plea of guilty of murder in the second degree and permit a life sentence. As Richeson stands before the law, he is indicted of murder in the first degree in taking the life of Miss Linnell by giving her cyanide potassium."

"Unbelievable," Jake said. "Cyanide."

"Read this," the Captain said, handing over a second, undated (and headline-less), photocopy of a news clipping. Jake read, "Clarence V.T. Richeson, age 36, charged with murder, was executed by electrocution in Massachusetts on Tuesday, May 21, 1912. The former minister was electrocuted for the murder of Miss Avis Linnell, a Hyannis Port girl to whom he had been engaged."

"Keep those," Cunningham told Jake, now turning to go out. "They might come in handy."

Now Barrow was on the phone, asking questions. Jake again explained what the mayor had said about eliminating the museum. "Eliminate the *museum*," Wallace fumed. "That's going too far. I had thought the worst we'd face would be we'd have to let Audrey go and – what's her name? The little girl in the back." (Sixty-year-old Mary Tuchlein.)

"Mary."

"Yes. Mary. And leave you upstairs and the girl downstairs – what's her name, the Stanton girl?" (Julia Seymour-Stanton, fifty.)

"Julia."

"Yes. The Stanton girl. I thought they'd at least leave us the two positions."

The next evening, on Tuesday, Captain Cunningham said frankly, "I trust you understand, Jake, to try to keep the museum open, Carlena Lagorio wants to see you you *unemployed*. How am I supposed to stop her? You ought to be thinking very seriously about finding another job."

"What is the Association going to do?" Jake asked.

"What is the Association going to *do*?" the Captain echoed. He shrugged his shoulders.

On Saturday, Ben Mulvane told Jake he'd talked with The Captain. "Things look grim," he said. "Do you know that Cunningham's not going to do anything about this? He's got his own agenda. As I understand it, he's going to let the museum be closed down. He's going to say nothing, do nothing! Do you believe it? He's got the notion he'll just let it close. The staff is going to be let go. You will go. The Captain will run it. They'll keep the place open a few hours a week. The Captain will be in there. He'll have his own little private museum to play with. He'll be in seventh heaven. We've got to do something."

Alice Armour Armstrong wrote in the Camperdene Daily Journal of cash being in short supply "should Town Meeting members follow the Finance Committee's recommendation to allocate zero funding for The Museum of the Year 1912 next year. The jobs of the four full-time employees and the part-time custodian, paid by the town, will go. Lobbying with Town Meeting members for support of the museum is tricky. The museum's status as a 'non-profit' agency means its Corporation members cannot engage in lobbying.

Powderkeg Cunningham was out and about, telling folks the museum would remain open *no matter what* – even if the museum lost town funding. He told Jake he was against any tax hike – he would sooner see the museum close down than that he should pay more taxes.

The Camperdene Daily Journal printed "An Open Letter" from Association member Ben Mulvane: "Last week I read alarming news in the local papers. Mayor Driscoll has proposed 'eliminating Town funding for the Museum of the Year 1912.' He proposed this course of action because he feels the institution 'could survive independently.' Another newspaper has quoted Mayor Driscoll's saying 'The parks and recreation department and the Museum of the Year 1912 have the best chances for obtaining outside support. The museum has an alternative funding source.' I know the town faces some difficult economic times. But the Mayor's view, that the museum could survive without Town financial support is flawed. The Town needs the museum. The museum could not 'survive independently' without Town aid. The Museum Association simply cannot fund the museum's day-to-day expenses. Without Town finds (moneys that historically have provided staff salaries), the Association will have to cut museum hours and staffing. The Association will have no choice but authorize such painful cuts. Could we actually use the moneys from Association endowments, as the Mayor suggests? The Executive Board of the Museum Association ought to be hesitant about using such funds. These funds were not donated to the Association to pay for day-to-day operations; to do so would be a betrayal of a Trust, and would discourage future donations. I for one oppose the budget of the Town Administrator. If you feel strongly about this subject, as I do, please let me hear from you. We need to show our support. Also contact your elected Town Meeting representatives, and demand continued funding for The Museum of the Year 1912."

Ardent museum advocate Verononica Pillsbury responded, "As a fellow Corporator of the Museum of the Year 1912, I wish to state that I am entirely in agreement with Benjamin Mulvane's letter. Our Town faces difficult times, but we have met them before. To my knowledge, town funding for the museum has never before faced elimination. Instead of depriving our people of something so vital, let us rise up and meet the challenge this problem presents. It recently came to my attention that one of the first places a father took his children after they had moved to town was The Museum of the Year 1912. Would he have the same impression of our town if he had found the door locked; if he had been required to pay a fee or had been limited in any other way in the use of this museum?"

Association Treasurer Angela Perry responded with brevity and clarity, "The Mayor's proposal to eliminate town funding for the Museum of the Year 1912 is, indeed, alarming. As Ben Mulvane has told the press, Mayor Drsicoll has shown that he does not understand how our museum functions. I am opposed to any budget that eliminates funding for the museum. I plan to contact town meeting representatives to ask for their support."

Headline: "Camperdene Warned on Museum."

"Wallace Barrow, the President of the non-profit Corporation that owns the Museum of the Year 1912 said yesterday that the Mayor's proposal to eliminate town funding of the facility could result in layoffs and curtailed hours of operation. 'This could be a real setback,' said Barrow. He said the Executive Committee of the Association's board of directors would be meeting Thursday to discuss how to react to the potential cuts. 'We don't know if this will be the worst scenario (total loss of town funding) or if it will be something less,' said Barrow. 'We will probably take some steps Thursday night.' Two weeks ago Mayor Driscoll warned Millstonians that town funding for the museum may have to be eliminated. Barrow said yesterday that perhaps Driscoll mistakenly believes the Corporation's private endowments could enable it to continue running with minimal impact to its operation, should the town funding be cut. Barrow has said nothing about what devastation the cuts could bring."

The Executive Committee of the Museum Association met at the long tables near the display case for the 1912 Olympics. At the outset, Barrow asked Jake what he wished to report as curator. Jake said he only wished to know when he could expect his long-overdue performance appraisal; he said he would be glad to put everything else on the back-burner in order to get to the matter at hand. Barrow said Captain Cunningham would have something for Jake the following day. The phone rang. It was for Barrow.

Barrow was out of the room for about five minutes. He came back and said it had been Corporator Jennifer Sariff, who had received a letter from Ben Mulvane. Carlena Lagorio said, "Jennifer called me, too, and had asked me to say so. I guess I don't need to tell you, now, that she called. And I don't think I need to tell anybody here what Jennifer had to say."

They went around in circles, discussing how to react to the potential cuts. They resolved they'd go before the Finance Committee with the originally proposed budget.

Headline: "Superintendent Bonaventura Evaluated: F." Alice Armour Armstrong of the Camperdene Daily Journal wrote about the Superintendent of Schools, Michael Bonaventura, "The School Committee has evaluated Bonaventura's performance. While walking on water has rarely been a required skill for school superintendents, that doesn't mean Michael Bonaventura hasn't considered it. He told School Committee members this week that it also wouldn't hurt if he were stronger than a speeding bullet and able to leap tall buildings in a single bound."

Captain Cunningham called Jake to say he was going to come in with Jake's Performance Appraisal.

He was there within the hour. He sat my father down. He said that although he'd worked from the notes of others on the Board, the final draft of the document was his: "Performance Appraisal, Curator. Overall performance: above average. Interest in job: excellent. Responsibility: excellent. Knowledge of job: excellent. Punctuality: excellent. Appearance: excellent. Ability to follow instructions: good. Quality of work: good. Thoroughness: good. Cooperation: good. Accuracy: good. Disposition: over cheerful. General comments: Strong interest in public service, beyond job requirements. A latent tendency toward inaction. Re-hire: perhaps, *if* the position is *funded*."

CHAPTER SIXTEEN

The Mayor balked at Wheel Barrows' request that he sign a "Proclamation on Behalf of The Association" from the Town, acknowledging the beneficence of Museum benefactors Simon and Louisa Lagorio, "Stewards of God." Barrow said he was conducting a campaign on behalf of The Association, "a public relations effort" to "create sympathy" for the Corporation.

"Praise for the Museum of the Year 1912, but not exaltation," read the Camperdene Daily Journal headline. "The Museum Association should be thanked for its work, but dubbing its founders 'God's Stewards' is going a bit too far, the Mayor decided last night. 'Isn't it beyond my jurisdiction to proclaim anybody God's stewards?' Mayor Driscoll asked. 'I have a problem with any proclamation that does that'."

Barrow publicly denounced the "scoffing" attitude of the Mayor toward the Association's founders. The Finance Committee requested that a record of the private trust funds held by the Association be made available to the committee during its review of the museum's budget. A reporter from the Boston Globe called Jake at home, asking for the exact figure of the Museum Association's trust funds. Jake had no idea. The writer asked how much Association money went into the institution's total operating budget. Jake reminded the reporter he was calling him at home, where he was just then playing with his five-year-old son, and not at work, and that he didn't have those figures handy.

Front page news, Saturday edition, Boston Globe: "Camperdene's Museum of the Year 1912 Curator Jacob Friedman Wright has refused to release the exact figure of the Museum Association trust fund and failed to provide an estimate of how much money from the fund goes to the Museum's annual operating budget. 'So much the worse for him,' said Finance Committee Chairwoman Martha Stronkski. 'If you are going to ask the town for public money, you have to show the town what you have got. It has too long been a deep, dark secret.' According to Stronkski, the request may mark the first time the Finance Committee has asked the private Corporation that owns the museum to reveal the inner workings of its finances. The committee voted on the matter Wednesday. In a letter to Walllace Barrow, President of the Museum of the Year 1912 Association, the Finance Committee has asked for the latest audited statement of the Corporation's assets and liabilities, according to Stronkski. Barrow said yesterday that the holdings of the non-profit Corporation are a matter of public record. 'It amounts to a couple of hundred thousand dollars,' said Barrow, adding that the holdings of the Corporation could be readily found in the public records at the museum.

"Although the museum is privately owned, the town funds the salaries of museum employees. According to Barrow, the arrangement was established by Town meeting. 'We are not asking for anything from the town other than what town meeting granted years ago,' said Barrow. He has taken issue with Mayor Driscoll's statement that the Museum could rely on its private holdings to weather fiscal crisis. The museum curator has chastened Driscoll for 'creating an adversarial situation' within Camperdene.' For years, the town has picked up the cost of museum staff salaries and supplies. Without that money, said Wright, 'it would be a part-time, volunteer parody of a museum.' The actual building is owned by the Museum Association, a private non-profit Corporation. Corporation leaders say they are unwilling to use up investment principal to pay daily operating costs such as salaries. 'We could never do that,' said Wallace Barrow, President of the Association's executive committee. Barrow yesterday expressed confidence that Town

Meeting members would restore some funding for museum staff. If not, he said, the museum will remain open only a dozen or so hours a week, with volunteer labor.

On the day the trustees of The Museum of the Year 1912 were scheduled to go before the Town Finance Committee, Wheel Barrow and Captain Cunnigham arrived at the museum and sat together at a long table, whispering, before crossing the street with Jake to meet with the Finance Commitee. As they stood to go, Barrow said earnestly, "Now let's not say anything to embarass one another." The Captain had a coughing fit. The mortician offered, "Captain, get a grip on. You'll have to come see me about your coffin. We'll measure you."

Before entering the school room, Barrow looked in the window and saw Ben Mulvane was in there, so he grabbed Jake's elbow and told him to go in and pull Ben out – he needed to talk to him before the meeting got going.

At the meeting, the Committee Chairwoman, Martha Stronkski, asked Barrow for the Museum Association's papers, which she'd requested well in advance of the meeting. Wallace said "No, Martha. We're not handing over anything." Barrow immersed Chairwoman Stronski in his morass of details about money and the Museum Association. He told her nothing she did not know already. He said the members of the Fin Comm had to make an appointment and look at the papers at the Museum just like anybody else. Martha Stronski, exasperated, pointed out to Wallace Barrow that she and her colleagues were busy people. Barrow persisted. Ben Mulvane's eyes were rolling in his head.

Before leaving the room Jake remind the Committee, "I'm really between a rock and a hard place here. Just remember who really stands to lose in all this. The people of Camperdene."

Outside, Ben Mulvane was talking to himself: "*Fuckin A's,*" he spit it out. "Those fuckin' *pigs* don't care a fuck about the museum. Fuckin' A's."

"Take it easy, Ben," my unflappable, sanguine father said. "Go home, write a letter."

That same day Martha Stronski got a letter, via the editor of the Camperdene Daily Journal, from one Alex Brandt: "Dear Mrs. Stronski, I am writing in support of the Museum of the Year 1912. I moved to Camperdene just a year ago. The museum was one of the first great things I discovered about the town. Since then I have visited the museum many, many times. It is a tremendous resource for all of us who live here. The museum is particularly impressive given its small size. The curator and his staff seem personally dedicated to their work. I understand the museum is in danger of losing a significant portion of its funding. It would be a terrible blow to Camperdene to lose the museum. I strongly encourage you to explore all possibilities that would enable the museum to continue to operate at full budget. Please let me know if there is anything I can do as a Camperdene resident to ensure that the Museum of the Year 1912 remains open, staffed, and fully functioning as the important resource that it is."

On March 14, Martha Stronski responded to Mr. Brandt: "As a native of this town and one who has spent nearly all of her 77 years in the town I am well acquainted with the Museum's value to our citizens. I am sure you must be aware that funding sources for Massachusetts municipalities and state agencies and services have been threatened with major cuts for the forthcoming fiscal year. Maybe *you* can tell us what the possibilities for saving and cutting are. Would you keep the museum open but fire firemen? Would you fund the museum but desist from picking up curbside trash? There seems to be a huge lack of understanding in town of how our assorted community services are paid for. I had *hoped* to clear up the lack of knowledge on the part of this committee of the museum's support other than town funding. Unfortunately, the response by Museum President Wallace Barrow to the members of this committee did little to erase that lack. The Finance Committee at this time is meeting twice a week – trying to come up with a reasonable plan to fund all town services and most of our departments have been very helpful in supplying for us any information we have requested. Most of us do not have the time to go out searching for information needed to make our report to Town meeting members.

There is not enough revenue to fund all of our departments. If we are to continue to provide needed services to our citizens there must be a clearer understanding on the part of citizens as to what problems we are facing. We meet every Tuesday and Thursday evening. Our meetings are open to the public. However, the public does not seem to be interested until they hear that their favorite town service is to be cut."

Later, back at the museum, Jake met with the Executive Committee of the Museum Association. Wallace Barrow told him that now only a majority of the Committee could sign official museum papers. Carlena Lagorio, Barrow, and The Captain next carried the meeting into a riotous discussion of a regular museum visitor, the former female minister of the Congregational Church, one Reverend Richeson, who had not too many years before been tarred and feathered and driven out of town after being charged by police for the molestation of a child. Eurydice Richeson, who still occasionally visited Camperdene, though she'd been cursed and driven like a dog from it, had the audacity to approach Wallace Barrow to ask if she could join the Museum Association: "Imagine! Eurodyce Richeson asking me if I would appoint her a Corporator of the Museum Corporation," Barrow hee-hawed.

Carlena Lagorio had a great howl over this, too – as did then the whole group. "Have you heard of her, Jake?" Barrow neighed, eager to tell him about Richeson, soliciting hoots, neighs, and oinks from his colleagues. Carlena Lagorio next told the assembled a story Audrey Morris had told her, of how Jake had recently spoke with the former minister. Audrey had told Lagorio of Jake's telling Richeson he would personally look into a certain matter for her. "So Mr. Wright here told Eurydice Richeson, the granddaughter of a murderer, herself under investigation, that he'd investigate. Oh, it is just too delicious." Oink! Oink! Oink! Oink! Oink!

Oinking all around – the Executive Committee oinked and oinked and oinked. I would have gone around the room and slapped each one of them twice upside the head, the oinking morons, but not my serene, self-possessed father. He just smiled and said, "Well, it was a good thing I was there. Audrey and Mary both told me afterwards they would not have served Richeson. But if *she* is turned away, will *bums* then also be? *Alcoholics*? The *illiterate*?" He then excused himself.

"I took care of Eurydice Richeson," Carlena Lagorio whispered. "She won't be back." Oink. Oink. Oink. *Oink*. Her swinish oinking certainly followed Jake out.

"He has to learn how to deal with women," Wheel Barrow whispered.

I think I would have got it over with once and for all and just smacked that smug, self-satisfied blubber mass right in the fat kisser. But not my father. Oh no, not him.

At home, Mark had an ear infection. He woke up repeatedly throughout the night, screaming. It was like he'd wrestled with the devil. He screamed at it – at the pain – at the phantom knife-like searing pain. "Go a-way!" he shouted. "Stop it! Leave!" My father was up with him all night.

Minna was wild, angry with her husband in the morning because he had remained in bed an extra hour after she'd got up, him holding Mark in his arms. Minna claimed he was *spoiling* the boy. Jake said the boy was in searing pain, and needed to be *held*. They needed to go to the doctor. Minna insisted, "No doctors." She told Jake he didn't know anything about *anything*. And doctors didn't know anything about *anything*. The piercing, sharp agony of Mark's pain was *good for him*, Minna insisted, saying his jerks and starts and screams acted like *medicine* for what ailed him. She was going to pour oil into his ear, but Jake protested. He said they should first let a doctor make a diagnosis. It could be something worse than a mere ear-ache, for which the *last* thing they ought to do would be *pour oil in*.

Jake was seriously far more concerned about Mark's pain than Minna's fury, so he dressed hurriedly and took Mark in his pajamas to the car. Only then did Minna agree to go with her family to the doctor. The doctor told Minna Mark had a blister in his ear caused by a particularly odd but not unknown virus infection. He did not recommend putting oil down Mark's ear. He insisted Mark would need an antibiotic. Minna agreed to it, and that was that. She afterwards refused to talk about any of this. It is all like ancient lore to me now – prehistorical myths and sagas – all these stories of the twists and turns of my family. What can you do when you're the low man on the totem pole when it comes to such dynamics in your family? You can scream so loud no sound comes out and grit your teeth and pull your hair – you can sit there like a time bomb ticking – that's what you can do.

After all that, Jake walked stoically to work in the rain. There he was greeted by the news: "Mayor Driscoll is prescribing stoicism for the town's ills. 'It's going to be an extremely lean year all around,' the Mayor said. 'Not everybody is going to be happy; probably not *anyone* is going to be happy'."

Jake went to his desk and wrote a letter – not to the mayor, but to Eurydice Richeson, the granddaughter of the cyanide poisoner, Clarence Richeson.

He hoped he would see her again, he wrote (he wouldn't). He told her all he knew about her grandfather's arrest and electrocution. He included copies of the two news articles that Captain Cunningham had recently pressed on him, the one, "The Hansboro Pioneer, North Dakota, January 12, 1912":

"Prominent Boston Pastor Confesses – Rev. C.V.T. Richeson, former pastor of Immanuel Baptist Church of Cambridge, Massachusetts, today made a written confession to the effect that he poisoned his former sweetheart, Miss Avis Linnell... he is indicted of murder in the first degree in taking the life of Miss Linnell by giving her cyanide potassium"

And the other unattributed account:

"Clarence V.T. Richeson, age 36, charged with murder, was executed by electrocution in Massachusetts on Tuesday, May 21, 1912. The former minister was electrocuted for the murder of Miss Avis Linnell, a Hyannis Port girl to whom he had been engaged. Richeson, originally from Virginian, had come to Massachusetts in 1906. After studying at the Newton Theological Seminary, he'd been called to be minister at the Hyannis Baptist Church, where he met the Linnell family of Hyannisport – mother, father and four beautiful daughters. Richeson fell for 17-year-old Avis, a fine soprano singer and a student at the new Hyannis State Teacher's College.

"Richeson was soon preaching in both Hyannis and Yarmouth. He had a Southern style of preaching, filled with exuberance and zeal – not to his conservative Cape Cod congregation's liking. In April 1910, he resigned. He had, meanwhile, given Avis a ring. The two were speaking of getting married in October. Richeson found new employment at Immanuel Baptist Church in Cambridge. He talked Avis, into applying for admission at the New England Conservatory of Music. In the early fall of 1910, she moved into the Y.W.C.A. in Boston to continue her education. The two never married. In early 1911, Avis told her mother she and Reverend Richeson were no longer seeing one another. In March, Richeson got engaged to a wealthy Brookline woman, Violet Edmands.

"On October 14, at the beginning of her second year in Boston, Avis committed suicide. They found her near-lifeless body in a Y.W.C.A. bathroom. Before anyone could call for an ambulance, she was dead. An autopsy revealed Avis was several weeks pregnant and that she had taken cyanide. Authorities wrote off the young woman's death as the suicide of one more good girl in a bad fix. In fact, Avis had been murdered by Richeson. Avis was carrying Richeson's baby, and earlier that day the minister had given the young woman a chemical preparation that he assured her would cause the fetus to abort. Instead it had killed her. Richeson would have gotten away with it, except for one small mistake. One of the matrons at the Y.W.C.A. had placed a call to the reverend less than two hours after Avis died. Richeson had demanded to know why he was being called when he barely knew the girl. 'We felt that, since you are her fiancé and that she was out to lunch with you during the day, it is right that we should notify you,' the matron replied. There was a pause on the other end. 'Did she say anything before she died?' Richeson asked. The matron replied Avis had not regained consciousness after her body had been discovered. The minister had assumed Avis had kept their affair secret. He was confident that no one could directly connect him with her death. But the Boston Post called for a deeper police investigation of Avis Linell's suicide. The Post found the druggist in Newton who had sold Clarence Richeson the cyanide. The Post called for Richeson's arrest, which occurred ten days after Avis's death. The Post, with its big front-page headlines, worked New Englanders into a fever pitch.

"After spending several months in jail and failing in a suicide attempt of his own (he tried to castrate himself with the sharp edge of a tin can lid), Richeson changed his plea to guilty and confessed. Judge George A. Sanderson of the Superior Court presided at the trial. He sentenced Richeson to death. On May 21, 1912, he was strapped to the electric chair."

On Saturday morning, Jake mailed his apologetic letter with the clippings. He took Mark along, and the two went out for breakfast. They walked along the railroad tracks and down Hart Street to The Golden Spoon restaurant. They planned their order along the route – hot chocolate, pancakes, pan-fries, wheat toast, and eggs. When it came time to order, however, Mark stumbled. Jake knew Mark wanted to be elegant and eloquent, placing the order on his own. But now he balked. Jake knew he had the words clear in his head, but they were not coming out as wished. He was at a loss for words, and it threw him for a loop. My father said he could see his boy's exasperation. Then Mark pulled himself together and famously addressed the waitress boldly, with sudden brightness gleaming in his eyes: "I know what I want. I want my egg cooked so that the sunshine's smiling at me."

My father later told me how special that was, that single simple bright morning, amid the general dark dullness of those times. It had struck him as so luminous and wonderful. Despite dramatic deathly global warming, there seemed to be, for my father, at that time and in that place, to be a general *chill* in the world – a deficit of sunshine.

CHAPTER SEVENTEEN

Around this time, the Captain took my father aside to enlighten him, "Martha Stronski wants to get control of the Association's money for her own purposes."

"No she doesn't," Jake said.

"She and Wallace Barrow go back a long way. They are like cat and dog."

"Obviously. He's arrogant to her, and she's preachy. And the townspeople are going to lose."

"No they're not. Where do you get these ideas?"

"I listen to people."

"You just don't get it. You're not from New England. You don't know how we are."

"I know how people are, Captain. What are you telling me?"

"Are you looking for other work?"

"No, I am not. I am trusting that enough money to see us through will come through."

"Jake, you really don't get it. There's not going to be enough money. There won't be need of professional staffing. We won't be needing a curator with a Master's degree."

My father recorded he was stunned. His heartbeat quickened. His thought his breathing stopped.

The Captain continued: "Do you know why the Corporation agreed to have a curator with a Master's degree in the first place?"

"To have an efficient, excellent museum?"

"No, not at all. Only in order to get additional funding from the town. The Commonwealth said the museum could only obtain additional funding from the town if a professional curator was hired. Now there won't be any aid coming – and so we won't be needing a professional curator. I am soft-spoken in this. You should hear the other Corporators."

"You lean in close and you stand there and you tell me these things – as if we were talking about brands of laundry soap or the weather. I'm hearing your words. I really can't believe my ears. You talk on and you persist. You're talking worse possible Museum trusteeship – botched stewardship – and yet you show the opposite of shame. I don't get it. I don't. You talk on, you're educating me, you're insisting Massachusetts people don't need professional museum services, I'm dumb not to seek work elsewhere, you're calmly trying to teach me that this is all quite reasonable and rational and, with a little bit of luck, I will come to understand this. Thanks so much for your patience with me, trying to get these strange views you hold through my thick skull."

"I look forward to round two," Captain Cunningham said calmly upon leaving, as Mary was turning out the lights.

In the morning, Jake got a call from Nick Wentworth. He asked about how things were going, museum-wise. Jake told him about Captain Cunningham's comments. "The man sounds simply inept," Wentworth said. "A goddamned busybody who wants to stir things up." Wentworth promised he'd call contacts – friends and reporters – to have the trustees be interviewed. "Let them be asked certain hard questions," Wentworth said. "And let them answer, for the record, at long last. I know the O'Daceys, a local lawyer and his daughter Marcy, our local representative in the State House. I know these people personally," Wentworth affirmed. "We can get these people interested in all this."

Jake asked Nick to wait. He needed to talk to Wallace Barrow regarding Captain Cunningham's comments on Friday. He called Barrow at about 11:00, and told him what Captain Cunningham had said, and asked him what was true and what was not. Wallace told Jake he really didn't know where the hell old Powderkeg was coming from.

"Jake, let me rest your mind," Wallace said. "What the Captain said simply is not so, and I don't have a clue as to why he would ever tell you those things. He's acting on his own initiative in talking to you like that. It is not the opinion of the Board, I can assure you. This is between you and me, Jake: I can promise you that even if we get only enough money to pay your salary, from whatever source, that money will be used to keep you at your job. And even if we get less than your salary, we will see to it that the difference is made up. There are ways of getting that money, and we will. Do you understand?"

"Can I get that in writing?"

"No, I can't sign anything apart from the Board. But listen: you have my word. You know I only want what's best for the museum, or I wouldn't even cross the street to help it out. I'm only trying to keep things straight. There's quite a mess emerging. You can't tell what's going to happen next. There are all kinds of factions. Did you know that there's a faction out there that only wants to see one of you stay on board at the museum?"

"One of whom?"

"One of your staff. There are people out there with assorted kinds of power and everybody's playing a different game. Some people are out there campaigning to keep just one of you working at the museum, at the expense of the rest of you. You didn't know this?"

Jake knew this too could be a ploy, creating further divisiveness. But there was something straightforward and frank in the way Wheel was speaking.

"I can't tell you who, but you can figure it out."

"Julia Seymour-Stanton?" (She has political connections, she's lived in Camperdene forever, people would certainly rally around her – I would, too.)

"I can't say," Wallace said. "You can figure it out. But I'll tell you again – and this is just between you and me: Captain Cunningham has got it backwards. I don't know why he told you what he did. I promise you: if there's any money at all for staffing at the museum come July, you'll be the last to go – not the first, as Powderkeg told you. Does that put you'r mind at rest?"

"It does. I just don't want this whole thing to blow up in our faces. The last thing I want to see is the museum become a battleground. Thank you for taking time to answer my questions, Wallace. I'm braced for the worst, but I'm going to campaign for the best."

"I know that. The Board thinks very highly of you. Why, just this morning," Barrow said merrily, "Veronica Pillsbury and I were talking about you. Veronica feels very bad about all this mess and thinks it's too bad and that you're a fine fellow. She says we New Englanders can't just come out and say what's what. Stuff gets hidden."

That evening, the Captain sauntered in and helped Jake close the museum. He then offered Jake a ride home. "Did you send those clippings to Eurydice Richeson?" he asked Jake along the way. When Jake said he had, the Captain paused, then asked, "Did you hear back from her?" When Jake said no, he hadn't, the Captain spoke ominously, "I doubt you will." When Jake got out of the car, Cunningham asked another pointed question – this one a rhetorical question which Jake could not answer: "What's the Latin for *Don't let the bastards wear you down*?"

CHAPTER EIGHTEEN

Jake shaved and showered in the morning, same as every other day. What he did not remember to remember was that this was April 1st – April Fool's day. My mother ran into the bathroom and, out of breath, said, "Jake, Wallace Barrow phoned. He said the museum's going to be closing down for good – starting today." Jake turned off the shower, wrapped a towel around himself, and went upstairs to call Wallace Barrow back. He was standing there near naked, wrapped in a towel. In my high chair, I was reported as having grinned delightedly right along. He was still dialing when Mark joined Minna, chirping, "April Fools!"

I think I never saw him so upset. If I remember rightly, he was crying. It seriously ruined my father's day.

When Carlena Lagorio came into the museum that morning and said haughtily, "I will be so sorry to see you have to leave this institution, Mister Wright," Jake responded with humility, "I also will be sorry when *you're* gone."

An old man came in, just in the nick of time, nicely dressed in a three-piece suit. He looked like a banker who wrote poetry on the side – calculating and compassionate. "I regret the botched job some of our town officials are doing," he apologized. He told Jake how it was a shame the museum potentially faced zero-funding. He'd been hearing what an excellent place the museum had become since Jake had come aboard. He was praising the services of the museum's helpful staff and....

Jake could see Carlena Lagorio couldn't stand it. She was turning purple. She suddenly intruded, "We do our best. We..."

The sweet man looked at her as at a bad abstract painting. "Who are *you*?" he asked. "I was talking to Mr. Wright."

"I am Carlena Lagorio, a distinguished Corporator of this museum — a direct descendant of its founders."

"Ah," the man said, sizing her up as he reached out a hand to shake Jake's. "You will see to it Mr. Wright keeps his job?"

My father said Lagorio looked like she wanted to put the man into a bottle and throw him in the ocean. Me, I think I would have wanted to put Lagorio into a bottle to throw her into a black hole. A complete and total utter nut case. Adios. She left in a huff.

Later that day, Julia Seymour-Stanton arrived and took Jake aside, asking, "Do we have, or have we ever had, anything in the museum indicating in any way that Barton Driscoll is a 'tyrant'? Mayor Driscoll told me this morning that his son told him we'd posted materials here that say his father, Mr. Driscoll, is a 'tyrant'."

Jake called Mr. Driscoll's office. Babs, one of his two secretaries, informed Jake, "The mayor is at a meeting." When Jake called later, Babs said, "The Mayor has gone out of his office. He'll be back at 4:15." Jake left a message, "We need to clear up a misunderstanding, should you want to clear it up." Then Jake sat down and typed a letter. Minna came in at 4:00 to fetch Jake home for dinner. They stopped by the bank to cash his pay check, then crossed the street to enter Town Hall, where my father put his letter to Mayor Driscoll right on his desk.

"Mayor Driscoll," Jake had written, "Qualified professional people are needed to run the Museum of the Year 1912. We are dedicated, and cost-effective. Any political constituency can afford what it really wants to have. Professional curators play a key role in dealing with the increasing complexity of an education- and information-conscious society. I'm sad to see the difficult situation we are in together degenerate into a losing situation for our townspeople. My conduct has not included maligning you; it has included being kind and patient."

Mayor Driscoll called Jake the next morning, saying "Jake, you're making a Goddamn mountain out of a molehill."

"Maybe," my father said, and invited the Mayor to go in and actually *see* the museum some time.

Wheel Barrow showed up and took Jake aside, asking, "What's this I hear about you being a *tyrant*? I was just downtown and somebody came up and told me there's a rumor going around that you're a *tyrant*." And Barrow had other concerns: "Jake, I'm also hearing that some of the people in the Museum Friends group are talking about getting into the Museum Association." His voice was now quaking. He was shaking visibly.

"I was myself thinking that would be a good by-product of the present difficult situation – wouldn't it? There could be some good people coming up, concerned people who might be of help to the Association."

"Have you mentioned this to anyone else?"

"Maybe. Just in expressing my hope that some good may come of our present plight."

"Don't go any further in that," Barrow commanded. "The Association takes care of itself. Don't get mixed up about this. It's *our* domain, not *yours*. You got that? Don't you go and make me *angry* on this."

"You misunderstand me," my father said. "I'm saying you should keep your eyes open, you know, keep an eye out for good people coming up. Tap them for the Museum Association. That's straightforward. That's a good thing."

"*We'll* tap them as *we* see fit. *You* just stay out of the Association's business."

A few days later, on a blue and sunny warm morning, while my mother was out looking at houses for sale – optimistically in search of a next Wright family home, despite their very precarious financial situation – my father was in the backyard with little Ethan, from next-door, and me, pulling us around in Mark's red wooden wagon while Mark was busy working in a little Chinese moss garden behind the apartment – the phone rang. The head of the Massachusetts chapter of the Guild of Bookcrafters, Arthur Westcott, was *frantic*. He had received word from somebody named Bowlegged Cottageham, or something like that, that the Guild of Bookcrafters was being turned down for their meeting at the museum, which Jake had himself scheduled, months before, for a Saturday in mid-April. Art was all apologies, believing it was the *Guild's* fault. He just *had* to have the meeting at the museum. What would he *do* if he couldn't get permission to use the museum at this late date? It had all been printed up, announced in the Guild newsletter, and on and on. Jake assured Westcott, "I'll find out what's going on and I'll get back to you."

My father phoned Wallace Barrow and explained that, apparently, Captain Cunningham was intervening against the use of the museum for an event which Jake had scheduled months before. Jake said he needed Barrow's approval for the Guild of Bookcrafters to meet at the museum.

"Wait," Barrow said. "Who – who wants to use the museum?"

"The Massachusetts chapter of the Guild of Bookcrafters."

"*Book*crafters? Who are *they*? Where are these people coming from?"

"Worcester."

"So what do they want with *Camperdene*?"

"Well, you know we have this community of book arts people in Camperdene, Nicholas Wentworth, for one – the President of the Friends."

"Oh yeah. Wentworth. What day?"

"Saturday, mid-April, at 2:00 p.m."

"You want to be there and open and close the museum for them?"

"Sure, I wouldn't mind."

"You know you're going to owe me *big time* if I do this for you?"

"I understand."

"Well, okay. Go ahead. You have my word. It's okay. But just remember. You owe me."

A few days later, Mr. Infinite Patience, my undaunted father, called on Wallace Barrow. He was not at the funeral home, but rather at his gravestone shop on Banyan Street. Jake asked him if he would sign the payroll that week. Barrow promised he'd swing by later. But Jake had some errands to run anyway, and it was a beautiful day, so he took a chance and just showed up at Barrow Monuments.

Peering in through the front windows, he could see Barrow in his office, feet up, reading the newspaper. He looked up, saw Jake, got his feet off the desk, folded the paper, and jumped up. "Jake," he said flatly, and started talking away just like some caught-out schoolboy eagerly aiming to influence a discussion in his favor. Standing, he said he wanted Jake to see a beautiful tombstone decorated with a Fawn in a Glen scene. "This would look good on you," Barrow said.

"Wallace," my father gently declared, "I'm not going to let you bury me."

"Fine," Barrow spat it out. "I'll cremate you instead."

CHAPTER NINETEEN

Minna had big news. She had found the cutest little bungalow, she said, for us to live in. It had been built in 1912, of course. She said it looked like a single-level beach bungalow from the outside, but that it was huge inside – long, like a tunnel, and under the tunnel-long bungalow was a huge basement to match, with the same amount of abundant space in the cellar as on the ground level.

Mary Tuchlein called that night. She said she wouldn't be in to work in the morning. She had thrown her back out. Minna was livid when she heard this, furious. She had wanted to go shopping in the morning – alone – without children. It was not on the schedule posted on the refrigerator door that Jake should go to work in the morning, she complained. Now he would have to go in. Jake told Minna that Mary Tuchlein had thrown her back out and *could not* be there in the morning. he would *have to* go in and work. Sometimes that's just how it is.

"With you," she said bitterly, "that's how it is – *always*. Here I am, I work all day, looking everyhere for a house for us to live in and I want to have just a little bit of time for myself, to go out shopping, maybe I just get a little something nice for myself, but *no*. No, I can't go. *Jake* has got to go to *work*. Work, work, work, work, *work*." Indignant, she stomped off to bed. For all that, Jake *still* had to go in to work in the morning.

It was a very busy morning. People were spinning in and rolling out all day – wearing summery Bermuda shorts, T-shirts, floozy blouses,

Panama hats. Audrey was in on time, at noon. "It's unseasonably warm, isn't it?" she said. Downtown, there was a heated meeting of Town Department Heads. Sweating bullets, glum Barton Driscoll said he'd had a meeting with Martha Stronski. "Some money *could* be coming in from the state, and the museum *could* be the first in line to get restored funding – *if* the money does come in."

Back at work, Wheel Barrow called. "Jake, I just got a call from, ah, Arnstrom – Alicia Avery Arnstrom – the reporter."

"Alice Armour Armstrong."

"Yes. Over at the paper. She wants to know about our money. She asked me some questions I thought had been answered. Somebody put her up to this. I said, 'Do you go asking the sponsors or the owners of your newspaper how much or from where the money comes in for the paper in order for you to get your job done'?"

After an ominous pause, Barrow said, "Somebody's out to get us. Martha Stronski wants us to use up all our trust money on operational costs, and she's putting somebody up to this. And I don't like it."

"You know my opinion on this," Jake reminded him. "I've said again and again that you don't use up Trust funds on operational costs. That is, in fact, a betrayal of the Trust."

"Jake, you don't know of anybody in the Friends of the Museum who would be feeding this Arnsberg girl this line," he asked. He said he was angry that everybody was not happy after he *had gone out of his way* to be open.

What with the New England chapter of the Guild of Bookcrafters meeting coming up in mid-April, Nick Wentworth volunteered to put in a display of Japanese papers and book arts materials through to the end of the month. Jake called Roland of the Artfacts Committee to get permission to for Nick's putting in his display. He said, "No, no no. I am scheduled to put in my collection of model cars, trains, and planes this afternoon."

In the evening, Jake went over to the high school for a meeting of the Task Force for Quality Schools in Camperdene and, after, returned to the museum to help Audrey close. "What if Mary can't be in in the morning?" Audrey asked. She had an appointment with a doctor in the morning, and she and Mary had arranged for Mary to cover for her.

"Well, then *I'll* just have to come in again, won't I?"

At home, Mark was up, in bed, looking at a book. Minna was apparently putting me to bed. I was crying and Minna was late for a meeting of her *Goddess* group. She went off, leaving me still crying. Jake came in to soothe me, letting me stay awake a little longer. I turned gleeful. Little by little I made my way upstairs to Mark's room. Jake had closed the door. Mark was asleep. I just wanted in. I rattled the door knob. I cried out. Jake gently eased me from the door, but I went straight back and rattled the door knob some more. I cried out again. I woke Mark up. Mark started crying. I remember our father sang us both to sleep, right and left of him on the front room couch.

Mr. Tuchlein woke the three of us, phoning my father just to say that Mary at work had *seriously* wrenched her back out, and *definitely* would not be in in the morning. "She can't even come to the phone," Mr. Tuchlein emphasized.

And so, in the morning, Jake walked to work and opened up the museum and got the lights and computers and air conditioning all up and running, and not five minutes passed but the phone rang. Martha Stronski, Chair of the Finance Committee, famously had called to ask my father, "How could you have betrayed me?"

"*What?* I betrayed you?"

"I'm hearing you're telling people I'm a *tyrant!*"

"Martha, that's not true."

Stronski said she could see now Jake was clearly *in cahoots* with Wallace Barrow. Jake told Stronski that all he was interested in was what he thought was good for the museum and for the people that it was there for.

Stronski contemplated that a moment, then said she had an idea and she wanted Jake's opinion on it: "Jake, If I can put together a group of representatives from the Finance Committee – and I can assure you I wouldn't be on it – who could they go and talk with? Is there anybody on the Board of the Association who isn't hypnotized by Wallace Barrow?"

Jake mentioned Angela Perry, Association Treasurer.

"Yes, but – Angela Perry. Isn't she the mother of the girl that married Wheel's son?"

"Right."

"What about Captain Cunningham?"

Silence. Jake said nothing.

"Is there *anybody*?" Martha said, despairing. "Well, I'm going to go ahead with this," she closed. "Some of us will be meeting with some of them and hopefully they can work something out, so that the museum can get something out of this."

"I hope it truly, Martha."

Audrey came in at 11:00. Jake crossed the street to the Barrow manor. Reggie was there – and a guest. Wallace was on the phone. He hung up and said, "What do you want? – Speak."

"In private," Jake requested. Barrow ushered him into the neighboring room.

"I'm being squeezed," Jake began, and spoke of the pain that the mischief and the animosity in the air brought to him.

"Animosity?" Wallace faked befuddlement. "I have no feelings of animosity," he said.

Jake could see it was useless to get to any better side of Barrow. *That* just wasn't *there*.

Barrow volunteered the information that he was *deeply* upset about the Museum Support Group. He said, "They're up to something. They're going to try to trip us up."

"Trip up *what*?" Jake said. "What's to trip up?"

Barrow leaned in close to Jake's face and said Jake was *very* close to making him angry, and Jake had best not make him angry.

"I'm only concerned for the museum" Jake said.

"You still don't get it, Jake. It's *our* museum –the Association's. It belongs to *us*. When are you ever going to see that?"

The next day, early in the morning, my brother Mark awoke my father and took him by the hand and led him outside, though they were was still in their pajamas, to show him there was a teepee in the backyard. It was Mark's sixth birthday and, on this cool and windy lovely day, there was to be a thematic party – cowboys and Indians. Half a dozen kids would show up – little Annie Oakleys, Davy Crocketts, Sitting Bulls.

Next thing, Reggie Barrow was phoning my father at home and asking him *where the hell* he was. "Everybody's at the museum," Barrow said, "waiting for you. You'd better get in here *pronto*," he said, or there'll be *hell* to pay." When Jake got there, out of breath, the first thing he saw, in the plush old chair by the fireplace, was Camperdene Daily Journal reporter Alice Armour Armstrong. She had come in to look at the Association's records – those which Wallace had handpicked for her.

At 2:30, Martha Stronski came in with her special subcommittee to meet with a special subcommittee of the Executive Committee of the Museum Association – Wheel, Powderkeg, and Carlena Lagorio. There was laughter – gaiety. Wallace Barrow was charming them – disarming them. The *real* problems weren't going to be addressed. They'd be trussed up, obfuscated, and then buried under Barrow's slippery leering laughter.

On the radio the next morning came the first report: the Finance Committee was recommending funding for three of the four-and-a-half positions at the museum.

Audrey departed that morning for a four week Florida vacation.

My father got a call from the Chairwoman of the Public Relations Committee of the Massachusetts Museums Association: "You've won the PR award, Jake – for the year's best museum PR Campaign'." Seriously. That was nice.

CHAPTER TWENTY

At the next meeting of the Executive Committee of the Museum Association, the assembled Corporators were at the long tables: gossip, whispering. At 8:00 Jake went over. He took payment papers to them, to be signed.

Wallace Barrow had mentioned at the previous meeting that Jake would be receiving instructions from the Town Accountant: a number of members of the committee would, in future, be required to sign. Here they all were, and Wheel announced they were ready to sign. The papers were passed around. All signed. Carlena Lagorio instructed Captain Cunningham, "Put a line down that column so that no-one can add to it." The Captain said, "It's not in my job description."

What job? What had Jake missed?

Barrow asked Jake if he had any new business. Jake deferred, due to the financial crisis, but mentioned his wish to attend the upcoming Massachusetts Museums Association conference. Jake told them he'd been asked to come to receive, on behalf of The Museum of the Year 1912, a PR award. Wheel scoffed aloud at the idea. "Imagine a bunch of curators gathering at a conference," he bellows. "Ha ha! *What would they talk about?*"

"Of the many museums in the Commonwealth of Massachusetts, big and small, *we've* been chosen to receive this year's award for 'Best Public Relations campaign'."

"That's a feather in our cap," Carlena Lagorio said.

"Yes it is."

"*You* will go to receive this award?" Lagorio asked scornfully.

"Yes."

"So it's a feather in *your* cap," Carlena scowled.

"Is that not okay?"

"It is not for me to say," Lagorio said, sniffing the air.

Wallace Barrow said, "Well, it is important *we* stay in the background. Still, it is *we* who provide you, Jake, with the museum in which you receive these awards."

"It's an honor for all," Jake said. "Let's just accept it."

No further discussion. Jake was dismissed. As he went out, he could hear loose-lipped Carlena Lagorio recalling the good old days at the Museum when you couldn't even talk – you had to whisper – *or else.*

The next day, Wheel Barrow came in wearing his black mortician's overcoat and said, "Jake, do you know when to keep quiet and when to speak?"

"In terms of what?" he answered cautiously.

"Just: do you know when to keep quiet and when to speak?" he repeated.

By then I'm sure I would have grabbed that ass Barrow by the neck and strangled him, or kicked him once and for all in his cuckoo clock, but my father – oh my father – he just stood there, taking it. "I know to speak my mind if need be," he said, "and I know to shut up, if need be."

Barrow gestured Jake over to the couch by the fireplace. As he sat down, Barrow pulled from his coat's inner pocket a copy of the Association's papers of Incorporation. He pointed out a clause stating, "So long as said Corporation shall allow the inhabitants of the town of Camperdene free access to The Museum of the Year 1912 at reasonable hours, for the purpose of using the same on the premises, said town may appropriate money for the purpose of defraying the expenses of maintaining said museum."

At that point I would have seriously disturbed that vile man Barrow's intimidating grand airs where it hurts worst but, no, not my unruffled father. My father just sat there and took it.

"Do you know when to keep quiet and when to speak?" Barrow repeated yet again, rhetorically. "Not that *I* know anything," he said." *You're* the *curator.*"

CHAPTER TWENTY-ONE

A bombshell fell now, in the form of a new Camperdene Daily Journal article: "Museum-Town at a crossroads. The Museum of the Year 1912 told to open its books!

"It's a centuries-old New England tradition: a private museum owned by a private Corporation. But with Camperdene's finances stretched thin, the tradition is in jeopardy. When Camperdene Mayor Barton Driscoll unveiled a budget proposal last month that eliminated all public funding to the Museum of the Year 1912, some residents began a crash course in how the institution is run. During the intervening weeks, a philosophical difference has come to light between members of the Museum Association – the group charged in the institution's bylaws with maintaining the museum – and the public. Members of the Association say they run the museum like a business and maintain a hands-off policy when it comes to local politics. But members of a support group who joined an effort to save the museum say the association should take a public stand and fight for the institution. The trustee's attitude of caution has been taken by museum supporters as indifference, and sometimes as secrecy. Nonsense, the association's president counters. At the same time, the town's own Finance committee has worked to determine if the museum could survive on its endowment – a process the panel's chair calls frustrating.

"Like several other museums, Camperdene's is partially funded by the town but, according to its bylaws, its destiny lies in the hands of the private Corporation, The Museum of the Year 1912 Association. Though it is a public resource, the museum's roots are in the private sector. Exercising a power that is comparable to that available to the board of a business Corporation, the Association board governs the independent, not-for-profit museum with an iron fist. The executive committee of the Association oversees the funding and maintenance of the building and grounds and hires and fires employees, according to the museum's bylaws, first drafted in 1913. Within budgetary constraints, they can open or close facilities, expand or contract the staff, increase or decrease the budgetary allocation available for expanding the collections. Financial resources available to the museum remain within the museum. They are not vulnerable to reallocation to other city or county departments. Conversely, nowhere is it written that the town has any obligation to foot any portion of the bill. However, Town meetings have voted through the years to give money to the museum to make it free and open to the public, says museum curator Jake Wright.

"Camperdene's Mayor Driscoll's rationale for ending town funding is that The Museum of the Year 1912 has a private endowment that could easily keep the museum open without any outside help. But with no funding from the town, the museum would have to resort to volunteer staffing, and would probably have to cut its hours of operation. Without a paid, professional full-time curator, the town would also lose state funds for the museum.

"The Finance Committee this month proposed including some funding for the museum in the budget. That recommendation came after a large public outcry to save the museum, and after updated budget information, which adds state aid revenues to Camperdene's fiscal picture. Neither the finance panel's budget, which includes some $90,000 in funding for the museum, nor the Mayor's budget, which offers no tax dollars to the museum, meets the budget request of the institution. Even if the Finance Committee's alternative budget passes, Museum Association President Wallace Barrow says the Trust would be hard pressed to make up the gap. Barrow says trustees are disinclined to comment on what the museum's fate will be. 'How well the museum is run depends on how the trustees see themselves,' said Nicholas Wentworth, a bookbinder on Banyan Street, a museum supporter. 'Do they see themselves as stewards of a public trust? Would they do everything in their power to see that the museum is a great place?' Barrow insists the answer to that is yes, but that it is not the Association's place to take political stands. 'We're not a town entity. We have plans.' Despite charges that he appears ready to accept having a volunteer staff at the museum, Barrow said, 'It's a very poor thing for our employees not to be funded.'

"For as long as the Association fills its mandate of providing the building and keeping it open, the trust may receive funds from the town to defray expenses of running the museum, the bylaw says. 'The museum should be a partnership between the town and the museum's trustees,' said Finance Committee Chairwoman Martha Stronski. But getting the financial statements they needed to make an informed decision about how to allocate the limited funds at their disposal was no easy task, said Stronski.'The trustees ignored our public hearing, they ignored our requests for their financial picture. Yet they'd be devastated if we took away all of their funding,' Stronski criticized. Stronski noted that other private Corporations that the Finance Committee funds, such as the survival center and the community center, voluntarily submit their budgets to the panel.

"'The idea that the Museum Corporation is sitting on a pile of private funds is misguided, Barrow said. But, the value of stocks and bonds held by the Trust added up to some $380,000, according to a recent financial report. Barrow said, 'We'd be derelict in doing anything with our principal.' The trustees only spend interest accrued on the endowment funds. Wentworth said that even after the financial problems are settled for this year's museum funding, there is more work to do. 'We may look, top to bottom, into how the Museum Association is organized and look for ways to get more town involvement in running the museum,' he said. There was talk that 'the Association might have political or ego motives to try to undermine the museum,' Wentworth said, adding, 'We'd like not to believe those rumors.'

"Some have speculated that the Association's vice-president, Captain Richard Cunningham, himself is interested in running the museum. He said that is not true; while he enjoys conducting historical research there, he doesn't want to take on the time commitment of overseeing day-to-day museum operations. Museum curator Jake Wright, though literally an insider, is a man caught in the middle. He claims not to know all the institution's financial facts. At meetings during the past month, in which town department heads discussed Camperdene's budget, Wright had little information on museum finances. Wright, whose salary is paid by the town – but who work for the private Museum Association, says he is not privy to the fiscal accounts of the institution he oversees.

"Museum expert Martin T. Gleason, author of the book 'Politics and the Small Museum: A Management Guide,' noted, 'the many town and city museums scattered through the country all have a variety of governance structures. Some fall under the jurisdiction of city or county government and have no board of curators at all, only an advisory board. Other museums are departments of city or county government and have a policy-making board as well. Another kind of museum governance sees the museum operating as an independent, not-for-profit Corporation, with or without independent taxing authority. Finally, there are those village, town, or city museums falling under the jurisdiction of state government. In every case, the problem is that all of these museums ultimately depend on benefactors from the business world, where even the best-intentioned people sometimes have difficulty separating philanthropic and fiduciary activities from personal business interests, intervening in the running of the museums in often highly improper ways. The conflict of interest inherent in the situation often degenerates into abuse,' Gleason said. 'Normally, the board makes policy and the curator hired by the trustees manages the institution, carrying out the policies established by the board. When confusion about these roles arises between boards and curators, the affected institution and its staff and the community are cast into a kind of hell. Obviously, a museum should be the most inviting, interesting, elevating place in any village or city, attracting visitors and then holding their attention.

But what sometimes happens instead is that museum trustees, clothing themselves in cloaks of privacy, degenerate into a self-perpetuating group of deluded individuals meeting in private, plotting ways to keep people *out*. Trustee accountability sinks to null. Trustees cease keeping public records, fail to reveal accounts of their doings, deny the press access to information concerning their activities'.

"Just so, museum curator Jake Wright claims he has 'long since' ceased to be included in the decision-making process. 'I nudge them, I persuade them, I talk to them, but the situation has sunk low.' Wright's every move must first be filtered first through his trustees. 'I have no idea what either their aims or their resources are,' Wright said. 'It's like trying to get Doctor Frankenstein's monster to sing.' The uncertain situation has provided at least one bright spot for the curator: the public outcry against eliminating funding for the museum has created a fertile ground for conversation, where condemnation of the cloak-and-dagger board gives way to flowering praise of Wright, reassuring him he's been doing very well what work has been allowed him.

"Letters have flowed daily to Selectmen and the Finance Chairwoman pleading to keep the museum open and functioning at least at its current level. Dozens of people have come together to form a support group to make strategy to keep the museum afloat. More – almost 750 people – have signed petitions in support of the museum. 'What they're finding out now is that the people do care,' Wright said. 'If it weren't for the public outcry, nothing would have happened,' he said. 'It was like a test'."

Jake was reading this news on a fine, sunny Saturday morning while enjoying a pancake breakfast at the counter of the Golden Spoon when Wheel Barrow suddenly appeared, taking a seat on the stool next to him. He was obviously distraught. He leaned in close, whispering, pointing out the "stupidity" of members of the Friends of the Museum Association Support Group, people who would "interfere" with Museum Association matters. "They may or may not be happy with the Association," Barrow said, "but if there are problems, then they're problems of the Association, and the Association has to deal with them, not these people. They're internal matters, none of their business. You're making me angry," Barrow warned, lowering his voice. "You watch out about your loyalty – *or else*. Believe me, you don't want to say *too much* to your Friends in the Support Group," he warned.

"Everything you ever told me that was confidential, just between you and me, I've kept confidential, between you and me – and my diary."

Barrow stood to go. Scowling at Jake, he said firmly, deliberately, "I don't trust *anybody* who writes *anything* down," then he turned and went out.

The Artifacts Committee, scheduled to meet that day, didn't show up – except for Veronica Pillsbury. No one had told Committee member Veronica that the Artifacts Committee wasn't going to be meeting. She crossed the street to the Barrow Funeral home and learned from Wheel that'd he'd instructed the committee not to meet until the new fiscal year, starting in July. He said it was an oversight that Veronica hadn't been notified.

"I told him you were *also* hurt," Veronica told Jake after. "He told me, 'Jake does not need to know everything'."

On Mother's day, with our father's help, Mark and I filled our home with festive decorations and served Minna breakfast in bed. In the afternoon, we all walked down the railroad tracks around the Town Pond to the Fire Station, where the firemen were holding a fireman's festival. My father was at his best, joking around and laughing and shaking everybody's hands, putting all his troubles aside and obviously just enjoying the day immensely. Mayor Driscoll was there also, dancing like Zorba the Greek, holding the Ouzo bottle high, grinning wickedly.

The next day, Monday – *Black Monday* – *all* the museum staff received pink slips.

Jake phoned Wallace Barrow. He was not in. Around 4:00, Jake saw him arriving home. He went over and buttonholed him. The two went into Barrow's dark back office. He was wearing sunglasses. Jake couldn't see his eyes. "It is done," Barrow said, and turned away.

Back at the museum, a visitor sat on the front steps – a droll, hungover Mayor Driscoll. "You said I should come see the museum personally," he reminded Jake. He told Jake that Town Attorney Robert Carson had ruled that the "intent to remove" employees from the Museum of the Year 1912 had to be issued jointly by the Museum Association and the Mayor. The Mayor promised he would get for Jake a copy of the Town Counsel's letter. "I want you to know," he carefully emphasized, fixing his eyes on Jake's, "I am recommending that it not be *you* who loses his job. I am *for* the museum."

The next day, my father with heavy heart walked over to Town Hall to pick up the promised copy of Town Counsel's ruling on the "intent to remove" museum employees. The Mayor was on the front steps. Wistfully, he said, "It's in there. Tell the Association *three* positions are to be cut – all *but* the Director."

Julia Seymour-Stanton Mary Tuchlein had already begun packing their things. Only Audrey Morris, Hayden Brown, and Jake were present at the emergency staff meeting Wheel Barrow had called to order. He read Mayor Driscoll's letter aloud:

"This coming fiscal year's adopted Town budget substantially reduces funding to the Museum of the Year 1912. A reduction in personnel will be required. All museum employees to be affected by this budget reduction should be notified by June 11. The last day of the pay period is June 25th. Museum employees to be laid off cannot work beyond this date. The Town Attorney has indicated that the Executive Committee of the Museum Association and the Mayor are the joint appointing authority. It is requested that a joint meeting be scheduled to discuss what steps are to be taken for reduction in staff. Please inform this office regarding convenient dates and times."

Hayden Brown stood and went out. Wallace Barrow's eyes followed him out. He then held up a fresh page of paper. "This is a letter to Mayor Driscoll from Town Attorney Carson." He read:

"You have requested information as to the correct procedure to be followed when laying off town employees because of budgetary considerations. The procedure that must be followed is outlined in the Camperdene Charter under Chapter 7, Section 7-11. This section provides, in summary, that any appointed employee may be removed from the duties by the appointing authority. The process involves a written notice of intent to remove and a statement of the cause therefore to be delivered in hand to the employee or by registered or certified mail. The employee then has five days to request a hearing. The written notice of intent to remove is issued by the appointing authority of the employee. An additional point must be made with reference to the town employees who work in the Museum of the Year 1912. Because said employees are town employees and since the executive committee of the Museum Association is empowered to hire and discharge employees, it is my opinion that the notice of intent to remove must be jointly issued by the Mayor and the Executive Committee of the Museum Association."

Barrow said, "There is not money enough to fund more than one position. The half-time custodial position will go. Mr. Wright is aware he will become responsible for light housekeeping." Barrow requested that Jake should meet with his staff directly after he left, to discuss the matters that had come up at this meeting and to report to the Executive Committee in one week. Grinning hugely, Barrow closed the meeting.

Audrey went to the plush chair by the fireplace to sulk. Jake went over and sat down on the couch across from her. After a few minutes thick with her silence, she volunteered, "The Mayor is an idiot." She felt Wallace Barrow was being a perfect gentleman. She told Jake that Barrow had recommended to her, in private, that she should show no kindness toward the Town for what they were doing to her. The two now closed the museum and went out. Audrey was crying.

The next day, the Artifacts Committee met. Reggie Barrow was there. Veronica Pillsbury was not. Reggie informed Jake that he was now a member of this committee. He had been appointed to the post by his father, Wheel, Association President and Chairman of the Executive Committee.

On Monday, Jake marched alone in the Memorial Day Parade. Nick Wentworth, President of The Friends of the Museum, had recommended

Jake should go out in comfortable pants, suspenders, a red-and-white striped shirt, and a straw hat, looking like Uncle Sam himself. "You go out there and stand tall," Wentworth said, delivering a pep talk. "Like most people, I've had plenty of opportunity to sit by and watch corruption from the sidelines. Every now and then, however, we get pushed to the middle of things, where we must stand up. Too much sitting by and it's not long before your butt falls asleep. Also your head and heart. Now you go out there into that parade and you stand tall and tell people what you stand for and what you won't stand for."

On Tuesday, the Association's Executive Committee met with Jake at the long table by the air-conditioner. Jake presented a proposal for reduced hours in diminished circumstances. A merry Wallace Barrow declared, "It just shows we never needed even one staff person, doesn't it?"

Jake submitted, for the occasion, a "dress code for staff and volunteers" and suggested the Association should purchase an answering machine.

The Captain intently studied his copy of Jake's handout. Then he turned to him and said, "We'll take this under advisement." Jake went and fetched papers that needed their signatures. As the papers were handed around, Jake noticed Carlena Lagorio was frowning disdainfully at Wallace Barrow (eyebrows furrowed, her nose high). "Carlena?" Barrow said, "There is something you want to say?"

Carlena Lagorio held up a letter sent to Wallace Barrow from the President of the Friends of the Museum Association, Nicholas Wentworth. Her voice was shrill. *She* had not received a *courtesy copy* of Nick Wentworth's letter. *Captain Cunningham* had received a courtesy copy, she pointed out, but *she had not*. "How *come* I didn't get one of these?" Lagorio cried out. "Who else *did* get one? *Who* determines who gets what and who doesn't?" she demanded to know.

Greeted by puzzled looks and silence, Carlena Lagorio read the letter aloud:

"The Friends of The Museum of the Year 1912 have plans to begin raising money both from private and public contributions – including town businesses, industries, non-profit and fraternal organizations, and door-to-door canvassing – for the express purpose of building a brand new Museum of the Year 1912, from the ground up, in the town of Camperdene."

Ably, cunningly, Barrow and Captain Cunningham began loudly bickering, effectively shutting out Lagorio from the conversation, maneuvering the meeting to a confusing, bitter close. It was all in the newspaper the next day.

CHAPTER TWENTY-TWO

The Camperdene Daily Journal headline the next day was this: "New Museum Battle."

"Museum of the Year 1912 Association insiders say the members of the Executive Board of the Museum Corporation traded barbs over the motives of each other last night. Association president Wallace Barrow and Vice President Richard Cunningham said *both* wanted to be Board Chairman. As a means of forcing the issue, Cunningham distributed a release to the media saying why *he* should be President and why Barrow should *not*. Barrow charged Cunningham with 'grandstanding' to impugn his character, casting doubt regarding his ability to serve as Association President.

"In related news, the President of The Friends of the Museum Association, Nicholas Wentworth, has announced his group's plan to begin raising money from private and public contributions for the express purpose of building a new Museum of the Year 1912 in the town. Association President Wallace Barrow last night said he did not think such money could be raised, nor does he believe the money could be legally 'transferred' to the Town for the building of a new museum. He warned the Friends organization against any such fund-raising effort. 'If they intend to go ahead with this,' Association Vice President Richard Cunningham warned, 'they had better have their ducks in a row, and all the proper papers, including a soliciting permit.'

"Executive Committee member Carlena Lagorio expressed concern about the proposal that T-shirts could be sold at the Museum. 'There is concern all around,' she noted, 'about the words and/or picture to appear on the T-shirts. The Executive Committee wants to see the final design for the Friends' T-shirts, and to have the final say before any are printed'."

The Wright family celebrated the Fourth of July at the Town Picnic held in Camperdene's Central Park. At night, the fireworks flew. Songs were sung, and dances danced. I was happy. Curious and perplexed, Mark was like bread in soup, soaking it up. On the fifth of July, the Wrights signed papers, purchasing a house – the 1912 Craftsman bungalow Minna had set her heart on. The Wrights moved into their new home in mid-August.

Once moved into our new digs, the four of us slept together, that first night, in a new, enormous family bed. I got up first the next morning, already out and about exploring the house. Mark stayed in bed, snuggling close to Jake and Minna, demanding stories be read. He wrapped his arms around Minna who, I remember, was wearing a blue-and-white-striped one-piece bathing suit. "Do you like my nightclothes?" she asked. "Yes, mom," Mark said famously. "And your meat and bones and loving heart." I re-emerged in the room, cooing "foo-foo" and "Bee-o Bye-o." My trademark expression was "new-o" ("no"). I had my own language. To anything anybody asked, I answered, "New-o." In bed that morning, Jake tried to trick me. I was on a "new-o" bender, so Jake snuck in the question, "Are you the brightest, the smartest in the family?" I paused, looked at Jake cutely but intently, and famously said, "Yes."

On the following hot August night, with us two kids tucked into our own beds, Minna took Jake by the hand and led him out back of the house, to the garden, where they stood holding hands, looking up at the full moon a long while, before she finally pulled him down to her and caused them both, as Mark would later remember, "considerable ecstasy." Then they came back into the house to check on Mark and me. What with all the commotion, I had awoken and was crying. Minna tried to calm me – to no avail. In the living room, Jake moved a stack of books from a chair and sat down. He listened and waited. Finally Minna came down, discouraged. "I give up," she said. I was still crying. Jake recommended Minna let me come downstairs. He read to me from a book about gardens. Apparently I listened intently, then wandered around the disheveled house. Finally – satiated, exhausted – I was ready for sleep. The three of us went up to bed together.

Merriment filled the house and yard and neighborhood all the next day. Friends of the Museum President Nick Wentworth had organized a surprise housewarming party for us Wrights. He brought along a friend, Cal Winston, an Oriental Classics scholar who sang Oklahoma cowboy songs. After a few glasses of bourbon and several bottles of pale ale, Nick gave a short speech before passing out: "All are familiar with the legendary long-standing moronic bickering, back-biting behavior of the Museum Corporators through several years, and of the dire consequences for curators. If that behavior could be ended by so-called insubordination by the current curator and by public attendance at Corporator's meetings, then I say 'Go for it!' I happen to know the current curator is an able and creative person who is sincerely interested only in working cooperatively with other people – anybody – for the good of, and for the future of, not only the Museum of the Year 1912 but of our entire backwards community, of backwards-looking Camperdene. He makes mistakes and learns from his mistakes and remains hopeful, able, and eager to move ahead. Diligent and honest people who don't accept bribes should be *thanked*, not beheaded. Let people know what you stand for and what you won't stand for, Jake! Tear down the old bridge, people! Build a new bridge!"

Wentworth was resolved to build a new bridge between the Corporation and the appointed Board; between the Board and the staff; between the Board and the Friends of the Museum of the Year 1912 organization, even if that meant burning every bridge there had ever been behind him.

The Friends of the Museum were scheduled to meet with the Executive Committee of the Museum Association the next evening, but a furious August storm arose, with a hurricane warning. The winds were high; rain poured down; the museum windows were rattling. At half past eleven, Jake got a call from the new acting Mayor, Martha Stronski, who told him that all non-essential town employees should go home. Jake insisted it was *essential to him*, after all he'd been through, having fought so hard for so many months to remain at the helm of the museum, to stay – to not leave the museum in the middle of the day, even with a hurricane approaching. "Jake," Martha Stronski said, "admit it. A museum curator is not *essential* in a *hurricane*."

Jake secured the museum and went home. While the storm raged around them, the Wrights unpacked boxes, settling further into their new home. In the evening, Jake picked up that day's Camperdene Daily Journal. There was an article on page three illuminating "The Tenth Anniversary of the Temple of *The Ordo Templi Anodopetalum*."

Alice Armour Armstrong noted there hadn't been much talk in advance about the *reason* for this gathering, "and there was no speech-making, nor reminiscing at their secret dinner, touted as a Celebration for their Beloved Building's Tenth anniversary," she reported. "The order's collections – secret papers, precious jewels, medallions that members of the Higher Orders wear around their necks during meetings – were all housed far away from admiring eyes, in a heavy wooden chest. Wallace Barrow, four-time Past Master, said the notion of secrets dates back to the building of the Egyptian pyramids. This place where local members of *The Ordo Templi Anodopetalum* meet is the *Templi* – the Temple. Past Master Barrow told the Camperdene Daily Journal that the fraternal organization dates back to the building of the Temple of King Solomon. When asked why there was so much secrecy around the celebration tonight, Barrow leaned in close to this reporter and offered: 'Ours is not a *secret* group. We are, however, a group with certain *secrets*.'"

Chapter
Twenty-Three

"Be strong in the Lord and in the strength of his might," Camperdene's Congregational minister Simon Metcalf preached one bright, cool Sunday morning early in September, reading from Ephesians. "Put on the whole armor of God, that you may be able to stand against the wiles of the devil."

After the sermon and hymns and our communal prayers, Jake dropped off Minna and us kids at home and went over to the Golden Spoon for some pancakes and to read the Sunday paper. Sitting at the counter, as immersed in the news as the pancakes were drenched in maple syrup, Jake was startled from his reverie by Wheel Barrow, appearing suddenly, glaring. He leaned in close and whispered, "Listen, Wright. There'll be a new man working at the museum. He starts tomorrow." No mincing of words. "He'll be paid by the Association."

"Just so it's not Captain Cunningham," Jake said, kidding Barrow.

"It *is* Captain Cunningham," Barrow said.

Silence. About ten seconds of silence.

"You don't see any problems with that?" Jake said.

"No," Barrow answered. "Why?"

"Well," my unflappable father said, "I'm the curator, and he's the Vice President of the Corporation. Having the curator be the boss of the Association Vice President could be worse than a little awkward.

And we're talking about Powderkeg Cunningham. Based on his past performance, it seems to me we could be into some real trouble here."

"You won't be the boss of him," Barrow said firmly. "It won't be a problem."

"What will his schedule be?"

"He'll work twenty hours a week," Barrow explained. "You can work out a schedule with him tomorrow."

"Anything else I wanted to tell you?" Barrow asked himself. "No – I guess that's it," he said, and departed from the Golden Spoon grinning.

Usurpations, wrongs, offenses – *and yet ever increasing* usurpations, wrongs, and offenses. Gads, were it me, I think I would have torn all their hearts out with my bare hands. Would have plucked their eyes out! I would have strung them along on chains hanging out the backs of Jeeps! But not my father, Mr. Peaceable Kingdom. He seemed to take it all in his stride. Despite these terrible usurpations, wrongs, offenses! This private Corporation, created from and endowed by a trust, was *obviously* totally corrupt! I would have damned these usurpators, wrong-doers, offenders, to eternal hell. They deserved it. But my father? No. Unshaken, he never even raised his voice. Not my father, Mr. Saint Francis of Camperdene for crying out loud.

Back at the house, my mother was packing – but just for an afternoon picnic as it turned out, not leaving for good. Whew. Mark's new first grade classmates and their parents were gathering together at the mountaintop home of Mark's stuttering pal, Solomon. Mark would be starting first grade at a private school in the fall. Minna would be teaching German part-time. It was a fun day, but my father was seriously preoccupied with thoughts of Barrow's pressing revelations. That night, he began composing a letter to his new best friend at the museum, the President of the Friends group, Camperdene bookbinder Nick Wentworth.

"Dear Nick: Whoever cares ever more deeply for the fate of The Museum of the Year 1912 is ever a better friend of mine. Thank you for your concern. I trust that only good will come of it. I have lately come to have the opinion that a crime is itself, the punishment. I believe that conscience brings to each of us exactly such a punishment as we earn. Corruptions have occured that must cause certain individuals some awful, sleepless nights. So be it. You will remember that I made your acquaintance in the first place through my dedication to having good things happening at the museum. Though the series 'The Art of the Book in Camperdene,' of which your display was a part, would be immensely successful in the end, it early on faced opposition – from the President of the Museum Association and the Chairman of the Museum Artifacts Committee. You have recognized that the Museum Association has repeatedly malappropriated the display cases for the improper distribution of misinformation. So far as it is right for me to do so, I apologize for them. I have been careful to proceed in the most optimistic and productive manner possible – under the circumstances. I have been optimistic and forward-looking – and diplomatic, and patient, and cautious – in working with the Executive Committee of the Museum Association. Unfortunately, certain members of it – only a few, I must emphasize – have crossed the lines of civility. I trust formal apologies will be forthcoming soon. I trust justice will catch up with those who've abused their opportunities and the public's trust. I am eagerly awaiting a change in the current atmosphere, looking forward to a new Museum of the Year 1912. Anybody who also cares to see this happen is a friend of mine."

On the first Monday morning in September, my father walked to the museum and found, out front, Wallace Barrow chumming it up with former Mayor Barton Driscoll. Wheel was guffawing, regaling Driscoll with a story, then they were both braying – hee-haw, hee-haw, hee-haw. Jake went up the steps smiling, greeting them. Driscoll moved quickly toward Jake to take his hand, and shook it vigorously. Hands deep in his pockets now, Barrow was frowning. Jake asked for a second of his time. Driscoll said, "Excuse me, gentleman," and went across the lawn to depart in his new silver Audi convertible.

"What is it now?" Barrow asked.

My father told him he had given the matter of Captain Cunningham's impending employment much thought. He requested the Captain either be asked to step down as Vice President, or that the Executive Board reconsider its decision to make him a salaried employee of the Association. Jake repeated what he'd said the day before, that he couldn't see The Captain's being both under his authority even as The Captain had authority over him. Jake asked Barrow, couldn't he *see* how wrong it was for a museum trustee to be given a salaried post as a museum assistant? He searched desperately for a metaphor. "If one of your dying potential customers said he'd let you bury him only on the condition you let him have sex with your wife before he died, would you *sponsor* that?" Would that be *ethical*? Hiring a museum trustee, the Captain, to work for money at the museum – is that *ethical*?

"You're calling me a *pimp*?" old Wallace famously hollered out loud so that everybody in the neighborhood could hear. So that everybody in the *town* could hear. "Why, you *troublemaker*! You should get your *head examined*! I hope you have your resume out there because – you are *out of a job*!"

I would have told old Barrow to take his job and cram it or just slugged him in the guts and left him writhing on the ground, the bastard. But not my ethical, amicable father. He just stood there, waiting for the next thing to happen.

Indignant Barrow turned on his heels and marched away. What a showman! As if the whole world turned on this, he stomped across the street, stomped up his drive, and entered his funerary office, slamming the door behind him.

My father went back at his leisure into the museum and started making phone calls. He phoned the Commission of Museums in the Commonwealth of Massachusetts, Acting Mayor Martha Driscoll, and Alice Armour Armstong at the Camperdene Daily Journal. Tuesday's morning headline would read: "Museum of the Year 1912 Curator Not Pleased with New Staff Choice."

Chapter
Twenty-Four

"The museum's governing body has hired its own Vice President to assist the museum curator," Alice Armour Armstrong reported in the Camperdene Daily Journal. "Museum curator Jacob Friedman Wright said he was notified Sunday that the museum's private Corporation had hired its own Vice president, Richard Cunningham. Wright called the move unethical and said it puts him in the strange position of overseeing the work of one of his bosses. Richard Cunningham will be paid from the Association's own fund, which consists of the interest on a private trust.

"The museum, like many such New England institutions, is owned by a private Corporation and may or may not receive funding from the municipality. 'Bringing Cunningham on board is a matter of practicality,' said Wallace Barrow, President of the Museum Association. 'We need him,' he said. Barrow pointed out that Cunningham is willing to work for low wages, but did not say how much he will be paid. Cunningham, who will work twenty hours per week, declined to say how much he would be paid. He said serving as Vice President of the Association and working in the museum shouldn't be a problem. 'It's reasonably common in Corporations,' he said. Barrow and other museum Corporators said yesterday they saw nothing wrong with the move which is to be funded by the Corporation and not taxpayers. 'I look at it this way,' said Barrow: 'Banks can have presidents who often also are trustees.' Cunningham called it 'a non-issue,' adding he has worked as a volunteer at the museum for eleven years. 'I am going to be doing what I have been doing already for essentially no pay.'

"'As a professional curator with more than twenty years of experience, I don't think I can work with him both as Association Vice President and as a staff assistant,' Wright insisted. 'Being Vice President of a museum Corporation should not be a ticket to obtaining museum employment'. There have been rumors," Armstrong closed, "that Cunningham would like to run the museum."

In a separate article that same day: "Support Group Starts Drive to Build New Museum":

"A group of Museum of the Year 1912 supporters yesterday announced they will turn to old-fashioned fund-raisers to fund the building of a new museum. Over the next 10 months, members of The Friends of the Museum of the Year1912 say they hope to come up with more than $700,000.00 'to build a new museum building appropriate for the 21st Century.' One proposal is that it be built on Lake Street, on grounds fronting Camperdene Pond. 'The new museum,' said Friends' President Nicholas Wentworth, 'will provide programs and services in a welcoming environment which will promote inquiry and learning while lending entertaining and informational materials in a variety of formats for persons of all ages. It will be a community information center, a child's door opening to learning, an independent studies center, a formal education spport center, an outreach provider, a community activities center. This is possible,' Wentworth stated emphatically. 'We are going ahead with this proposal – we are going to build this new museum.' At present, the Friends group counts about 100 members. The Museum Association has not yet shared with this reporter their position on this issue."

"Dear Camperdene Resident," the newly formed Museum of the Year 1912 Building Support Subcommittee of the Friends of the New Museum began, "We are writing to ask for your help with a project that is of the utmost importance to the future of our town, the construction of a new Museum of the Year 1912. Our goal is to raise $900,000.00. Substantial pledges of $10,000.00 each have been received from assorted community banks and businesses. We enclose a pledge card for your convenience. Specifically, we ask you to pledge all you can in support of the capital fund drive for construction of a new Museum of the Year 1912. Sincerely, Nicholas Wentworth, President, Friends of the Museum of the Year 1912."

Jan Bundy, proprietor of the Golden Spoon Restaurant, was the first to sign on. This too was in the news: "Golden Spoon Restaurant Puts New Museum on Friday Menu": "The Golden Spoon Restaurant, at 37 Banyan Street, will offer its patrons an opportunity to support The Museum of the Year 1912 support group in its effort to raise funds for a new museum while they dine. From now through October, The Golden Spoon will donate 10 % of every meal purchased on a Friday to the museum support group. Owner Jan Bundy will work with Friends of The Museum president Nicholas Wentworth to host book displays at the restaurant. Bundy said the fundraiser is one way the restaurant can support the community."

On September 5th, in the afternoon, at about 2:30, Martha Stronski phoned Jake. "Your head is going to roll," she assured him. "The Association is in the process of having you removed from your position. Just so you know." She urged Jake to hire a lawyer.

I would have liked to have socked every sucker in that Association in the nose. What a bunch of jerks. Now my father was supposed to go and get a lawyer. Jerks! I'm so glad I was just a little kid and didn't know what was going on. Under those circumstances, knowing myself, unlike my father, I probably would have done some serious damage to somebody. I'm pretty sure. You never know what you're capable of sometimes.

My unflustered father recorded that Carlena Lagorio arrived at the museum at 4:00 p.m. sharp. She said to him, "I need to look in the files for Executive Committee minutes," and just went right on into the back room. Then she left, just five minutes before the museum closed at 5:00 p.m.

After closing the museum, Jake famously went to the office and found that Carlena Lagorio had gone through his desk and papers, including the contents of his personal briefcase. Further inspection of the premises revealed that the keys to every display case or cabinet in the building had been removed. Among the papers missing from Jake's briefcase was a note he'd written to himself: "Thursday, September 5th: Martha Stronski phoned to say the Museum Association is in the process of removing me and that I'd better get a lawyer."

CHAPTER TWENTY-FIVE

Captain Cunningham came in the next morning with Association member Roland Henselmeier to install an exhibit of postage stamps bearing George Washington's visage. Jake asked the Captain if he knew the whereabouts of the keys to the assorted locked cases, which were suddenly missing. Cunningham said he didn't know, and held up an empty wooden box for Jake to see. "My key was in this box," he said. He put down the box and held up his hand for Jake to see: he was holding his own key.

Jake had learned later that, in fact, the Executive Board of the Association had appointed the Captain official keeper of the keys. Mary Tuchlein observed, "Just when you think the Association has reached the bottom, they surprise you. They just keep going down."

At the Lutheran Church that Sunday, reading from Mark 7:31-37, Pastor Metcalf cried out, "*Ephphatha*! – Be opened!" The closing prayer was exceptionally long, touching on the theme of suffering, especially "for people in periods of transition", and "facing tough choices." During the hymns, my father sang his heart out. After the service, he took a walk around the town with Mark and me. Wallace Barrow was out front of his funeral manse, clipping the hedges with buzzing electric hedge-cutters. He waved Jake over. He turned off the cutters. Taking his children's hands in his, Jake approached.

"I warned you not to cross me," a stern Barrow said fiercely, right in front of Mark and me. "I will squash you like a *bug*."

"Let's go, kids," my father said softly, ignoring Barrow and shepherding us away.

"I will crush you like an *insect*!" old Barrow screamed at Jake's back, letting his hedge shears rip.

"Daddy," Mark said thoughtfully, after we'd walked about a quarter mile. "Does this mean you're going to lose your job?"

"No," Jake assured Mark. "It means we're going to get a better museum so I can do a better job without that man to stop me." In the back of his mind, Jake was already composing a letter of resignation:

"I have heard, and do not doubt, it is the will of the Executive Committee of the Museum of the Year 1912 Association that I should no longer serve as Director. I would comply, except I remember that I came to Camperdene for a reason: to be of service, and to be of some value, to this community. I am not inclined to let myself be so simply turned away. Like it or not, we are together now – whether together or apart – entering a new phase."

The Superintendent of Schools, Michael Bonaventura, had meanwhile written to Barrow, "While I clearly do not know the complete story, I would like to be on record as agreeing with Jake Wright that the Museum Association Executive Board's hiring of Association Vice President Richard Cunningham is entirely inappropriate – and, in fact, seems purposefully confrontational. I don't know the Association's By-laws (though I should), but it is certainly considered usual for Boards of nonprofit charitable organizations to stay at the policy (not practice) level, confining their hands-on impulses to approving the overall budget, supporting institutional development, and hiring a curator to run the organization. Explaining the rationale of the crucial division of responsibility and authority between Board members and the curator would be to belabor my point. Suffice it to say this recent action undermines trust, creates barriers, and demeans the Museum Board. This is a matter of principle. I could not let it pass without comment."

In mid-September came powerful headline news, Alice Armour Armstrong reporting: "Seven Million Dollars for The Museum of the Year 1912."

"An anonymous donation of six million dollars has been made toward securing the building of a new museum in Camperdene. Nicholas Wentworth, local bookbinder and President of the Friends of the Museum of the Year 1912 and its Museum Building Support Group, said he yesterday received a direct transfer in that amount from a private account into the only recently created New Museum Building account. The donor, rumored to be a long-time supporter of the Museum of the Year 1912 Association, 'has asked to remain anonymous,' Wentworth disclosed. 'There are just two conditions, stipulations,' Wentworth added: '(1) there can be *no* money from the fund that shall go to standing or special displays at the New Museum featuring 'The Pujo Committee' which, in 1912, made investigations into allegations that the entire financial industry was being controlled by just a few wealthy individuals; and (2) *all* money allocated for the building of a *new* Museum of the Year 1912 must respect that the façade architecture of the new museum shall be based on that of The Beaney House of Art and Knowledge in Canterbury, England.'

"'These conditions do seem a little eccentric,' Wentworth acknowledged. 'But I'm so accustomed to being so blindsided by so much more deeply incomprehensible demands so far worse. This is Easy Street. The donor's idea is that Camperdene and Canterbury should be 'sister cities', Wentworth said. 'I like that'."

"The Mayor of Canterbury had laid the foundation stone for the Beaney Institute in September 1897; the building had been completed in September 1899.

"The astonishing anonymous contribution brings Camperdene's New 1912 Museum Building Fund to a whopping seven million dollars.

"Sidestepping the issue of the ongoing conflict between the Museum Association and its Director, Jacob Wright, Wentworth said he hopes Wright will consider serving at the helm of the new museum operation, 'steering a bold, fresh course'."

The news carried my father into a splendid season of hope and love and friendship, I think. He seemed hungry every morning – famished! – and he sang in the shower. And he sang all day. Seriously. I just loved it. I remember this. It was just a season of singing and singing and singing.

CHAPTER TWENTY-SIX

Captain Cunningham was furious when Jake phoned him at home, saying a number of people had been in, all wanting to see special materials in the museum collection. "A gentleman from California was in, wanting to know if we had any historical records mentioning one Solomon Albert Kendall, born in 1912. Perhaps Camperdene's Kendall Street was named for him? Unfortunately, the keys to all of our locked cases have been removed from the office. I have notified Association President Wallace Barrow of our need for the immediate return of the keys. If he or you can't find out about the whereabouts of the keys, we'd better begin an investigation into what happened to them! Thanks."

On Friday the 13th, Jake got a call from Ben Mulvane: "Hi Jake. I got a call last night – late last night – and I was told that all the keys are in a cabinet in the museum somewhere – and there's a key to the cabinet in question in plain sight, but I don't have it."

"Don't have what?"

"The key."

"To the cabinet?"

"Right."

"Wait a minute, Ben. The keys are all here, in the museum?"

"I guess. In a cabinet, or in plain sight."

"Okay, Ben. Fine. When you find out where to get the key to open the cabinet to get the keys to the cabinets, or you find out where, in plain sight, the key to the historical collections cabinet is, you'll let me know?"

"Yes."

Later that day, a young woman arrived with an envelope to deliver to Jake. She was from the firm Leventhal, Leventhal & Harper, Attorneys-at-Law, 46 Allston Street, Boston, Massachusetts. "Are you Jacob Wright? she asked politely.

"Yes."

"This is for you," she said, and handed Jake the envelope and turned and went out.

"Dear Mr. Wright," Mr. Kevin F. Harper had written. "I represent the Executive Committee of The Museum of the Year 1912 Association. They have asked that I review your Letter of Resignation. On their behalf and in their name I respond as follows: 1. Your resignation is accepted; 2. The Board is anxious to minimize the impact of your job change on you and your family. For that reason the Board will make sure that your income will continue as curator until December 31st. If this is acceptable, we will determine what the sum total of your accrued vacation and other benefits and establish a termination date prior to December 31st that will allow you to receive income through December 31st. In no event will the termination date be prior to October 15th; 3. Should you find a new position prior to the termination date you may terminate your position sooner, at which time you will be due all your accrued benefits."

That night, Jake answered Kevin Harper: "Thank you for your letter, dated today and delivered to me at The Museum of the Year 1912 this afternoon. I am surprised to learn that you reviewed any resignation letter of mine, for I did not write one. I am attaching a copy of a note I sent to members of the Executive Committee of the Museum Association that may have been mistaken, by them, for a letter of resignation but, please be assured, I did not resign. Most Association members have emphatically been asking me not to leave my post until such time as the Association itself, as a body, has looked into the Board's acts and intentions in both the matter of Captain

Cunningham's gainful employment at the museum and its curious conjunction with my potentially being dismissed."

At the end of the week Jake joined members of the Friends of the New Museum of the Year 1912 in an inspection of the proposed grounds, near Camperdene's Lake Street Park, for the new museum. The land was owned, most serendipitously, by the very benefactor who had already infused several million dollars into the Museum Building fund.

In the following week, Jake learned from Ben Mulvane that Ben and Veronica Pillsbury and other dispirited Corporators of the old Museum Association – mutineers – were bailing out. "Wallace Barrow is saying you slandered Captain Cunningham, calling him a pimp whose wife 'did tricks' for men at night in the museum."

"He did? I did?"

"Barrow is saying so. For all I know, there may be truth in it. Still, I don't even want to know what you actually did say to him. Captain Powderkeg is calling all around the town to tell Association Corporators that if you say you didn't say what Barrow says you said, you're lying."

"So what else is new?"

Ben was angry, but reflective. He felt Jake should be" the highest paid employee of the town": "I know what you're earning. They should pay you three times that for the job you do and another four times that for what you have to put up with!"

After a three-day heat-wave, with lightning and thunder ripping the heavens, bringing in cool air and heavy showers, the news came that the New Museum of the Year 1912 Building Committee had named its architects, Aldred, Hutton, and Campbell in Brookline, and that the proposed Lake Street property fronting Camperdene Pond was deeded over to the New Museum of the Year 1912 Board by the same anonymous benefactor who had already contributed millions to the project.

Captain Powderkeg was now spending many afternoons at Wallace Barrow's – brewing up something. One afternoon, Barrow and The

Captain were joined in the funeral parlor by Carlena Lagorio, Roland Henselmeier, Angela Perry, and others.

Jake had meanwhile taken the new Mayor's advice, and hired a lawyer. Jake's attorney, Andrew Coffey, had sent a letter to Kevin F. Harper, Esquire: "Dear Mr. Harper, I am representing Jacob Wright in the matter of his present position of employment with The Museum of the Year 1912 Association. I have reviewed your letter of September 13th as well as the text of the document which you apparently misinterpreted as a 'resignation'. I am sure that upon re-reading in light of this letter you will realize that this communication was in response to a recent outburst of Association President Wallace Barrow on September 3rd. At that time, he advised Mr. Jake, in effect, that he was out of his job; probably a misunderstanding as well.

"I believe that the trigger for the outburst had to do with the suggestion that the Museum of the Year 1912 Association's Executive Committee had acted inappropriately by hiring one of its own number as staff of the museum. While expressing no opinion of my own upon the subject, it is certainly true that a public trust such as that of the museum trustee used so that it inures to the benefit of one of its fiduciaries, is often regarded as possibly unethical in a variety of settings. I conclude that such concerns expressed by Mr. Wright was at the least a principled, professional, and appropriate matter for discussion between the curator of the museum and its Executive Committee.

"I have received communications from other citizens in the community who I know to be highly regarded – highly ethical and responsible people – who have indicated that they agree with the position taken by Mr. Wright on the matter of hiring Richard Cunningham. Once again, without taking a position of my own, it is my judgment that raising the issue was an appropriate and prudent act by Mr. Wright as the Executive Committee's employee. The outburst by Mr. Barrow could be regarded as retaliatory. I am concerned that the measured and thoughtful and obviously anguished communication of Mr. Wright should be tortuously misconstrued as a formal resignation. It was not; it does not say that it is.

"As a man of words your careful review will indicate that Mr. Wright was 'resigned' to a fate of certain severance from the Board to whom he addressed the letter, but it was after a denunciation and declaration by Mr. Barrow which occurred on Tuesday, September 3rd and was not initiated by him as an act of termination or separation. As nearly as I am able to determine from reviewing the by-laws and documents relative to the Museum of the Year 1912 Association under the terms of his employment his present term extends through June 30th. If your actions are to be interpreted to be the actions of the Corporation's Executive Committee, then this is a formal reply that you requested to put you and your client on notice that Mr. Wright does not feel he has resigned, nor has any legally sufficient official step been taken to terminate him. I suggest that all parties deliberately and dispassionately review the recent events and consider whether Mr. Wright was in fact acting professionally and responsibly to call attention to the Board (by which he is employed) that there was a potential problem with an action they had taken that merited further consideration. Perhaps a reasonable observer will conclude that the appointment was not unethical, illegal, or improper. That does not make raising the question evil; it is, rather, prudent.

"I hope that the reply you have required by September 18th, and which this letter confirms (I will have called you), will be understood not as a cannon or a salvo, but rather an olive branch. Even if our respective clients must separate there does not seem to be any sound reason that they should do so with a letting of blood or a trashing of a neighborhood. I would rather resolve this matter in a peaceful and measured way. I seek to enlist your help in that course. Very truly yours, Andrew R. Coffey."

With a copy of this letter, Mr. Coffey sent a copy of a short note sent to School Superintendent Bonaventura: "Enclosed please find a blind copy of a letter I have written to Kevin F. Harper in an effort to assist in cooling tempers and moving this matter back into a more appropriate perspective. I certainly cannot tell whether it will work, and

I am sending this in the hopes that perhaps with this knowledge you will be able to assist."

Later in the month, a lady arrived at The Museum of the Year 1912 from Rochester, New York, looking for information about her ancestors which she believed she could find among the museum's archival materials. She said she was in town only for this one day. Jake called Captain Cunningham. "Hello, Captain."

"Hello."

"A lady is in all the way from Rochester, New York, and she wants to look at our historical materials."

"So?"

"So, can you come in and help her?"

"I don't have the key."

"You don't have the key?"

"I think you know that. And I think you know why."

"No, I don't know. Can you tell me?"

"Look in the Camperdene Daily Journal"

"Today's?"

"No. Last week."

"*When* last week?"

"I think you know."

"I don't know, Captain. Can you tell me?"

"You know. And you will pay."

"I'm being punished? The keys have been removed to punish me?" The Captain hung up.

Jake tried to explain the situation to the lady from Rochester, who was sympathetic to his plight. "I assume you're looking for work elsewhere," she said.

Reverend Metcalf, also sympathetic, left a note for Jake, saying, "I just want you to know you have been in my thoughts (even in a prayer or two) this week. Hope you are hanging in there and able to feel life's marvelously crisp edge. Keep the faith. Reverend Metcalf."

As the Association bowed out of participating in the Annual Fall Festival, the Friends of the New Museum of the Year 1912 showed up, advancing the "Build the New Museum" campaign. Jake was at the Festival at assorted hours throughout the weekend, helping out at the "New Museum" booth, showing off the architectural firm Aldred, Hutton, and Campbell's designs. I was happy to run around barefoot at the festival, under clear blue skies, delighted amid all the people and all the bustle and activity. I remember Mark was wild about the airbag-trampoline ride and the burgers and the hot dogs.

Association treasurer Joan Perry-Barrow was working at the Hamburgers and Hot Dogs stand. She said, frankly, that she felt for Jake in his plight. She said she really didn't know what was going on, but she said she knew he'd got himself into some kind of trouble and she said she knew he'd come out all right one way or another. It was Joan in her food truck who offered Jake and Mark and me a ride home (Mark, hauled home from a festival in a pick-up truck full of hamburgers and hot dogs, was thrilled; me not so much).

At the end of the month, my father wrote a letter to Ellis Bolton, the editor of the Camperdene Daily Journal: "My name is Jake Wright. I am the curator of the Museum of the Year 1912. I am as glad in doing my job as I was when I came here – and as committed to following the ethics of my profession as when I entered the profession in the first place. On September 3rd, I urged the President of the private museum Corporation to call on the Vice-President to step down from the Executive Board, or to have the Executive Board re-consider its having hired him to a salaried post. As a result I was told by the President of the Museum Association (before ever he conferred with his associates) that I was out of a job.

"Even as these events unfolded, a different group of Camperdene citizens have been engaged in seeking funds for the building of a wholly *different* museum, The *New* Museum of the Year 1912. Seven million dollars have been raised. We will be seeing here, in our community, soon, the kind of Museum that is not only due, but overdue. I will work closely with the New Museum Building branch of the recently established Friends of the New Museum of the Year 1912 as a team member. With the approval of town officials, and the backing of the

Friends' seven million dollar fund, we will be moving forward toward the creation of a healthy institution doing a good job, free of such treachery and insult as has been customary in that withered, musty, almost byzantine institution, The Museum of the Year 1912 Association."

Early in October came an "informal" meeting, so called, of the Association's Executive Committee – the "Treason Hearing," as it would later be called. The Corporation's lawyer, Mr. Harper, was present. Jake's lawyer was not. The motley crew met with Jake at the familiar long tables amid the magazines and newspapers. The atmosphere was extraordinarily chilled: Carlena Lagorio seemed to choose her place carefully: next to Jake, her chair pushed sideways so that she faced him 100% – 100% of the time – scowling, nose high, looking down at him (she'd obviously been coached, or she had trained herself, prior to this evening, in the fine art of making people feel small in a tight spot). But Jake found her stance quite predictable – even humorous. He avoided looking at her.

In the course of the meeting, Vice President Cunningham spoke not at all. Treasurer Angela Perry was also silent (except when Mr. Barrow asked Jake if he had not had a certain conversation with her. Jake had, and he said so. He said he'd written it out longhand, and had then thrown his notes away, because the conversation indeed had been "confidential."

"It still is," Angela said (so how come Mr. Barrow knew all about it?).

Carlena Lagorio was openly hostile. At one point, Carlena Lagorio's intent to "do damage" to Jake was introduced into the conversation – then the matter of Wallace Barrow's having taken him into a room in his funeral home where a body was on the bier, where Mr. Barrow had explained that Carlena Lagorio had a drinking problem. Mr. Barrow led Lagorio to the Director's office to see whether or not she wanted that discussed any further. She did not.

Roland Henselmeier was bold, making assorted off-the-wall assertions. He said Jake had been told to keep his hands off the display cases, and yet Jake had gone ahead, without permission, and organized and curated the successful series of displays and workshops/programs concerning "The Art of the Book in Camperdene,'" featuring local artisans.

Wheel Barrow appeared as stately, elegant, and charming as ever, presiding over the kangaroo court. He had begun by asking Jake if he recognized the "validity" of the Association's by-laws, and followed with all kinds of questions and accusations (expressly stated or insinuated) concerning the "danger" Jake had placed the Museum Association in, and the "damage" Jake had done – and was still doing – to it – to them.

I would have stood up and walked over and socked that clown Barrow on the jaw, but not my father. No, he just sat there all silence and subservience, like a Quaker in his pew.

The Association's newest member, the Captain's daughter, Association Secretary and Clerk Lizzie Cunningham, sitting across the table from Jake, spoke boldly and often, and clearly in support of Mr. Barrow's points. This surprised Jake, as she had inquired, early in the discussion, as to whether or not Jake felt that members of the board had minds of their own and could think independently. Jake had said he felt indeed that members of the board had minds of their own and could think independently. Nonetheless, here she was, the secretary, taking notes, aping Barrow's points and views, though almost all the matters under discussion had preceded her presence on the board or had transpired without her being involved.

Lizzie Cunningham wondered aloud four or five times in the course of the evening as to why Jake made so many "errors of judgment in recent weeks," asking why he hadn't immediately, after his morning confrontation with Mr. Barrow, called a special meeting with the Board (Jake had never called a "special meeting" with the board before; nor did he know he could do so; nor did he think it would have done him any good). "I didn't think to," Jake said each time, in response to Lizzie's repeated refrain. "Why didn't the Board call a special meeting with me?"

In the company of his colleagues and their attorney, Barrow made a striking closing remark: he recommended that Jake cease to associate with "that seven million dollar infidel on Banyan Street," the President of the Friends of the New Museum of the Year 1912 and the New Museum Building Committee, bookbinder Nicholas Wentworth.

Their attorney, Mr. Harper, was not hostile. He did snicker and orate copiously, helping along the "kangaroo court" atmosphere of the session. The word "collusion" comes to mind. He obviously enjoyed his own command of legalese and displayed a clear, deep pleasure in his own voice (almost non-stop talk) and abundant rhetorical flourishes. (Interestingly, Jake was no more impressed or intimidated by all that than he was by Carlena Lagorio's harsh, hate-filled-stare trick.) Harper stated quite clearly, in any case, that his clients felt Jake had, in his words and actions, "damaged" the Museum of the Year 1912, "threatened" its security and well-being, and done "irreconcilable harm" to the institution, which his clients were obliged to safeguard.

Jake politely disagreed.

Mr. Harper informed Jake that the Association secretary would be writing up the minutes of the meeting longhand, and he would be asked to sign them in witness of their veracity. He said he would be contacting Jake's attorney sometime soon. The meeting was adjourned.

A few days after that, Mayor Martha Stronski met with the Association's Executive Board. Barrow was as cunning, accomodating, and slimy as he could possibly be. But, no matter. Martha Stronski was working closely, in the meantime, with Town Attorney Carson, writing up Jake's contract with the town, and a job description.

Barrow was doing everything in his power to de-rail the forthcoming transition – Jake's leaving the employ of the Association to become curator of the New Museum of the Year 1912 – but the Association was already fast becoming but a footnote in the annals of local history, as the people of Camperdene forged ahead with the building of their grand new forward-looking museum.

On October 22nd, a Camperdenian, Bonnie Patterson, came to the museum in hopes of looking at some historical materials. Per Captain Cunningham's orders, Jake told her she would have to contact him. She did. She called Cunningham and then returned, later in the day, angry and shaking, to tell Jake of the conversation she'd had with old

Powderkeg. She was told, among other absurdities, that "Mr. Wright doesn't come from here. He's just making trouble. Soon he'll be gone."

Jake called his attorney, Andrew Coffey, on November 3rd to let him know that Captain Cunningham had called him to say Cunningham would be starting work at the museum the next day, and that the Association's Treasurer, Angela Perry, had quit the Board (in disgust). She'd felt such urgency, she'd gone to Jake's home to tell him. Though her daughter had married Barrow's son Reggie, she had just realized *enough was enough*. She said the final straw was something her colleague on the board, Carlena Lagorio, had said. "It was just incredible," Angela Perry told Jake, without divulging the insult. "I just stood up and told them, 'I'm through,' and I walked out of the museum."

The next day, Captain Cunningham started work at the Museum of the Year 1912, whether Jake – or anybody else – liked it or not.

Then, one sunny, cold morning when Jake was out front of the museum, talking with Art McCaffrey, a wonderful, humble, outspoken mailman, Powderkeg's purple-faced daughter Lizzie Cunningham walked up with scowling, furious-faced Carlena Lagorio. Talk about spoiling a day. The two settled in at the end of a long table near the 1912 Olympics display case. Sun streaked in. They called Jake over to review some papers. He moved to sit down in the chair next to Lizzie's. She said, "Why don't you sit across from me?" This put Jake next to nose-high, skulking Carlena Lagorio. Lizzie pushed a stack of papers across the table toward Jake.

"These are?" he inquired.

"The minutes. We thought you wanted to see them."

"I had asked you, simply, to send a copy to my lawyer."

"I thought you had said you wanted to go over them with me first."

At that point, I would have slugged her in the guts, I think. But not my father. No, he didn't bat an eyelash. "No. Not today," my father said. "You can just send them as they are."

Lizzie was visibly angry and in pain. Carlena Lagorio banged her chair against Jake's and scraped it along the floor a little ways and then dropped it, all just to create for an invisible audience some added ruckus of noise and extra drama.

"Sorry about the misunderstanding, Lizzie," Jake said (Seriously) as the two departed.

You might think things could not possibly have gotten worse at that point, but they did. A "spontaneous' demonstration took place that same evening. On the Museum lawn an unruly crowd of protestors showed up wearing sandwich boards and carrying torches, pitchforks, shovels, rakes, and protest signs:

"Liar, Liar, Pants on Fire"
"Jake Must Go"
"Jacob Wake Up"
"Wright Is Wrong"

I can just see them. In my mind's ear I can just hear this lynching rabble chanting:

"He'll cause mayhem you will see, if we simply let him be!"
"Beware: he'll stalk you in the night, with his monster appetite!"
"We aren't done with him at all; we'll mount his head upon a wall!"

They hoisted banners:

"He's Not Like Us"
"We Won't Take No More Jake"
"We See the Light, No More Wright"
"He's Not Sorry"

Just plain nuts!

On the surface, my father may have been laughing at all this concocted weird commotion but I think, deep down, this must have been the last straw – must at last have hurt his dignity, his sense of pride. I think in secret he was weeping, wailing, crying. I don't know. At that time, maybe not.

All I know for certain is that, after the angry mob finally dispersed in the night, Jake sat down, pen in hand, and calmly composed a handwritten letter to the Association:

"Dear Museum Association Members, In compliance with your Executive Committee's October 3rd Executive order, declaring me to be ineligible as a candidate for the position of curator of the Museum of the Year 1912, I have sought employment elsewhere, and have found it."

Next, news came of a formal Resolution adopted by the Mayor: "Museum management shall not be private. Administration of the New Museum of the Year 1912 shall be conducted with openness and accountability to the citizens of Camperdene. Museum administrators shall show a willingness to cooperate with any people or groups working to improve museum services."

On November 9th, Alice Armour Armstrong reported in the Camperdene Daily Journal, "Richard Cunningham has quietly stepped down from his post as Vice President of the Museum of the Year 1912 Association. The Corporation's President, Wallace Barrow, confirmed Cunningham's resignation yesterday. 'Of course he stepped down,' said Barrow. 'It was the obvious thing to do.'"

Jake's lawyer, Attorney and Counsellor At Law Andrew Coffey, let him know, "We've won."

Soon, all the streets and shady lanes of Camperdene were riddled with campaign placards. The Board of the New Museum of the Year 1912 was to consist of six members. The special election outcome was not surprising. Three of the new Board members were former Corporation Executive Committee members – Wallace Barrow, Roland Henselmeier, and Carlena Lagorio – and three were "new" faces – Ben Mulvane, Veronica Pillsbury, and Michael Bonaventura.

Of course it wasn't very long until the Camperdene Daily Journal headline appeared, "1912 Museum Battle."

"The Board Trustees of the New Museum of the Year 1912 will again attempt to elect a chairman tonight," Alice Armour Armstrong reported, "as the top contenders traded barbs over the motives of each other. Both Wallace Barrow and Carlena Lagorio have said they want to be Board Chairman. Each has two backers. This leaves the six-member board in a deadlock. As a means of forcing the issue, Barrow distributed a release to the media saying why he should be Chairman and why he feels Lagorio should not."

The next day, the town was taken by surprise by the Camperdene Daily Journal headline: "Benjamin Mulvane Chairman of New Museum Board" – "Bowing to the fact that past museum struggles have tarnished the image of Museum Trusteeship in the town of Camperdene," wrote Alice Armour Armstrong, "the New Museum of the Year 1912 C, which includes three representatives from the old Museum of the Year 1912 Association, last night unanimously elected neophyte Benjamin Mulvane as its chairman. But the Board was divided in its support of museum curator Jacob Wright, former curator of the old Museum of the Year 1912, now run by Museum Association past President and Vice President, Richard Cunningham. Mulvane, Trustee Veronica Pillsbury, and School Superintendent Michael Bonaventura, another new member of the recently created New Museum of the Year 1912 Trustee Board, all had only the highest praise for museum curator Wright, but the Association's representatives to the new Board – Wallace Barrow and Roland Henselmeier – expressed doubts, while their colleague, Carlena Lagorio, could not be reached for comment.

"Local bookbinder Nick Wentworth, named Chairman of the New Museum of the Year 1912 Building Committee, joined Ben Mulvane, Museum Project Manager, in viewing the architectural firm Aldred, Hutton, and Campbell's museum blueprints at Camperdene Town Hall last night. Mulvane told reporters. 'We've got a green light – it's "all systems go" – for the New Museum of the Year 1912'."

CHAPTER
TWENTY-SEVEN

Now came a season of still more heated battle – both formal and informal, both rigid and formed on the fly. The meetings involved mostly Mayor Stronski, Town Attorney Carson, the Town Council, the Superintendent of Schools Michael Bonaventura, New Museum of the Year 1912 Building Committee Chairman Nick Wentworth, and Project Manager Ben Mulvane. All were up to their eyeballs in the labyrinthical transition.

The lawyers from each faction wrangled over the collections to be handed over from the one institution to the other. Powderkeg Cunningham's inventory listing the old museum's holdings sent impartial investigators out to break the locks on the doors of a dozen or more different secret storage units throughout Camperdene and its neighboring environs, them attempting to get their hands on whatever they could from the old museum's widely distributed hidden contents:

A collection of ten hobo wooden nickels and twenty carved nickels; rocks and shells collected in India, Corfu, Egypt, Yugoslavia, Rhodes, Cyprus, and the south of France by Simon and Louisa Lagorio; miscellaneous American Indian artifacts. 1912 railroad depots, terminals, tracks, change makers, and tickets paraphernalia; advertising (idyllic families, cherubic children, fairytale ladies; all promising beauty, love, and miraculous cures); a packet of seeds for cherry trees like those sent from Tokyo to Washington, D.C. on March 27, 1912; assorted 1912 novelties; soaps, perfumes, foods, patent medicines, and items for leisure activities; a dozen harmonicas; an accordion; a guitar that had been owned by blues singer and guitarist Lightnin' Hopkins; hundreds of assorted children's games and toys; playing cards; Tarot cards; a box filled with cigars that belonged either to anarchist Ben Tucker or anarchist Ben Reitman; a meerschbaum pipe that had been Henry Miller's; pipes that had belonged to Freud, Jung, and Eric Sevareid; a Scoville Heating Unit testing system apparatus; a bat, ball, and glove that had belonged to Red Sox pitcher Joe Wood; a single (empty) Cracker Jack Caramel Coated Popcorn & Peanuts package carrying the message "A Prize in Every Box," and eighty-seven different accompanying Cracker Jack prizes; a package of Crane's Peppermint Life Savers; a Whitman's Chocolates Sampler box; Lorna Doone cookies; Nabisco Oreo cookies; a carton of Morton's Table Salt; a jar of Cape Cod Cranberry Company Ocean Spray Cape Cod Cranberry Sauce; a jar of Hellmann's mayonnaise; a roll of cellophane from Switzerland; a hamburger buns; bread loaves; sliced bread; roses; dollar bills; a Navy torpedo patented in 1912 by B.A. Fiske; a bayonette; a machine gun; Bullets; a dozen sticks of (powderless, fuseless, and disabled) dynamite; chains; Cumming and Carberry handcuffs; a pair of Al Jolson's shoes, one of his kneepads, and a blackface makeup kit; a pair of Eleanor Powell's tap dance shoes; the shoes Pierre Teilhard de Chardin had worn when he'd been ordained as a priest; shoes said to have been cobbled together by Italian American laborers Ettor, Giovannitti, Caruso, Tresca, Galleani, Sacco, and Vanzetti; a wide-brimmed felt hat that had belonged to Charles Fletcher Lummis; a straw hat with a price tag hanging on it that had belonged to Minnie Pearl; two "simultaneous dresses" designed by painter Robert Delaunay's wife Sonia for actress Gloria Swanson, both successfully echoing the peasant Russian costumes of her childhood while illuminating her avant-garde theories of non-representational color abstraction; a colorful, striped dress that had belonged to Edith Schiele, wife of Austrian Expressionist painter Egon Schiele; a chess set that had belonged to Alan Turing; four different

1912 birth control devices; a medical kit that had belonged to Clara Barton, the founder of the American Red Cross; William Carlos Williams' empty doctor's bag; Albert Schweitzer's doctor's bag (with pills and ointments for curing malaria, sleeping sickness, leprosy, elephantiasis, heart complaints, osteomyelitis, tropical dysentery, hernias, pleurisy, whooping cough, and venereal diseases); ribbons, pins, sashes, miscellaneous ephemera, and confetti collected at the New York City parade honoring the return from the Swedish Summer Olympics of the 24-year-old American Indian, Jim Thorpe who, after winning the the pentathlon and decathlon, had been dubbed "the greatest athlete in the world" by the Swedish King, Gustav V (Thorpe had replied, "Thanks, King"); ribbons, pins, sashes, and other ephemera from the 1910 New Jersey Democratic Gubernatorial Convention, from which Woodrow Wilson had gone on to become Governor of New Jersey and President of the U.S.; ribbons, pins, sashes, and other ephemera from the Industrial Workers of the World and the Socialist Party collected at the 1912 Socialist's convention held in Indianapolis; similar stuff collected at the Democratic, Republican, Progressive, and several other 1912 Conventions; one of Eugene V. Debs' own handkerchiefs; spectacles that had belonged to Teddy Roosevelt; fob watches belonging to Teddy Roosevelt, William Howard Taft, Uncle Joe Cannon, Robert LaFollette, Elihu Root, Warren G. Harding, William Jennings Bryan, Eugene Chafin, Oscar Underwood, Champ Clark, Woodrow Wilson, and Sigmund Freud; one of Freud's morphine vials; a pair of cufflinks that had been Gustav Carl Jung's; a wedding ring that had belonged to Otto Rank; a pair of woolen hiker's breeches that had been George Bernard Shaw's; other assorted woolen goods; a loom; a parachute that had belonged to Captain Albert Berry, the first man ever to descend from an aircraft to the earth by parachute (from a height of 1,500 feet, in Missouri); one of Louis Armstrong's first cornets, with the mouthpiece notched all around, because Armstrong believed this improved his embouchure ("bouche" means "mouth"), giving maximum sound with minimum effort and play without pain (on a note attached by a string to the instrument: "only Louis Armstrong notched a cornet like that");

an oil lamp and a twisted metal scrap from a dogsled used by Roald Amundsen in his journey to the South Pole; a lucky horseshoe that had been owned by Robert F. Scott atop a facsimile copy of Scott's South Pole expedition diary; a propeller from the first amphibious aircraft, Grover Loening's "aeroboat" concocted from an old speedboat and a Blériot fuselage, prop chain-driven, the motor mounted in the hull (Loening had gone on to work for the Wilbur and Orville Wright Company); a chain-driven twin engine Harley-Davidson X8E motorcycle; a Victrola phonograph and a cylinder carrying the voices of Atlantic City Council grafters accepting $5,000 bribes from undercover detectives; a "Blue Amberol" cylinder manufactured by Thomas A. Edison, Inc.; an Edison kinetoscope; two bags of Edison Portland cement; a concrete specimen from the Aswan Dam on the Nile; an extra bone that had been removed from the Piltdown man; a replica of the bust of Queen Nefertete found in El-Amarna, Egypt; souvenirs from Sir Lawrence Alma-Tadema's Egyptian travels, with one of his paint palettes; painter's palettes having belonged to John Sloan, Henri Matisse, Juan Gris, Georges Bracques, Pablo Picasso, Ande Derain, Emil Nolde, and Maurice Vlaminck; a replica of Eric Gill's sulpture "Mother and Child" accompanied by a photograph of the sculptor-writer also known for his drawings, bas-reliefs, engravings, hand lettering, and typeface designs; six Gustav Stickley bookshelves and assorted other furniture from Stickley Associated Cabinetmakers; a foot-pedal operated dentist drill and dentist's chair from the office of the western writer Zane Grey; te actual electric chair in which Reverend C.V.T. Richeson was electrocuted, in 1912, for having poisoned his former fiancé, Avis Linnell, with cyanide potassium; a duplicate 1" hick hull shell plate as would have been used in the building of the Titanic; a duplicates of decorative and practical accessories that would have been aboard the Titanic, in the styles of Empire, Adams, Italian Renaissance, Louis Quatorze, Louis Quinze, Louis Seize, Georgian, Regency, Queen Anne, Modern Dutch, and Old Dutch; duplicates of automated shampooing and drying appliances that would have been available for all classes on the Titanic's C-Deck; duplicates of darkroom equipment that would have been available for amateur photographers in the darkroom aboard the Titanic; a duplicate 5-kilowatt Marconi wireless radio station that would have been available to passengers on the Titanic's Boat-Deck, for sending and receiving telegrams; a duplicate fifty-phone switchboard like the one that would have been aboard the Titanic for intra-ship calls; duplicate Titanic blankets, table cloths, bed covers, eiderdown quilts, bath towels, fine towels, roller towels, pillow-cases, toothpaste, tennis balls, table cloths, table napkins, wine glasses, tea cups, dinner plates, ice cream plates, soufflé dishes, pudding dishes, finger bowls, egg spoons, grape scissors, asparagus tongs, nut crackers, oyster forks, and salt and pepper shakers; a photograph of Japan's Emperor Meiji and his son Yoshihito, who would accede him to the throne (the Meiji era ended; the Taisho era began); original drawings of "The Katzenjammer Kids," Hans and Fritz, by Rudolph Dirks and Harold Knerr; two original drawings by Charles Addams for cartoons that appeared in the New Yorker; drawings and cels from Disney animators Ollie Johnston and Frank Thomas from early short works like "Mickey's Elephant" and "The Brave Little Tailor" to feature films "Snow White and the Seven Dwarfs", "Pinocchio", "Bambi", and "Peter Pan"; a poster advertising the 1912 Olympics held in Stockholm, Sweden; two Will Bradley posters, one advertising "Will Bradley's Art Service for Advertisers" and the other "Will Bradley's Print Shop"; a poster advertising George M. Cohan in "Broadway Jones"; a poster advertising Giacomo Puccini's "Tosca" playing in the old Boston Opera House; a poster advertising the Irish Players production of Synge's "The Playboy of the Western World" at the Adelphi Theatre in Philadelphia; a poster for the 1912 Ziegfeld Follies; a poster advertising Winsor McCay's animated film "Gertie" ("Greatest Animal Act in the World: she's a scream. She eats, drinks and breathes! She laughs and cries. Dances the tango, answers questions and obeys every command!"); a poster advertising Deutsche Bioscop's Babelsberg glass studios film "Der Totentanz" ("The Death Dance"); a poster advertising the first foreign feature film exhibited in the U.S. (in New York), "Queen Elizabeth"; a poster advertising "Richard III," one of the first feature films ever made

Oppenheimer and his rocket scientist brother Robert Oppenheimer; a carefully written note by Alexander Graham Bell, apparently a draft version of a telegram sent to N.C. Kingsbury, vice president of the American Telephone and Telegraph Company in New York ("I was very much touched by the action of the board of Directors in electing me a Director of the American Bell Telephone Company but found myself unable to accept. A facsimile copy of Kingsbury's return telegraph: "We regret exceedingly that you have found yourself unable to accept the position of Director of the American Telephone & Telegraph Company."); a copy of the September 21, 1912 issue of "Electrical Review and Western Electrician," carrying a story about "Phonographic Music Transmitted by Telephone," announcing "The New York Magnaphone & Music Company has inaugurated the central-station generation and distribution of music, thus carrying out a scheme proposed by Edward Bellamy in his book 'Looking Backward'."; an April 9, 1912 dedication program from the opening of Boston's Fenway Park (at which the Red Sox defeated the New York Highlanders before 27,000 fans, 7-6, in 11 innings), and four separate newspaper acccounts about the new ballpark and the opening game; seventeen copies of The New York Times, each carrying a review, by Carl Van Vechten, of a ballet or modern dance performance; five pages filled with scribblings from the hand of Henri Poincaré, puzzling over chaotic motions that had arisen in a standard celestial mechanics experiment (three matching objects had been launched from three different positions and their orbits had taken three different paths); seven pages scientific data from a diary kept by the German meteorologist Alfred Wegener during an expedition that found him on the northeast coast of Greenland climbing a moving glacier; a sheet of indecipherable scribblings attributed to the Swedish author August Strindberg; two hand written letters by the Norwegian explorer Fridtjof Nansen (one beginning "Untrodden under their unmarked mantle of ice the polar regions have slept the sleep of death since the dawn of time," and the other his declining to becoming the next Norwegian president); hand-drawn maps of Greenland, Spitzbergen, and Novaya Zemlya, also by Nansen; a facsimile copy of Robert Scott's

Antarctic diary; a letter from art critic Bernard Berenson to Henry Duveen of the New York office of the Duveen Brothers ("I want to be absolutely aboveboard. It would be fatal to cheapen me to the rank of salesman. I practice business only as a means to an end. The end is not to enlarge my business and pile up money but to pile up understanding"); correspondence between Harvard Professor of Surgery Harvey Cushing, the Polish scientist Casimir Funk, and the English biochemist Frederick Gowland Hopkins, discussing obesity, diet, good health, and vitamins; an original, handwritten copy of Vachel Lindsay's "General William Booth Enters into Heaven"; a facsimile copy of Salvation Army founder Booth's notes for a speech delivered on May 9, 1912 at London's Royal Albert Hall; thirteen pages of correspondence between Hull-House founder Jane Addams and her friend Ellen Starr (exchanging views on Hull-House, philanthropy, political action, widespread indifference, and the real needs of the poor); an invitation to Virginia Stephen's August 10, 1912 marriage to Leonard Woolf; a letter to William James from George Santayana confessing an increasing desire to resign from Harvard in order to move to Europe to devote himself to writing; fifteen short letters variously exchanged between Irving J. Gill, John Charles Olmsted, Frederick Law Olmstead, Jr., Frank P. Allen, Jr., and Bertram Grosvenor Goodhue (each touching on either the experimental industrial community of Torrance, California or the Panama-California Exposition in San Diego); unused 1912 stationery from the Beverly Hills Hotel; a copy of Samuel B. Flagg's brochure, "City Smoke Ordinances and Smoke Abatement," published by the U.S. Bureau of Mines; a dozen copies of the Daily Worker, all with articles contributed by Woody Guthrie in his regular column, "Woody Sez"; a letter sent to Woody Guthrie by TV personality Art Linkletter; a menu from the Thirteenth Annual Convention of the National Negro Business League in Chicago, signed and inscribed by Madame C.J. Walker, the nation's first Black millionaire ("Shirley, I am not ashamed of my humble beginnings"); an official press release, on "National Association of Rotary Clubs" stationery, announcing the Club's reorganization, on April 13, 1912 in Duluth, Minnesota, into the International Association of Rotary Clubs;

a facsimile Chinese document written on the Order of the Chinese president Yuan Shikai declaring, in 1912, that the Republic of China would henceforth consist of mainland China and ("as Nationals of the Republic") Mongolia, Tibet, Huijiang, and the Huis in Xinjiang; four handwritten invitations by pioneer Zionist Henrietta Szold to the study circle meeting at the Temple Emanu-El in New York City (at which Szold would urge her colleagues to embrace "practical Zionism," forming "The Hadassah chapter of the Daughters of Zion"); authentic Masonic documents telling of certain "Antient and Primitive Rite of Mizraim," the "Oriental Order of Memphis," and the making of "a magickal child" or "homonculus" through prescribed esoteric practices; a facsimile copy of a charter issued by a Masonic Order, "The Illuminati," granting "Theodore Reuss," the "Sovereign Grand Inspector General" of the German "Societas Rosicruciana High Council" authority to form lodges of masons under his "Obedience" both in and out of Germany; eight letters written to Reuss by Rudolf Steiner in Berlin, seeking "to renew the Eleusinian Mysteries" by combining "the Terrestrial with the Celestial and the Visible with the Invisible" through saving, for the future, the Masonic "Misraim-Dienst"; correspondence exchanged between Massachusetts lawyers Arthur Thad Smith, Harvey H. Pratt, Jeremiah S. Sullivan, and Charles W. Bartlett concerning the trial of Chester S. Jordan, convicted of murder in the first degree and sentenced to death (his lawyers argued their plaintiff had been denied due process of law under the 14th Amendment, as he'd been tried by a jury that had included Willis A. White, whose sanity they questioned. The Supreme Court would find juror White's mental capacity sufficient, concluding that Jordan, not having been denied due process of law, would have to pony up, and be electrocuted); several scrapbooks with newspaper clippings about a former pastor of Immanuel Baptist Church of Cambridge Massachusetts, Reverend C.V.T. Richeson who, after confessing to poisoning with cyanide potassium his former fiance, Avis Linnell, was indicted of murder in the first degree and subsequently electrocuted; copies of Edwin Grozier's Boston Post investigating Avis Linell's "suicide" (including the issue in which reporters announced their discovering the druggist in Newton that had sold Clarence Richeson cyanide and, and calling for Reverend Richeson's arrest); a copy of "True Detective Stories from the New England Police Annals," issue 5:2 (carrying John W. English's story, "Avis Linnell and her murder by Reverend Clarence V.T. Richeson"); a copy of Sir Arthur Conan Doyle's pamphlet, "The Case of Oscar Slater" (arguing that Oscar, the operator of an illegal London gambling operation convicted of stealing a brooch from an elderly woman, Miss Marion Gilchrist, prior to bludgeoning her to death and leaving the country, was innocent. A medical examiner at the crime scene had declared a large chair dripping with blood must have been the murder weapon, but Slater stood accused of having used a ball-peen hammer. "The whole case will," Conan Doyle wrote, "remain immortal in the classics of crime as the supreme example of official incompetence and obstinacy." Conan Doyle and others gave money to Slater for legal fees. Slater was finally cleared of all charges, and awarded compensation. When Slater refused to reimburse Conan Doyle, or even to thank him, the author wrote Slater, "you are the most ungrateful as well as the most foolish person whom I have ever known.") a copy of a 1948 newspaper notice regarding Oscar Slater's death ("Oscar Slater Dead at 78; Reprieved Murderer; Friend of A. Conan Doyle."); a note from D.H. Lawrence, apparently to Frieda Weekley ("I love you and you love me. You are the most wonderful woman in all England."); an unsigned hand-colored pen and ink drawing of Chief Luther Standing Bear of the Oglala Sioux who had moved from Sioux City, Iowa to Hollywood, California in 1912 (he would be elected president of the Indian Actors' Association); two artist's notebooks full of drawings and writings from young Khalil Gibran (with transcendental esoteric jottings in both Syriac and Arabic describing naked women, swirling cedars, rugged cliffs, cascading waterfalls); eleven pages of correspondence between William Butler Yeats and Ezra Pound (who'd introduced Yeats to Japanese Noh drama, enormously influencing Yeats's work in the Irish theater); two fliers, one promoting Sonia Delaunay's "Casa Sonia" shop for interior decoration and accessories, and the other promoting her Paris shop, "L'atelier Simultané"; two fliers, one announcing the

CHAPTER TWENTY-EIGHT

Even as Wallace Barrow was busy debunking my father and his friend Nicholas Wentworth, Wentworth was busy making arrangements to lease the Majestic Movie House, an abandoned theater on Banyan Street, next to The Golden Spoon restaurant, as a temporary dwelling for The New Museum of the Year 1912.

The Mayor had formulated a Resolution concerning the town's portion of annual funding for the new museum – that is, the museum's annual piece of the pie. Alice Armour Armstrong quoted her, in the Camperdene Daily Journal: "The New Museum of the Year 1912 Board must realize that an unresolved dichotomy may paralyze operations, and they must work to resolve the issues and build consensus. Dissent is a fact of life that provokes discussion and warrants respect, but it is harmful if it paralyzes action. Camperdene's New Museum of the Year 1912 Board should understand that museums must adapt to changing needs and constraints and have qualified personnel and clear lines of responsibility in order to carry on existing business, to be aware of new service possibilities and to move forward in implementing appropriate courses of action."

Early in November, on a brisk and windy Saturday morning, state senators, town officials, department heads, school officials, assorted Board members, and Camperdene's townspeople all gathered for ground-breaking ceremonies for the new museum. Jake's boy Mark was particularly pleased and impressed, hobnobbing with senators, constables, the police chief, and the fire chief.

Soon, Fusaro Corporation workers began their work at the Lake Street property, clearing trees to prepare the site for blasting and concrete work, big front-lift caterpillars and trucks busy scooping the earth, leveling out the ruts and rolling sweeps, creating the foundations. Mounds of dirt were set all around. The museum was built in interlocking blocks built on top of each other. Concrete was delivered to the blocks in buckets. After each bucket was delivered, four or five men called puddlers would tromp around, packing down the concrete, making sure there were no airholes. One rainy day, Jake and his son Mark went down and joined in, puddling to their heart's content. The rainwater swept down along newly dug ruts, draining into the rising Pond.

Jake began interviewing for New Museum of the Year 1912 staff, asking candidates to summarize their work history. Any previous experience in public service? Museum service? What attracted you to this position? Assets/Liabilities you think you'd bring to this particular position? Summarize your experience with computers and with computer automation. How do you relate to co-workers? What knowledge or attitude do you find most useful, when working closely with the public? How do you deal with stress? How do you defuse potentially 'explosive' situations? What kind of supervision most effectively motivates you? Hobbies, foreign languages, reading interests? Anything else about yourself that you'd like us to be aware of? Why do you feel you could be the best candidate for the position? Any questions?

Likewise, Jake had questions for the candidates' references. How long have you known the candidate? What capacity/working relationship? How does the candidate relate to the public? How does the candidate relate to co-workers? Attitude? Responsibility? Flexibility? React under stress? Work quality? Work quantity? And so on.

Negotiations began with the Camperdene Association of Paraprofessional Employees (M.A.P.E.).

A performance evaluation process was put in place: "I, the undersigned new employee of the New Museum of the Year 1912, understand that I am subject to a ninety-day probationary period, at which time my performance will be evaluated. If at that time my job performance does not meet the expectations of the curator of the New Museum of the Year 1912, I understand I may be subject to the termination of my employment."

By mid-February, the staff was known: curator, Jake Wright; Collections Development, Audrey Morris; Exhibitions Curator Assistant (MAPE), Lizzie Cunningham; Curatorial Assistant I (MAPE), Mary Tuchlein; Curatorial Assistant I (MAPE), Frannie Micheline; Curatorial Assistant II (MAPE), Patty Stenikaan; Curatorial Assistant II (MAPE), Colleen McCartney; Curatorial Assistant II (MAPE), Francie Marshall Hearst (proposed); Archivist I, Francie Marshall Hearst; Archivist II, Susan Sanderson; Archivist III, Don Underwood; Director of Educational Outreach, Julia Seymour-Stanton; Educational Outreach Assistant, Debbie Joss; Maintenance Supervisor, Hayden Brown; and part-time help, three positions (to be determined).

Once the temporary museum was in place at the Majestic Theater, Jake kept busy at all hours filling out government procurement documents and placing orders by the fistfuls. Soon, furniture, shelving, supplies, and artifacts were coming in by the truckloads. It was a good, wild time my mother later told me. Despite their troubled relationship, Minna was eager to conceive child number three. Seriously. She said that once the kids were put to bed she put on silk and lace. She and Jake apparently emerged from all-night love-fests to diligently shower, dress, and make breakfast for us kids. I remember Mark and I bouncing through the rooms in the morning as if to mimic the night bouncing of our parents.

Work on the museum went forward that winter also at fever pitch. Drilling and blasting at the site went on amid the screams of warning sirens until the foundation outline, the building footprint, was achieved. It wasn't very long before work started on the storm drains and basic plumbing and the fundamental electrical and mechanical stuff. It was not at the new museum but, rather, at the Majestic, that a ludicrous problem now sprang up. Museum staffer Lizzie Cunningham showed up at work wearing "transparent underclothes," as Board Chair Michael Bonaventura protested – "only cellophane, actually – and bra-less to boot – an inexcusably obscene outfit." Insisting she was only "in synch with current fashions," Lizzie filed a formal grievance with the clerical union.

Reporter Alice Armour Armstrong wrote in Camperdene Daily Journal, "Some members of the New Museum of the Year 1912 Board are outraged because details of their decision regarding a grievance filed by a museum employee have been leaked out to interested parties prior to the decision being sent in writing to the union representing her. It has been leaked out and is being played in the papers,' said angry Board member Ben Mulvane. On Monday night the New Museum of the Year 1912 Board met in closed door executive session to discuss the weighty issue of the Exhibitions Curator Assistant's clothing, hearing the grievance Lizzie Cunningham has filed against museum trustee chairman Michael Bonaventura and museum curator Jake Wright.

"'It was fine. Everybody was fine,' Trustee Chairman Michael Bonaventura said. 'There was no yelling or screaming or hostility'. The trustees unanimously rejected museum worker Lizzie Cunningham's charge that she was constantly harassed by the museum curator. Fran Micheline, president of the Camperdene Association of Paraprofessional Employees (M.A.P.E.) says Wright contends Cunningham 'was altogether off the mark, off the wall – out of line'."

Obviously, Barrow and Cunningham had this all planned out ahead of time and, luckily, their stupid shenanigans fell through – or at least fizzled out... for a while.

In the next issue of the Camperdene Daily Journal came the news that "employee Lizzie Cunningham is considering an appeal of the trustees' finding that New Museum of the Year 1912 curator Jake Oppenheimer Wright did not unfairly single her out for her choice of clothes at work, Milford's Association of Paraprofessional Employees

(M.A.P.E.) President Fran Micheline said, declining to discuss the Board's decision, saying the issue has been 'blown out of proportion'."

If I met her today I would blow Lizzie Cunningham out of proportion, all right. Wouldn't I have just *loved* to blow *her* house down. But, as it happened, her father would take care of that.

CHAPTER
TWENTY-NINE

In mi-April, the Fusaro Construction Company announced the roof-beam-raising was coming soon for the new museum. The structural steel for the building was substantially complete. The roof-deck was complete. Welding was in progress. Deck pours on the first and second floors were complete. The main electrical work in the basement was complete. The main electrical equipment was operable. Mechanical, electrical, and plumbing preparation on the upper floor was in progress. The ductwork was all rigged. The initial fireproofing process was completed. Access work on Banyan Street was started, and work on the Lake Street curb layout and the parking lot had begun.

Then came this news, reported by Alice Armour Armstrong in the local paper: "New Museum of the Year 1912 Exhibitions Curatorial Assistant Lizzie Cunningham is alleging that Trustee Ben Mulvane 'initiated a smear campaign' in an effort to destroy her reputation, according to a letter from her lawyer, Kevin Harper. A museum visitor and an unnamed town official allegedly heard the remarks attributed to Mulvane and repeated them to a museum employee, who later told Cunningham. Cunningham claims she has lost weight and has had trouble sleeping since the alleged remarks began. She decided to threaten legal action to clear her reputation, according to Harper."

In May, the underlying work for all the new museum's stairs was complete. Stud framing was complete throughout. The roofing work was underway. All of the brickwork was completed, except on the southwest, more boldly-windowed side. The telecommunications wiring was all done. The permanent electrical power was in operation. All the site's outdoor pole lights were functioning beautifully. By June, all of the sheetrock wall and plastering was complete. The plumbing was just about completed. All the sprinkler systems – both in the building and across the lawns – were installed and functioning.

In essence – to the eye – the New Museum of the Year 1912 was ripe to be moved into.

A Mission Statement was formulated by the Board of Museum Trustees: "The New Museum of the Year 1912 will provide high-interest collections and services in a variety of formats for persons of all ages, stimulating interest and appreciation for culture, soicety, the arts, and learning."

Then Camperdene Daily Journal reporter Alice Armour Armstrong reported, "Museum Troubles Resume."

"A female New Museum of the Year 1912 employee has charged a museum trustee with harassment. The latest charge was made by museum employee Mary Tuchlein. Tuchlein told the Daily Journal this morning, 'the crux of the issue' was interference by Trustee Wallace Barrow. Tuchlein said, 'the constant interference of the Trustees in administrative matters,' as having influenced her decision to depart the museum. Likewise, she belabored 'their disruption of the chain of command through personal relationships with some members of the staff and intimidation of others, making the New Museum of the Year 1912 an impossible place to work'."

So there they were. Jake had to count on the graciousness, dedication, and expertise of Curatorial Assistants Frannie Micheline and Colleen McCartney to go forward. Various responsibilities needed to be delegated between the two of them as time permitted. "If I've forgotten something, let me know," Jake told them. "We'll come out okay. You have every right to be confident. You're doing fine work."

My father sent off a note to Ben Mulvane: "Ben, Michael Bonaventura phoned this afternoon to consent to my going ahead with sending the job ads for the vacated post. He said it is fine with him to go ahead and fill it. He says he will not vote approval on my recommendation for filling the position until after a discussion of Mary Tuchlein's allegations occurs. I feel strongly a special meeting should be held, in the company of a mediator (to keep the discussion on track)." Ben was very familiar with the ways in which some people could derail reasonable discussion of just about anything they chose to.

In his Director's Report to the Trustees, Jake wrote, "Some of us bring with us, from the past, terrible personal pain. Despite the arduous task of my interviewing candidates to fill vacant museum positions, and though we have been understaffed and busy, I have not enjoyed a finer month of work and pleased patrons than in this last month at the Majestic – I mean, the Museum."

At the next meeting of the Trustees, Chairman Ben Mulvane proposed offering new staff members "a general orientation to museum services, with a gentle immersion in the history and purpose of museums (e.g. purpose/function of board of curators), with an introduction to trustee lines of authority, staff answering of telephones, directing calls, handling complaints, and so on. It would be equally helpful to review some of the problems in staff-trustee dynamics: resistance to change, constructive versus destructive criticism, how to deal with stress, and so forth."

Then the six trustees battled over Jake's choice of who should fill the staff vacancy. They were split three to three, and then they were split three-three over the matter of whether or not the trustees even had any say in the Director's choice as to who should or shouldn't fill a staff vacancy – cunningly and successfully delaying the filling of the vacant position, half of them wearing down the other half. Ultimately, the candidate for the job just walked away from it. Lana Staufelder turned down the job, and Jake re-opened the search.

The feuding trustees continued to be in a deadlock over the open post. By and by, it became clear that three trustees were pulling for ~~my~~ *his* promoting staffer Francie Marshall Hearst to the post. But then Wheel Barrow announced Francie Hearst could not be under consideration for the vacant post, as "everyone knew" she was dating Board Chairman Ben Mulvane.

In fact, the Chairman of the Board of Curators, Ben, had been leaning hard on Jake to appoint her to the job. Jake had seen that she in fact had the pedigree, but he felt she lacked appropriate professional experience – or he would have appointed her to the post at the outset. Now the rumor was abroad that she was sleeping with the Chairman, and Jake wished he'd never brought her on board in the first place. Ben should have been facilitating her resignation, not calling on Jake to get her promoted. After all they'd been through, he just should have known better.

Of course the "other half" of the Board of Curators – the "Association" half – scoffed openly at the idea of "the Hearst girl" getting the job. "I'm sure she's good in some positions," Wheel Barrow said mischievously, looking at scarlet-faced Ben Mulvane out of the corner of his eye, "but she's not going to get in this one."

A steaming angry Francie Hearst stormed into the museum the next day and, an inch from Jake's face, told him she was going to keep the job she had and that she would sleep with whomever she pleased.

The Supervisory post remained vacant.

Ben Mulvane, who kept busy micromanaging the construction of the new museum, was furious. One day he called Jake on the phone to tell him he was crazy. This was Ben Mulvane, who I had thought so highly of. Now he was as much a raving moron as anyone. He said he'd previously truly appreciated Jake's clear-headed, resolute stands on issues back when the "nuthouse nuts" were in control, but now, obviously, Jake had *gone over* to *the other side.*

"I had thought you were my friend," Ben mourned.

My father had thought Ben was *his* friend. Now he was getting beat up even by Ben Mulvane. I swear, sometimes I can hardly stand it how everybody gets so all mixed up all the time. What can you do?

CHAPTER THIRTY

The work of filling the new museum on Lake Street with furniture and books and shelves began in earnest on June 1 – also the big move from the old Majestic Theater to the New Museum of the Year 1912. Staffer Frannie Micheline asked for extra hours to help in doing this work. Jake wrote her, "Frannie, I appreciate your offering to take on extra hours beyond your regular hour work week, to help get the museum moved. I have shared your letter with the Board and we are in agreement that there should be no extra staff hours offered. Thanks."

"No thanks needed," Frannie wrote back. "Just doing my job."

"Just doing my job" my ass. It turned out Frannie was an item with Ben Mulvane, may the two rot in hell.

My plodding father filled the museum's vacant post with one Louise Pynchon, eminently qualified. Her title was upgraded to Technology Implementation Coordinator. Information about the museum's program would be advertised over local cable television. Press Releases would be made available to all area newspapers.

Jake worked closely with Veronica Pillsbury on a gayla "Grand Opening" party for the new museum. A Grand Opening Committee had been formed and a free-for-all brainstorming session held. Some of Camperdene's best, most illustrious, and creative townspeople were there, making for a rambunctious session. It was decided that food for the shindig would be catered by The Golden Spoon restaurant. Former Massachusetts Governor Chub Peabody was invited – also the current

Governor, the Lieutenant Governor, State Representatives and Senators, past and present Regional Administrators, CEOs of Companies, and just plain folks. They aimed to have a thousand people show up. Why not? Everyone would be invited – librarians, trustees, dignitaries, museum *afficionados* – anybody who wanted to come. Strangely, no complaint or insult was issued or hurled by ferocious, aristocratic Carlena Lagorio. Jake's guess was that Barrow had successfully imposed his gag rule over her – him with his "way with women."

At the Grand Opening were Bluegrass musicians, a palm reader, a handwriting analyst, a caricaturist, a DJ with hits from the 60s. Jake enjoyed memorable conversations over drinks and a very good dinner with bursts of laughter throughout the evening. He got to see old colleagues and got to know some new people. He was shaking hands with everybody, telling jokes, obviously having a grand good time. Veronica Pillsbury was wild with glee, throwing her arms around Jake's neck, planting kisses with loose abandon on his cheeks and neck.

Wheel Barrow saw that and, almost as if on cue, went over and presented Jake with his sketch for New Museum Emergency and Evacuation Procedures: "A Supervisor should report the Emergency. If no supervisor is present, report the emergency yourself. Act quickly. Remain calm. One person should place a call to the police. Notify other staff of the emergency, and of the calls placed...." and so on. "After evacuating the building, all museum staff will meet in the staff parking lot."

Barrow also provided Jake with his notes on standards for patron behavior: "No Loitering on museum premises is permitted. The front steps and entrance must be kept clear to allow easy access to the museum. NO SMOKING, NO FOOD (NO GUM, NO CANDY, NO DRINKS in the museum. Any conduct deemed to be inconsistent with the orderly operation of the museum will not be permitted. Respect other people's right to privacy. Harassment of any kind, whether by obnoxious or threatening language or behavior, is not allowed. Anyone found damaging/defacing museum property will be prosecuted. Removing any material is THEFT, and will be prosecuted as such. The museum reserves the right to search any bags or parcels. No solicitation of any kind may take place on museum property. Appropriate footwear and attire are required in the museum. Parents are responsible for the behavior and supervision of their children. Bicycles must be left outside the museum in the racks provided. Pets are not allowed in the museum."

Wheel Barrow! I swear I'd like to pull his nose so hard his ears would bleed. Jake had long indulged him his grandstanding. He'd long indulged him his harangues. It had often been said that Jake had let him down. *Of course* he had let him down! What good was it to do work one loved where one was used and abused, where one constantly faced losing one's sense of humor? – which was far worse than losing one's job.

After the Grand Opening of the New Museum of the Year 1912, Barrow began yet *another* smear campaign, telling people around town that Jake was having an affair with Veronica Pillsbury. When my father denied that, he next got wind of Board Chairman Ben Mulvane's going around Town cruelly spreading a lie, mischievously telling people – this rat! – "Jake is a liar."

At the next meeting of the Board of Museum Trustees, Jake wanted to talk about that, so he asked that an executive session be called to discuss the allegation that he was "a liar." This newly pompous rat Ben Mulvane took Jake's proposal "under advisement."

The next morning, Technology Implementation Coordinator Louisa Pynchon stepped up to him and handed him an envelope, and remained standing – in obvious expectation that Jake should read the contents. My father smiled, opened the envelope, and began reading Louisa Pynchon's typed letter: "I realize you're trying to do a good job under both internal and external pressure," she had written, "but there are areas of your performance that you are not doing well in: You need to schedule time to work in all of the departments; you need to experience firsthand what personnel both do and are up against; you should never suspect any staff member of being motivated by anything other than pure and simple devotion to public service."

Jake told Louisa Pynchon he would give her observations careful, honest, sincere consideration.

"Go to hell!" Louisa Pynchon blurted out.

Now my father didn't want people to think like him, be like him, be "yessir-sayers, brown-nosers. He no more wanted those kinds of staffers around him than he wanted to be such a one himself. I know this much about him. He was no more going to stand for being scalded or insulted by anybody who simply and inexplicably and compulsively had that *need*.

Jake had the weekend to digest and contemplate these things. He came up with a "plan of action." He restored his old use of a "block schedule" which showed the museum work schedule hour by hour, day by day, showing (proving) his presence and involvement at the front lines of all of the departments.

Ben Mulvane recommended Jake explain the situation to the Trustees, illuminating why a staff member, hired by Jake, with trust and faith in her personality and abilities, had emerged with so great and furious spite in so short a space of time. He said Jake could not effectively do his job until all the players, from the simply cunning to the utterly deceitful, laid some cards on the table.

My famously naïve father again started getting weird anonymous threats at work and at home. Threats – strange, untraceable phone calls, harangues. But he just kept on keeping on, acting as if nothing fundamental was terribly wrong. Seriously, what would it take to be the curator of the New Museum of the Year 1912? – devilish cunning? A suit of armor? A lobotomy? He had thought the old Museum Corporation Board was hell to pay. Now all that looked to him like *warm-up sessions*.

"It seems the New Museum of the Year 1912, though the building is new, has an entrenched, long familiar history of bickering and politics," wrote one Natalie Rossi (apparently a newcomer to local politics) to the editor of the Daily Journal. She correctly identified "an insidious culture of in-house fighting."

There was just nothing that came to the attention of the Trustees that did not then come to the attention of the entire community via the media. Once a Trustee knew of it, it was all over town. My father was receiving letters in confidence from Trustees and MAPE union members, only to hear and see the information on the radio and in the news the next day.

CHAPTER THIRTY-ONE

"At their next meeting," Alice Armour Armstrong reported in the Camperdene Daily Journal, "the Trustee Board of The New Museum of the Year 1912 will address a proposal made by member Veronica Pillsbury calling for self-policing as a means of creating better morale for the museum staff. Pillsbury said a variety of past incidents affecting the New Museum of the Year 1912 and its Board of Curators had made her aware that still clearer museum goals and objectives would be needed."

In July came the headline, "The War of 1912." Alice Armour Armstrong reported on "Personnel problems brewing at the Museum of the Year 1912, this time between curator Jake Wright and Technology Implementation Coordinator Louisa Pynchon. Last week Wright took a whack at 'bad news' museum trustees, taking issue with the fact that one had called him a liar. He chastised the Board for 'brow-beatings, strong-armings and endless harangues.' In concluding, the curator said, 'I would be a stupid man if I continued to act as if nothing fundamental was terribly wrong here'."

"In an unrelated matter," Armstrong wrote, "Wright refuted charges that he had kicked a one-year old girl, waiting for her father, off museum property in September. The father charged Jake with frightening the child so badly, she left. The father searched frantically for forty minutes before finding the girl at a friend's house – crying." Armstrong closed: "Wright told the Camperdene Daily Journal he did not remember the incident. He further stated he does not raise his voice at anyone."

At last, one true thing. Alas, it fell through the cracks.

The next Camperdene Daily Journal headline was: "The War of 1912 Continues": "New Museum of 1912 Curator Jake Wright has accused Museum Technology Implementation Coordinator Louisa Pynchon of three instances of 'improper language and gestures," Alice Armour Armstrong reported, divulging the name of Pynchon's lawyer, Kevin Harper.

"Under grilling by New Museum of the Year 1912 Trustee Wallace Barrow," Armstrong reported in the following week, "Wright admitted he had not documented the incidents in the supervisor's file. 'It's your word against hers,' Barrow told him. Jake took a swat at what he termed the museum's 'fundamental problem' – 'Trustee micromanagement of the museum.' Local attorney Kevin Harper, representing Louisa Pynchon, said today that he will file a civil suit in County Superior Court against Wright and three of the six Trustees, who seem to be supporting Wright while scorning Pynchon. 'Who is next?' Trustee Wallace Barrow commented."

Then came the headline: "War of 1912 Rages On," Trustee Barrow volunteering the news that he was "disappointed in Jake Wright as a professional museum curator." At the hearing, however, Louisa Pynchon decided it would be in her best interest to resign her post. "If you have a loser for a case," commented Trustee Veronica Pillsbury to reporters, "you fold your tent and go away."

Attorney Kevin Harper went on cable television to tell area viewers that New Museum of the Year 1912 staff members had signed a document calling on Trustee Chair Ben Mulvane to share with his fellow Trustees information that had been compiled at the curator's request. The next day, the Daily Journal ran the headline: "New Museum of the Year 1912 Staffers Petition for 'Wright Action'." There was no mention in the article of Jake's having himself brought the "petition," so called, into existence.

Mark came home from school the next day and asked his father if he'd again been in the newspaper, for crying out loud. All the kids were saying their parents were reading about Jake and that Jake was a bad man. Seriously.

In August, this carefully crafted hideous cartoon was even further exaggerated when a "wrap-up" issue of the Daily Journal, stated, "Eight New Museum of the Year 1912 staffers petitioned for action against museum curator Jake Wright." It was put out there for consumption, just as if it were the truth.

My sanguine, unrelenting father worked hard, trying to get new candidates for the again vacant post, Technology Implementation Coordinator, but this seemed jinxed. People had got the word out about this job. Nobody wanted it.

Now Alice Armour Armstrong was reporting, in the Camperdene Daily Journal, "New Museum of the Year 1912 Issue Brings Threat from Union.

"The Camperdene Association of Paraprofessional Employees (MAPE) has asked the Board of New Museum of the Year 1912 Trustees to halt the alleged harassment of Curatorial Assistant Lizzie Cunningham by museum curator Jake Wright. In a strongly worded letter to the Trustees, MAPE President Fran Micheline called Wright 'a publicity seeker'."

This was proved when, at their September meeting, representatives of the member museums of the Massachusetts Museum Coalition voted a new slate of officers, naming my father chairman of the Coalition. "It's a real honor, and a privilege," Alice Armour Armstrong quoted Jake. "It's good to be recognized and appreciated'."

"You never know what's going to be in the papers," Armstrong had said in the course of interviewing Jake for that article.

My father's being so much in the news prompted him to wonder why he had heard nothing disparaging or ridiculous from Carlena Lagorio for many moons. Lagorio had often traveled, and everyone said simply she was probably off traveling again. Nobody knew where or when she'd last been seen. It was taken for granted she'd re-emerge soon enough – steaming, raging, neighing. But it didn't happen. There was no sign of her when the October campaigns for public office got underway. There were New Museum of the Year 1912 trustee placards all over the place – signs all over town: VOTE for Ben Mulvane; VOTE for Veronica Pillsbury; VOTE for Michael Bonaventure; VOTE for Wallace Barrow; VOTE for Roland Henselmeier; VOTE for Richard Cunningham.

Shortly before Thanksgiving, this headline appeared: "War of 1912 Explodes."

In her story, Alice Armour Armstrong wrote of Veronica Pillsbury's "plan that would provide a 'safe and harassment-free environment' for New Museum of the Year 1912 staff and visitors" which "exploded into a volley of accusations last night between New Museum of the Year 1912 Trustees Ben Mulvane and Wallace Barrow. The outburst by Mulvane was prompted by an anti-harassment proposal, submitted by New Museum of the Year 1912 Trustee Veronica Pillsbury to her fellow board members," Armstrong reported, "written to promote 'a high level of morale and mutual respect.' The proposal was defeated on a three to three vote," Armstrong reported, "with Wallace Barrow, Richard Cunningham, and Roland Henselmeier voting in the negative."

On Christmas morning, the Camperdene Daily Journal reported "A New Grievance" had been "booked by a paraprofessional Museum Aid. Museum curator Jake Wright has been hit with yet another grievance," Alice Armour Armstrong reported. "A letter of grievance came from Fran Micheline, President of the Camperdene Association of Paraprofessional Employees, filed on behalf of Lizzie Cunningham."

I would have slapped both those two dumb bitches silly, had it been me in that situation, but not my father. No, not him. He didn't hit back. He didn't get even. He plodded on stoically, doing the right thing. It was dawning on people that he too was probably as nuts as anyone, if not in one way, then in some other. You could cut the thing up every which way, but there was no way in which Jacob Wright, in his hard circumstances, did not come out appearing just as plain nuts as everyone else involved in this situation. This became clear to everyone.

Bad news on bad news piled up through the winter, right into springtime. If Jake knew anything by now, he knew this: there would never have been any degraded feuding or disgrace or furor to report in the local paper had not a certain trustee compulsively fueled the fires and fed the papers with it all, leading everyone nowhere but astray. Jake suddenly could see that, with the help of Powderkeg Cunningham, Wheel Barrow had been writing all the news articles all along – not Alice Armour Armstrong.

CHAPTER THIRTY-TWO

I remember my father telling me that, when he'd first come to Camperdene, it wasn't very long before Wheel Barrow was telling him, sardonically, "We hear you are a *spiritual* person. That's good, because I can tell you you'll be getting down on your knees, praying to God to get through what's coming your way. We don't pay you to be *happy*," Barrow had said, snarling. Jake had been lately hoping those days were over, but the revelation that Wallace Barrow had been behind all the recent ugly Camperdene news headlines now flew up and hit my father hard. He knew it to be true; and he knew it couldn't be proved.

It was New England mud time -- the dismal slump between winter and springtime. My father was scheduled to give a seriously dull Spring Report to the trustees of The New Museum of the Year 1912.

"The year speeds along," Jake wrote, lying through his teeth. "Here it is, April already. There's been plenty going on. In writing this report, I think of Mark Twain who once said about a letter, 'I'd have made it shorter if I'd had more time'..." and on and on he went, detailing programs and events, cake decorating workshops and a program for kids that compared classical and folk instruments from guitars and lutes and banjos to diverse percussion instruments including maracas, bongos, congos, and coffee cans. The Camperdene Art Guild had held their annual show – not a pretty sight.

In May, the New Museum of the Year 1912 Board Chair, Veronica Pillsbury, joined with Jake and past Chair Ben Mulvane, attending the

Massachusetts Museum Coalition sponsored Museums Legislative Day at the State House. The welcoming ceremonies were held in Doric Hall, with several speakers of passion and eloquence backing the two museum bills before the Governor and the General Court. Camperdene's state representative, Laura Mercer, told reporters, "Courage is not the absence of fear. Courage is doing right in the presence of fear." My father shook the hands of Senators and Representatives and followed up later with letters advocating for museums, asking the assorted legislators for more money.

As part of a package grant awarded to the town of Camperdene, the New Museum of the Year 1912 would reap still more munificence and benefaction. The State Department of Education gave out nine awards of $150,000 each to communities across the state for "family oriented" charitable services and programs. After Jake informed Museum of the Year 1912 trustees about that, and the Strategic Plan for the Future of Museum Services in Massachusetts, telling how the Information Networks were linking libraries and museums through existing automated resource sharing networks, enabling all of the networks to be linked to the Internet, growing the worldwide library/museum virtual catalog, Wheel Barrow raised the ire of his colleagues, saying, "Why, we'll be needing a still larger museum building for housing all this stuff. We'll have to add six or seven new Benjamin Mulvane Memorial Wings."

This last arose from a comment made at an earlier meeting, when it had been suggested by Ben Mulvane that trustees should not be competing to bring in new items for the museum's collections *by the truckloads*. The stuff was coming in faster than it could be stored, let alone *catalogued*, Mulvane ridiculed. The energy and passion of the feuding Board of New Museum of the Year 1912 Trustees could perhaps be focused, or waylaid, Mulvane proposed sardonically, *by adding another six wings to the existing structure* – one for each Trustee.

One night, my father had to leave just such a meeting to go take care of a situation that came up – two young guys racing through the museum, breaking display case glass and pulling precious artworks down from pedestals, screaming like banshees as they went. Three police officers showed up, but the kids got away.

It came almost as a shock to Jake one day when he realized, reflecting on it, that apparently he was free of any symptoms of burnout. He felt quite fit, in fact. Having endured so long amid mad people, he had to pinch himself to see if he was dreaming. He still had such good health, passion, energy, and peace of mind. He said he still could fall asleep so soon as his head touched the pillow at night, and he still felt eager to get out of bed on any given morning.

CHAPTER
THIRTY-THREE

A very dignified, soft-spoken, silver-haired lady wearing a pearl necklace came into the museum one evening and told Jake, "I'm very glad to meet you. I've been very disappointed about all this news about the museum, somebody or other misrepresenting things over the newspaper and radio. But when I come in, I can see for myself. This is a very good museum. You and your staff are doing great work – very generous and helpful."

This turned out to be Ellen Dunham, who followed up with a December letter to the editor of the Camperdene Daily Journal, saying, "I've been toying with the idea of giving a gift to the staff at The New Museum of the Year 1912 as a token of my appreciation for their hard work, cheerfulness, and knowledge. A museum is more than its contents. It's the museum staffer who can introduce you to a delightful artist or collections, opening up your world. So let my holiday gift to the museum staff be this public expression of thanks. And may a chorus of readers of this letter join in the next time they visit the New Museum of the Year 1912."

At this time, my father was wrapping up his term as chairman of the Regional Museums Coalition, and he told his colleagues he'd enjoyed not only the discussions of regional programs and services, but also the discussions of broader goals and trends within the museum profession, the sharing how they'd been coping with difficulties, keeping up with swift-paced change.

The next evening, a policeman came to the museum in pursuit of a young man who'd received either a stay-away order or a restraining order from a Massachusetts judge and had violated it, purportedly by stalking a certain young lady – in the museum. Lizzie Cunningham had entered Jake's office the day before, and had excitedly told him of there having been a young lady in the museum that afternoon who'd complained to Fran Micheline that a boy had been "waiting for her" with intentions of harming her.

I'm quite sure I would have, at that point, gladly tossed both Lizzie Cunningham and Fran Micheline into a dump truck heading straight to hell at that point, but not my father. No, not him, Mr. Peaceable Kingdom. Still, Jake knew he could not trust Fran Micheline or Lizzie Cunningham. He was *very* wary of either of them entering a room to speak with him alone without another person present. The lesson had been driven home to him that he was not to mention Lizzie's peculiarities in behavior to anyone, else she and her father and her father's friends would use their own words to prove Jake had a problem with her, and that this problem Jake had with her was *the* problem, and not any behavior or attitude of *hers*.

Jake had listened in silence to Lizzie's report. Lizzie had concluded by telling him about the differences between a court issued "stay away" order and court issued "restraining order". Her giving that lecture, which went on at considerable length, had made no sense to Jake. Finally, politely, he had thanked her. He'd said he would do what he felt was appropriate to the matter – on learning more. Lizzie had left the room clearly disgruntled.

My father had then phoned the police to make his own inquiry about "stay away" orders and "restraining orders" (both were court ordered, with the latter applied in domestic abuse cases, the former applied for all other cases of keeping particular people from harming other particular people). He had then spoken with Fran Micheline and asked that she write a short note of explanation to ~~me~~ him as to what was the matter, i.e., what had occurred. Fran had said there was nothing to write. It was just a girl who'd said a guy was in the museum who shouldn't be. She said she'd turned away, and when she turned back again, the girl had left. That was that, she said.

The next afternoon, Fran entered Jake's office with this same girl, who, she said, was afraid to leave the museum because she was sure she would get beat up. Jake asked the girl if there had been a formal court "stay away" or restraining order issued. She said no. Jake asked the girl if she wanted him to have the police come. She said yes. Jake phoned the police. He went upstairs with the girl and waited for the officer to get there. The officer arrived shortly, interviewed the girl, escorted her out of the building, and took her home. And that, as Fran liked to say, was that.

At noon, on December 21st, Friends President Nick Wentworth appeared at the museum with a high white chef's hat and seven huge salad bowls and treated the museum's staff to a surprise "Appreciation Luncheon" – which infuriated Wheel Barrow, as nobody had run it by him first. Anyway, while Jake could, he had a fine time at the celebration, cherishing the high spirits, laughter, and good conversation in the staff room. Wentworth was just giving a toast, quoting Flannery O'Connor ("Possibly the Lord just thinks all of this is funny. It is funny if you can stand it.") when Fran Micheline at the Circulation desk phoned down and asked Jake to please come up to the front entrance of the museum, immediately, to talk with an angry visitor.

The museum-goer was visibly upset. She was shaking. Jake sat down with her at a nearby table and asked her what was wrong. She said she'd never been treated so poorly by anyone. She said she couldn't believe the rude behavior of one of the museum's Circulation people. Jake asked her which person she was referring to She didn't know the name, and didn't want to point her finger at anyone, but she felt strongly that "someone should know how rudely her fourteen year old daughter had been treated by this person" whom she described as "tall, thin, pimply, with long, silky, mud-brown hair."

This was Lizzie Cunningham, certainly.

"This girl is probably efficient, it is obvious she is businesslike, but her treatment of human beings is, to say the least, very, very poor." The woman said the "other museum staffers are always pleasant and accommodating, but not this one."

Jake assured the woman he would do what he could to prevent the recurrence of such behavior. He told her a note from her stating her particular complaint would be helpful. She said she wanted to remain anonymous – "I don't want to cause any trouble. I just felt someone should know about this individual's bad attitude." Jake said he could appreciate that, apologized, and thanked her for speaking up.

At the end of the evening, after closing the museum and setting Hayden Brown into gear to do his night rounds, Jake considered writing a reprimand for Lizzie's file, but balked. He'd been sternly warned by Barrow about what could and could not be put into a staffer's file. Here they were, living in the midst of an information explosion and there Jake sat, tearing up the jottings he'd scrawled while listening to the patron's complaints about the "tall, thin, pimply" girl "with silky mud-brown hair."

Jake looked in vain for any other documentation in Lizzie's file that could show the drift and pattern of her behavior. He knew numerous papers had already been lifted from the file. Then, out of the corner of his eye, Jake noticed, atop one of several paper piles on his desk, a formal patron "Request for Reconsideration of a Museum Acquisition." This he now took in hand.

A few weeks before, my father had received just such a request, submitted by one Mrs. Marsha Wallace, which called for the removal of a controversial oil color picture painted by Wilburt Hayley in the year 1912. "We support," Jake had written, "the Freedom to View Foundation's principle that one of the museum's roles in a democracy is to provide a forum for the exchange of ideas, providing a wide range of artifacts, ensuring that individuals have access to artworks without others determining for them what they 'should' want to view or study. Our selection policy states, 'The New Museum of the Year 1912 strives to provide artifacts, exhibits, and programs for adults, juveniles, and children according to historical relevance and current popular demand'." Jake had noted he could share in Mrs. Wallace's reluctance to recommend the painting to anyone in terms of "good taste" but, as a professional museum curator, Jake was "duty bound to provide a wide array of materials to a diverse public."

Now this new "Request for Reconsideration of a Museum Acquisition" was on Jake's desk, submitted by a gentleman in the town, Richard Muller, calling for the removal of an artwork "that certainly must offend a great many." The sculpture, titled *The Artist's Mistress*, was obviously meant to provoke, right from the get-go. In 1912, the Viennese sculptor Heinrich Schimmel had divided a human form into several segments and re-assembled the pieces most curiously and (of course) provocatively.

I suppose that, had it been me, I would have simply told old Mr. Muller to go to hell and would have gone on ahead with whatever other things I had in front of me. But not my adamantly ethical almost Puritanical in stalwartness father. No, not him. The next morning, my father went in to work earlier than usual in order to contemplate the writing of a reasoned response to Mr. Muller's request.

Muller had maintained the sculpture *The Artist's Mistress* was "deeply misogynist," and had urged the curator to remove it *post-haste* from the museum. He had pointed out, rightly, that the New Museum of the Year 1912 was the "only museum" in that part of Massachusetts that owned a work by "this rotten Austrian junkman," Heinrich Schimmel. If Jake struggled against meanness and madness (and he did), advocating reason and honorable conduct (this too he did), then he must also want this mean, mad sculpture to go away. But censoring it was just an invitation to worse outrage. Not cops, columnists, librarians, or curators ought to lock up opinions.

It wasn't in my father's hands to decide. It was written in museum policy that it was up to the Board to deliberate and decide whether to keep or withdraw any acquisition. As if it mattered ultimately anyway – Jake knew by now that this issue would be *just so much fuel* for yet another fire – a trustee battle, a feud, a brouhaha. Mr. Muller would get no justice. Jake knew the entrenched, ridiculous, wild trustee donnybrook antics and mayhem would devour all.

At the Trustee meeting, Ben Mulvane delayed taking any action, insisting that Jake should first provide the board with an explanation of how the sculpture *The Artist's Mistress* came to be in The New Museum of the Year 1912 in the first place. For safekeeping, until the problem could be resolved, Ben had moved the piece into one of the storage areas.

Jake went wading through a knee-high maze of recklessly strewn artifacts and ephemera – recent acquisitions trucked in by at least six unidentified donors – sheet music for Mahalia Jackson's "God's Gonna Separate the Wheat from the Tares" and "Sometimes I Feel Like a Motherless Child"; correspondence between Mahalia Jackson and Isaac "Ike" Hockenhull, "Ike" trying to persuade Jackson to audition for the Works Projects Administration (WPA) Federal Theatre production of "Hot Mikado" by Gilbert and Sullivan ("Nobody can touch your voice. You've got a future in singing. It's not right for you to throw it away hollering in churches. Woman, you want to nickel and dime all your life?"); guitar strings, drumsticks, screws, nuts, bolts, dice, rubber bands, and a tambourine that had belonged to the composer John Cage; a pair of tap dance shoes that had belonged to Gene Kelly; a pair of ice-skates that had belonged to Olympic gold-winning figure skater Sonja Henie of Norway; a poster from the Chicago Repertory Theater noting, in small print, the appearance of one Studs Terkel; a poster advertising Jose Ferrer's starring on Broadway in "Cyrano De Bergerac"; a poster advertising the movie "Blow-up," directed by Michelangelo Antonioni; a letter from Truman Nelson to W.E.B. Du Bois regarding Harvard professor and literary critic F. O. Matthiesen's having helped Nelson break into print (Matthiesen, who'd been called to testify before a McCarthy committee, had declined and jumped out of a window to his death); a frying pan, two egg-beaters, and a large wooden spoon that had belonged to Pasadena, California chef and cookbook author Julia Child; rocks and shells collected by David Brower (conservationist, a recipient of the Blue Planet Prize awarded by the Asahi Glass Foundation of Japan, the richest environmental prize in the world) from his travels in

Kings Canyon, the North Cascades, the Redwoods, Dinosaur National Monument, the Yukon, the Grand Canyon, Yosemite, Yellowstone, New Mexico's Shiprock, Cape Cod, Fire Island, and Point Reyes, Olympic National Park, San Gorgonio, Mount Waddington (Canada), Thyangboche, and the Himalayan mountains; a souvenir miniature Statue of Liberty; and a pair of souvenir miniature Port Authority World Trade Center Twin Towers accompanied by a photograph of the architect who designed them, Minoru Yamasaki, standing not in front of the Towers but rather (for reasons not stated anywhere on the twenty-eight pages of accompanying documents describing Yamasaki's oeuvre) in front of the Empire State Building; the headlights of the car the painter Jackson Pollock had died in, as well as seven cans of paint left unopened in his garage at the time of his death; clippings from The New York Times and several other American newspapers announcing the death, in World War I, on the battlefield at Verdun, of Franz Marc; a painter's palette that had belonged to the German artist Emil Schumacher; the sculpture *The Artist's Mistress* by the Viennese artisan Heinrich Schimmel....

Someone had sandpapered the acquisition number off. Jake could find no record of it. He had no idea how it had come to be displayed in the Museum. When the trustees met, they voted unanimously to let Jake deaccession the item or re-accession the item as he pleased – "restore it, stash it, or trash it," Wheel Barrow allowed.

"I will begin with an apology," my father wrote Mr. Muller. "I appreciate your point of view concerning the statue *The Artist's Mistress*," he wrote, "which you requested we remove from our collection. I am hopeful you will understand and honor my position as a museum professional. This work, good or bad, will not be withdrawn. Our having an artwork in our collection does not mean that we endorse what's in it. It does mean we endorse the free flow of cultural information. One of the museum's roles in a democracy is to provide a wide range of materials so that people have access to culture without our determining for them what they 'should' want or 'ought to' reject."

Apparently, this just slayed him.

Ten days later, Jake read, in the Obituaries column of the Camperdene Daily Journal, that Mr. Muller, 83, had died. Jake's first thought, when he saw that, was that this was not the same man as Richard Muller, the museum visitor. Jake inquired of the Funeral Home, and learned that it was indeed him. He was told the Rabbi, in his remarks at the funeral, had made mention of Richard's enjoyment of the New Museum of the Year 1912, and of his having requested that a provocative sculpture housed there be removed.

My father was sad to learn of Mr. Muller's death. He was glad he had said, in his letter to Mr. Muller, that he believed Muller would understand and honor his position as a professional curator and would know how sincerely he respected him and appreciated his concern. Richard Muller had written back to Jake, saying, "Yes, it is better people should view such *dreck* and make up their own minds."

Jake now put into a frame a handwritten note sent to him by an anonymous scribbler the year before, and he set it on his desk in plain sight: "The world is divided into people who are right."

CHAPTER THIRTY-FOUR

In the spring, a new controversy was hatched from the head of Wallace Barrow. Veronica Pillsbury wrote a letter to my father that stood his hair on end.

"As Chairwoman of the Board of Curators of The New Museum of the Year 1912," she began, "I am obliged to inform you the Board requires you provide a simple statement as to what transpired as regards your establishing the holiday schedule for the weeks at the close of last year and the beginning of this year."

Jake got out his fat, wide carpenter's pencil and began scrawling words across the pages of a long, lined yellow pad: "(1) I was asked by Museum staffers, in early September, to inform them of the schedule for the coming holidays, to help them in making their personal holiday plans/arrangements; (2) I reviewed the Trustee Policy sheet, "Museum Hours As Impacted By Recognized Holidays"; (3) I reviewed past schedules; (4) I drafted my proposal for the winter schedule; (5) I shared the draft with staffers, calling on everyone – union and non-union employees alike – to notify me if anyone saw any inequity, impropriety, or error; (6) Suggestions were made only for shortening the memo. I shortened the memo. It was distributed on September 26th (attached); (7) Nothing was said to me of any problem with the schedules until I received your letter, now, formally calling the scheduling into question; (8) The schedules were constructed with the intent of following the guidelines of the official Trustee Policy, "Museum Hours As Impacted

By Recognized Holidays," and with the intent of providing equity and fairness to all employees per the norms and patterns of established museum scheduling practices; (9) Following the established pattern of many years, staff hours were distributed through the weeks of the holiday season in such a way that all would benefit equitably from the regularities and irregularities of both the holidays and the policy; (10) The memo, the policy, and the schedules are attached, along with the schedules of the preceding two years, which should speak for themselves; (11) There was no intention of not – or of improperly – observing the policy, or of not – or of improperly – observing the holidays. The intent was to properly observe both, and to be fair to all affected."

I would have told Veronica Pillsbury to get her dumb effing head out of her ass but my father, when he got wind of this, just quietly closed the door to his office to take a moment to contemplate a measured response to Veronica Pillsbury's letter. Now there came a thumping on that door. Trustee and School Superintendent Michael Bonaventura was calling through it, "What's this I hear of Francie Hearst calling one of our teachers a *bitch*? There are witnesses! I'd never tolerate anything like this from any of my staff! Are you in there? Who is running this show?"

Jake opened the door. He sat Bonaventure down and tried to calm him. Bonaventura asked Jake if staffer Francie Hearst had indeed said aloud that a teacher, one Mrs. Farrell, was a "*bitch*." He repeated himself, this time spelling the word for Jake: "Witnesses have told me personally that she called Mrs. Farrell, in front of the young people visiting the museum as a class, a B-I-T-C-H." He's going to bring in witnesses and, in the meantime, Bonaventura said as he went out, Jake could be contemplating "an appropriately serious reprimand."

The phone rang. Town Attorney Carson was returning Jake's call regarding the policy of the Trustees concerning public use of the museum's downstairs auditorium, which again was under discussion and review. At issue was the prohibition of the auditorium from groups requesting it for "partisan political purposes." The Board had initiated a policy decision to continue the prohibition in force, for obvious reason that "Once one group is let in," as Wheel Barrow had argued, "there will be no availability to exclude others." Trustee Ben Mulvane had called for a removal of the ban, quoting the Office of Campaign and Political Finance (in "A Guide to Political Activity for State, County and Municipal Employees"), to wit, "Using a public building or any part thereof for political campaign purposes is prohibited, unless equal access to the building is provided to any group wishing to use it, under the same terms and conditions as other groups. Under no circumstances may any political fundraising go in a public building or any part of a public building occupied for a state, county or municipal purpose."

Ben Mulvane believed a more reasonable and just museum policy would provide for "equal access to the building to any group wishing to use it, under the same terms and conditions as other groups. In reviewing the formal position statement of the American Museum Coalition, adopted by the American Museum Coalition Council. The council position was, "If any room in a museum supported by public funds is made available to the general public for any non-museum sponsored event, the museum may then not exclude any group based on the subject matter to be discussed or based on the ideas that the group advocates. For example, if a museum allows charities and sports clubs to discuss their activities in museum chambers, then the museum should not exclude partisan political or religious groups from discussing their activities in the same facilities. If a museum opens its rooms to a wide variety of civic organizations, then the museum may not deny access to a religious organization."

The Trustees had asked Jake to make a formal inquiry of the Town Attorney regarding all this, and now he had him on the line. Carson promised to gather together all the information he could concerning any decisions in this area that had been handed down by the courts in recent years, which could be brought to bear in further discussion of this issue – at his soonest opportunity.

It was now mid-May and my father was in way over his head in promises to keep with a program series he'd helped develop for the museum, an "Introduction to Orientalism in the Arts in the Year 1912," in cahoots with Liu Pan Li, formerly a physician in China who'd become, in America, a watercolorist and Tai Chi advocate. She'd presented "Orientalism in 1912," including a Tai Chi demonstration with Liu Pan Li and Melinda Swartzburg, an Austrian calligrapher and herbal health practitioner. The attendance was good and it looked like most people were pleased.

Toward the end of the evening program, Jake stood happily at the auditorium's entryway doors, eavesdropping on Liu Pan Li's telling anecdotes about one of her mentors, Thich Nhat Hahn. Relaxed by the soothing sing-song of her soft voice, he was stunned when the Fire Department stormed in. The newspaper reported they'd been "summoned to the scene by an unidentified caller to put a raging fire out."

CHAPTER THIRTY-FIVE

The morning headline: "Museum Up in Smoke – Curator Blocks Firefighters."

The Fire Chief had received an anonymous phone call informing him that smoke was filling the museum building. The truth was that an hour before the fire department swarmed upon the museum's auditorium, smokeless incense had been lit. As Jake would report to Board Chairperson Veronica Pillsbury, the arrival of the Firemen came as a complete surprise. "I was at the foot of the stairs, by the Meeting Room doors, when the furor of the many firemen spilled forth, filling the stairs with clamor, commotion, and the dozen or more dazzling yellow uniforms. I acted quickly, asking politely if any one fireman could please stand aside with me for one moment to clarify for me the reason for their being there. One did so. He moved with me from the staircase to the auditorium kitchen. I showed him the remains of the stick of incense that had been burned. It was there, in the kitchen, at this juncture, that the Chief appeared."

The newspaper article had closed with the comment, "At the Chief's direction, the source of the emergency was snuffed." The reporter could have written, in such a vein, that an elephant had been flying through the room.

The firemen had entered the museum through the front doors. Fran Micheline and Lizzie Cunningham, standing at the entrance, had efficiently waved them in and right on down the stairs. "After the firemen departed," Jake reported to Veronica, "Fran Micheline informed me a patron had told her there was smoke in the building, and that she and Lizzie had responded appropriately, telephoning the fire department. I mumbled, 'Yeah, yeah, yeah.' My memory tells me I mumbled 'Yeah, yeah, yeah' three times, not (as Fran now adamantly maintains) five times. It would be an exercise in futility to share the considerations in my mind at that moment, when I mumbled 'Yeah, yeah, yeah.' I did indeed sigh and look absently at the staff schedule, just as Fran maintains. And, as Fran insists, I did in silence turn away from the schedule and return to the auditorium. That Fran says she then expected I would order an evacuation of the building – that is news. At that point, with the firemen leaving, it would have made no sense to evacuate the building.

"As concerns the newspaper's quoting Fran's claiming that Hayden Brown told her I said somebody 'finally got even' with somebody for something," Jake reported to Veronica, "I have no control over what Fran says to Hayden, or what Hayden says to Fran, or what Fran says Hayden said. I do know that I did not say to Hayden what Fran says I said, and that Hayden says he didn't say what Fran is saying he said I said – for what that's worth. I insinuated nothing to anyone. I said plainly and frankly that I found it extraordinary that the Fire Department had showed up as they did, when they did. I may well have muttered, under my breath, something like, 'Here we go again'."

I would have told my father he'd be well-advised to rip off Fran's head to take to Hayden's ripped-off head to inform Veronica's ripped-off head of what Hayden's ripped-off head had said to Fran's and what Fran's had said to Hayden's and what Hayden's did or didn't ~~not~~ say in response to Fran's or what Fran's ~~said~~ did or didn't say to Hayden's or to the talking head of the chief of the entire fire department (a political appointment) and on and on. What a luxury that they were not all in hell together by then! They were flourishing in their agonies. It did feel as if some seed planted had been reaped, in the manner of so many other incidents and embarrassments through the years. Right down to all that exasperating newspaper bull that then also flourished (once more) on the heels of this event. "Firestorms Raging" – such nonsense an entrenched tradition now.

My father shrugged off such stuff. "There was always war," he wrote on a paper scrap I found among his papers. "There was always fighting going on somewhere."

"By the way," Jake wrote Veronica, "the Chief was *very* unhappy about his having to respond to the urgent call he'd received, only to snuff out a stick of smokeless incense. I told him I appreciated their consideration in not bringing stroke or heart failure to any of those in attendance at the program that was then in progress. The Chief is adamant that there should *never be smoke* or even anything *like* smoke in the building again, *ever*. He asked me if there was anywhere in the museum where there might be, or might have been, smoke," Jake reported. "I informed him that, yes, museum trustee Cunningham and maintenance man Hayden Brown smoked occasionally inside the building. Again the Chief warned me sternly, '*never* permit smoke or anything even resembling smoke in any part of this building *ever* again.' I said okay. By this we will abide.

"After that conversation," Jake continued, "the Chief and his men left the building. I heard nothing of what Mr. Barrow is now claiming transpired – some sort of 'obscenities' spoken? I know nothing of this. Concerning the Camperdene Daily Journal's report, I spoke with the Journal's editorial office and was told the Fire Chief indeed said these things to reporter Alice Armour Armstrong, who wrote the article. The Chief, however, contrarily told me he *never spoke with a reporter about it.*"

A few days passed, and Veronica got back to Jake, presenting him with a letter sent by Fran Micheline, asserting that Jake was "incompetent – and a pyromaniac."

"In light of my record of consistently encouraging and supporting Fran in her professional and leadership skills and growth," Jake responded, "her impassioned assertions of my incompetency and pyromania are very painful. The concoctions seem constructed in order to provoke – to elicit anger and perpetuate confusion."

In the days following, Fran took to parking her car in the space designated for the museum curator. In mid-June Jake wrote to Veronica Pillsbury, "I have given formal notice to all staff members that the curator's parking space is available to any staffer on the basis of 'space of last recourse' – when the other spaces are all filled. Anybody parking in the space when there are still other spaces available is missing the point." Jake also reported that, in the staff parking lot, just as one entered, the pavement had been sinking – apparently due to problems with an underlying sewer pipe. Hayden Brown had said he'd keep Jake informed of consultations with the Town Engineer and others concerning this problem. He'd seek three bids from different contractors able to make appropriate repairs.

It was at this juncture that Jake was told of yet another complaint. Lizzie Cunningham had told a museum visitor to "take a hike" fifteen minutes after Lizzie's noon lunch break had begun. The visitor had kept Lizzie busy till a quarter past noon. Instead of eating, Lizzie sat down and wrote a formal complaint to Jake, with a courtesy copy for the board of museum trustees.

"Obviously, this is an area of concern," Jake responded to Veronica Pillsbury's inquiry about Lizzie's returning 15 minutes late from lunch, and his filling in for her at the Circulation desk in her absence – and Lizzie's taking comp time for 15 minutes. "Quite apart from all this," Jake wrote, "what is your opinion of corrupt and mischievous people?"

One evening a kindly, soft-spoken, silver-haired old man came into the museum, sought out Jake and, looking left and then right of him, then looked straight into Jake's eyes and whispered, ominously, "My advice to you is, watch your back."

One night at midnight, while Jake's darling family slept, even as assorted museum trustees and staff slept or plotted fresh mischief, madness, and hardship, Jake got a call from Museum Board Chairwoman Pillsbury. She informed Jake the Trustees had, in Executive Session, voted to place a reprimand in his Personnel file, stemming from "discrepancies" in Jake's Christmas/NewYear's scheduling.

The next day, reporter Alice Armour Armstrong disclosed, on the front page of the Camperdene Daily Journal, that the Trustees had, in Executive Session, voted to place the reprimand in Jake's file. Museum trustee Wheel Barrow was quoted in the article, him saying "Mister Wright had again *done wrong*," displaying "utter professional incompetence in the execution of his administrative duties."

Jake later learned that Trustee Chairperson Pillsbury had issued a severe, angry reprimand to Trustee Barrow, decrying his passion for character assassination and media attention.

"Relative to Mr. Barrow's wrongful actions in this and related matters," Jake wrote to Veronica, "involving libelous, injurious patterns and practices, rest easy that no specific legal action will be taken by me – at this time." Jake informed Veronica of other issues, like his having entered the museum the day before via the Custodial area, there encountering Captain Cunningham smoking a pipe. "You'll remember the Fire Chief's recently giving me the sternest possible warning against there being smoke of any kind in any part of this building," Jake wrote, "and my agreeing with it – that we'd enforce it. Captain Cunningham should understand *there is to be no more smoking* inside the museum building. I am forwarding a courtesy copy of this letter to the Fire Chief. I want him to know he is being taken seriously, and that his demand is not being mocked, but enforced."

If this rebuke or slight affected Powderkeg one way or another, he did not let on. There were no immediate repercussions. It was not until autumn that the other shoe fell.

In mid-September, around four in the morning, my father got a phone call, at home, from the police. They had received an anonymous phone tip. The desk officer had called back, and had reached the museum's answering machine. Two patrol cars were in front of the museum, at that moment, awaiting Jake's arrival, to assist them. My father arose, dressed, and drove to the museum. There were two cruisers out front; three officers were already inside. They had entered the building through an emergency exit. The latch-bolt there had not been set securely in the doorjam receptacle – the door was not locked. The alarm had not gone off.

Jake switched off the alarm system and they together made a thorough search of the building, room by room. There were no signs of a break-in (and no "bum in the bathroom" as Wheel Barrow would later explain away the event). Jake re-secured the building, re-set the alarm, and left with the officers.

The next day, word came that the Governor of Massachusetts had appointed a new member to the trustee board of the Massachusetts Museums Coalition – Veronica Pillsbury.

"Congratulations," Jake wrote Veronica. "I am pleased by this news, though I'm sorry at your having to leave the Board of the New Museum of the Year 1912. Through several years now of questionable, most unprofessional (often blatantly unethical or just plain vile) words and deeds of at least one trustee and that trustee's mischievous circle of adherents, amid perpetual, contrived turmoil, you have stood your ground with clarity and dignity, offering valuable counsel and encouragement. I am grateful, and feel sincere appreciation, that you have served on the Board. I trust yours will continue to be a clear, strong voice, amid whatever debate or turmoil, advocating that Massachusetts museums will be among the finest in our nation, second to none. Good luck to you in your continuing journey."

My father arrived home that evening to find the house empty. Minna, Mark and I were gone. I shouldn't remember any of this, but I do. I mean, seriously, I was just a baby.

CHAPTER THIRTY-SIX

My father was seven the first time he'd seen the Grand Canyon. His mother had looked away as he strode confidently to the precipice. His father had seemed unconcerned, watching almost impartially as his son pranced astride the edge. It gave Jake goosebumps later, recollecting, he said. In his last days on earth he would tell me of how he'd developed, around that time, in Camperdene, a fear of falling into the Grand Canyon. He'd wake up in a sweat, on the verge of tumbling down and away, and away, and away.

Here was a new oblivion and openness and absence with which to contend. Jake had felt love and devotion, joy and contentment, passion and futurity. I know he now felt howling soreness of heart, melancholy, dismay. He was being torn through love's labors with tight-gripping pincers on his head. Both out of strength and out of weakness, my father resolved my mother should bear the burden of her decision. He would bear the burden of his. Let her go her way. Let her be her way.

What was Jake's way? To sweat and cry and pace. To think his thoughts and laugh out loud and then to sleep. To wake up from feverish sleep in the morning – glad to find himself still alive. Everything boiled down to that, he said.

There were ghosts about. The Camperdene Daily Journal had dubbed the unidentified caller who'd recently phoned the police at four in the morning – who'd got into the New Museum of the Year 1912 after hours and placed the phone call, then disappeared – the "Museum

Ghost." When, a couple weeks later, on a Friday, a burner on the stove in the auditorium kitchen was turned on and left on over a weekend, word arose that this was done by the "Museum Ghost." When someone snuck into the museum staff lounge and spun the microwave oven dial to high for the longest time allowed, with the ashes of burned books within, the word went out: this was done by the "Museum Ghost."

Then there was a "break-out" by an unidentified person shortly after the museum closed: the "Museum Ghost." The cars of five museum staffers were scratched (apparently by a key or screwdriver) across the sides, hoods, and trunks of their cars, parked in the museum staff parking area. The word went forth. The "Museum Ghost" had done it.

The new Chair of the Board of the New Museum of the Year 1912 Trustees, Ben Mulvane, very reasonably suggested these events were somehow tied into the possibility of a new appointment to the political post vacated recently by Veronica Pillsbury – museum trustee. There were already rumors of the post being filled by an outspoken anti-Museum-Ghost advocate. Ben Mulvane insisted the Board of New Museum of the Year 1912 Trustees should fill the trustee vacancy created by Veronica Pillsbury's resignation not with an appointment, but through the election process. And in this he did prevail.

Jake typed up a memo to the staff in which he welcomed their input regarding safety issues in closing and leaving the museum at night. He asked staff members to please check the Auditorium kitchen stove burners and oven and Staff Room stove/oven/microwave/coffeemaker when locking up, before going home.

The end of the year was fast approaching. Hayden Brown had put together a big artificial Christmas tree by the main entry doors, and had begun decorating it. He was there, at the museum, after it had closed, the night the police appeared to deal with a "break-out" that occured. Someone had been in the building after closing time, and had set off the alarm when leaving the building, even as Hayden Brown decorated the Christmas tree. Hayden told Jake that Fran Micheline remembered giving to a man ("homeless" in appearance) the key to the men's room shortly before closing time. Hayden surmised that this individual stayed has claimed, in the past, to be independent of Mr. Barrow's influence he has, on occasion, in similar circumstances, left the bills unsigned (though he has personally promised me that he would be in to sign). I understand he has explained these reversals by indicating Mr. Barrow had told him personally that he would sign the bills, and then did not. With Veronica Pillsbury no longer on the Board, we now have a New Museum of the Year 1912 Board of five, not six, members. Mr. Barrow's 'enemies,' the Board "majority," thus now consists of three, not four, members. Mr. Barrow asserts that Roland Henselmeier is 'with' him – I have no idea whether or not Mr. Hemselmeierer is 'with' anyone, or in outer space, or in the world at all. Mr. Barrow has likened this majority of four Board members to the Three Stooges. Mr. Barrow is entirely forward and outspoken about this work of his, to see 'The Four' disgraced, and me with them. His schemes and concoctions hatch usually as front-page news, his 'enemies' slammed in the local paper. The central most painful insult to me, however, was never in the papers. Mr. Barrow's assertion that 'the museum will be better off when Ben Mulvane is dead' was the clearest indication he had given me, up to that point, that in fact he has (instead of a reasonable sense of fiduciary responsibility) remarkable vanity tied to even more remarkable venomousness, absolutely breathtaking contempt, and a big mouth. I understand that Ben Mulvane, after learning from Mr. Barrow himself his deep hatred for him, which triggered my making my own inquiries, and my own personal value judgment, about him, and about Mr. Barrow, has heart troubles and has been in the hospital. With Ben Mulvane unable to come in, and with Roland Henselmeier promising to sign but not doing so, and with Mr. Barrow making his 'point' by refusing to sign the bills, we are left with just two trustees to sign the bills: Superintendent Bonaventura and Reverend Jack. By regulation of the Town Charter, two signatures are insufficient. Though Mr. Barrow is often in the museum, with even furniture and a space in a corner of the museum recognized as being 'his' – and with even some staff members generally recognized and identified as being 'his' – still he declines, even in these circumstances, to sign the warrant. Should not the Town of Camperdene, by way of Town Counsel, have an opinion in these matters? Is this open, oft-repeated show of fiduciary irresponsibility, this relentlessly arrogant attitude and conduct, acceptable? Can nothing be done? Must the New Museum of the Year 1912 curator, as Mr. Barrow has insisted, work for him alone in order to remain museum curator? Must those trustees who disagree with him come around to his way of thinking 'or else' – for example, the bills won't be paid? If this be a sign of 'leadership,' whether from a real or imagined 'majority' or 'minority' trustee, then may the electric company turn off the museum's lights so that the rest of us in the town will finally see Mr. Barrow's 'point.' Having myself been often threatened and slandered, in this entrenched tangle of political feuding and game-playing on the part of the self-announced current 'minority' Board membership, I obviously have no power, or influence, to effect a good outcome from 'his' war. In the coming week I will again actively solicit the required three trustee signatures to pay the museum's vendors, hoping to hold at bay the encroaching collection agents."

CHAPTER
THIRTY-SEVEN

My father had time to think on things over the holidays. The museum was closed on Christmas Day. Jake visited Nick Wentworth and other friends around town – presenting gifts, enjoying food and drink, and weeping copiously. Jake was desperate – wringing his hands, wrestling destiny, trying to put a straight-jacket of some kind or another on those ancient relentless twin demons, labyrinthical cunning and false representation.

The next day, Jake calmly wrote back to Town Attorney Carson to say thank you for a letter he'd written in response to a note Jake had sent to him. Carson had written back bluntly, "I will not be drawn into your personal or political battles."

Jake now wrote Carson, "Please *do* understand me when I say that your statement – 'I will not be drawn into your personal or political battles' – does best – *exactly* – describe my particular situation, and my inquiry. I came to Camperdene to be the curator of The old Museum of the Year 1912 – then curator of The New Museum of the Year 1912 – not to be drawn into the 'political battles' in which museum trustees have historically and traditionally been embroiled, not to be anyone's political pawn, and certainly not to be harassed by such abusive rhetoric and deeds as Mr. Mulvane or Mr. Barrow and his *people* have dumped on me. You do know exactly the situation which my letter addresses.

one commits many sins; a man's pride brings him low, but a man of lowly spirit gains honor.' I entered this profession, curatorship, out of youthful idealism. I left it for a short time, and returned to it because I could see nothing more I cared to do than to be a helper, a facilitator, in what I call the 'cultural conversation,' which is always ongoing, from community to community, from generation to generation. Museum professionals do not dictate what is to be viewed or talked about, but bring all the information available, equally, to all the participants in the conversation. This point of view, this ideal, makes all the more painful the recognition of what one particular Camperdene Daily Journal reporter has done – and has left undone. In purposefully mis-telling the news, she has misguided readers, the conversation participants. Whatever I have done, since being appointed curator of The old Museum of the Year 1912, and whether it was done well or poorly, has never been front page news. We have seen, printed as front page news, a vain 'minority' museum trustee again and again flinging his 'opinions' about 'mediocre' trustee colleagues and museum curators. We have seen his clique of people, who have regularly harassed the curator, accuse him of 'harassment.' Never could the headline have been, 'The truth be told.' We have seen this 'news' told from the same familiar, lopsided side of things, with that well-known, self-appointed demigod having obvious access to, and influence over, the local press. Such lopsidedness, the purposely leaving certain aspects of a story in while purposefully leaving other parts out, printed as viable 'news' stories is, I'm sure, 'standard procedure' in the news reporting business. But to be at the receiving end of the insult does make one want to comment on it, all the same. 'Standard procedure' or not, it is still an injury to the truth. I know there are reporters in the business solely to make money, share recipes, and keep their jobs, and that the business of the newspapers is to sell papers. But when an honest, hardworking person finds himself or herself taken down not once, but regularly, by concocted, wrongheaded, one-sided 'News' purveyed at the bidding of whatever irate, 'influential,' lying local politician and his circle ("Bribe her with little presents and she'll print anything you tell her to") – that hurts. It seems to be a comical old Camperdene tradition, this trustee unabashedly harassing curators, without consequence, 'connected' in such a way as to enable him to make them look like idiots in the press. But nothing about me is so colorful or interesting as the Daily Journal has led the community to believe. I have harassed nobody. Lord knows I have been harassed. Let's let bribery of reporters become truly old-fashioned, outdated – good riddance; let lying, comical, dictatorial megalomaniacs go unpublished; let them grow frustrated; let them just fade away. If a reporter can't do that, then she should at least attempt to tell the other side of the story. '*Ring out the old, ring in the new. Ring out the false, ring in the true*'."

Jake wrote this to Powderkeg Cunningham:

"When, you'll recall, the Camperdene Fire Department rushed to The New Museum of the Year 1912 after an anonymous caller informed them of smoke in the museum, it turned out to have been a piece of incense, which had been lit in the program room. Elsewhere in the building, you were smoking, as several people reported, your pipe. Camperdene's Fire Chief made it clear to me at that time that The New Museum of the Year 1912 curator could no more tolerate any smoke of any kind in the building – *ever*. This was told all museum patrons, Trustees, and staffers alike. Having come upon you smoking inside the museum, I wrote a letter to the Board Chair in which, I believe, I made it clear that the Fire Chief had ruled that smoking inside this facility is not acceptable. Just the other morning, in the aftermath of a Blizzard, in seeking out our Maintenance Superviser Hayden Brown 9:30 a.m. in order to enlist his aid in investigating leakage from the museum ceiling, I found you in the HVAC room, drinking coffee and smoking your pipe. Now, don't get me wrong. I understand your impulse to seek out a 'hiding place' in the museum in which to have a cup of hot coffee and a smoke on a cold morning. You will similarly understand that I must tell you that you can't smoke in the museum. It is no joke; it is not a laughing matter. Please don't smoke in this building again."

It was fairly evident from these writings that my father was on the verge of going nuts. Wheel Barrow and his people had been doing everything in their power to make the museum a place where secrets, bickering, backbiting, and blockage were not only acceptable, but rewarded. He had very ably made the museum a confusing, downright *scary* place to work. Jake was buckling.

When he was asked, "So why didn't you just leave?" Jake answered, "I feel obliged to stay and fix what's been maligned, injured, shattered." But, in point of fact – and Jake couldn't see this – he was intricately and perversely captivated by, and entwined with, his captors.

The New Museum of the Year 1912 should have been a place of respect, moderation, and civility. Instead there were Barrows' conflicts, duplicity, division, perplexity. Jake was not ready to accept such a low and ugly standard of personal behavior and professional performance – beneath even mediocrity. Jake vowed he was not going to continue to lie down and take it, to be buried in an ugly morass of Barrow's political game playing.

But no – the next thing he knew, staff sick leave policies were the avenue through which new outcry and mayhem arose. Suddenly trustee interest in museum staff sick leave policy was the rage. Jake felt it wise to share with the Board a highly unusual request that had come to him. Museum staffer Marcie Hearst, scheduled to work on a Saturday, per regular "Week One" scheduling, had asked a colleague to cover for her so that she could take a Saturday off and "work" on the following Wednesday instead. She had then formally requested of Jake that he grant her "Sick Leave" for the Wednesday – though Wednesdays had long and consistently been her regularly scheduled "Week One" day off.

Jake had not signed off on that. If there had been a precedent for such a request, Jake was unaware of it. He was quite perplexed by the request and wanted the trustees to consider its faults or merits before he reported back to Marcie on it one way or the other. It seemed to him that approving it would have created an unwanted precedent. If a staffer could take a Sick Day on his or her regularly designated day off, then he or she could also logically call in Sick on their day off and ask for Sick Leave credit, enabling him or her to take off a different day later in the same week. Under such logic, it would not be frivolous for a staffer to demand Sick or Personal time on a Snow Day, designating a different day in the week as the individual's private Snow Day, day off.

Jake now wrote to Marcie Hearst, "You need not report yourself sick on a Sunday, a snow day, or on your day off. If there is a precedent for doing so, I am unaware of it. If you are not working this Saturday, for which you are scheduled to work, please fill out the municipal 'Record of Absence' form, noting the date/reason. If you wish, you may appeal this before the Board of The New Museum of the Year 1912 Trustees at their next meeting."

To Ben Mulvane Jake wrote, "As concerns Marcie Hearst's 'Record of Absence' request for sick time on her regularly scheduled day off, which was under discusssion at the last Trustees' meeting, I have brought to her attention, 'You need not report yourself sick on a Sunday, a snow day, or on your day off.'"

Marcie now submitted a *second* "Record of Absence" form, identical to the first but dated after the fact, instead of prior to it. This raised an interesting question. It was *Marcie* who'd initiated the alteration of the regular schedule, so she would be "off" on her scheduled Saturday, Marcie having arranged with her reference colleague to "switch" Saturdays. Having arranged that "switch," Marcie had then requested the "Sick" time for Wednesday, January 10, her regularly scheduled day off. Had Marcie said nothing in advance, and simply submitted the form, as she did do after the Board meeting discussion and after Jake's letter to her, would that have been acceptable?

Jake's call. "No individual," he wrote, "should ask to take a formal 'Sick' day on one's day off, or to declare one's self 'Sick' on the day after the fact, without authentically having been sick – which is demonstrably the case here."

"Dear Mr. Jake," Ben Mulvane wrote, "I think you know that Marcie Hearst and I have got a special thing going, and I don't want you prying or messing with it any further than you have. I trust you get my meaning. Ben Mulvane."

"Dear Ben," Jake wrote back, "I get it – totally. Jake Wright."

The museum trustees, at their next meeting, voted favorably for Sick Time credit for time taken off on regularly scheduled Days off. In Executive Session, Trustee Chairman Mulvane led the Board in their discussion of what disciplinary action should be brought against Jake for his insubordination.

CHAPTER THIRTY-EIGHT

One day in March Lizzie Cunningham appeared, red-faced and out of breath, in Jake's office, accompanied by a calm, composed Fran Micheline, to tell Jake that a man had come into the museum at about 9:45 a.m. and had told Lizzie he was a truant officer and had asked if there were any truant kids in the museum. She described the man as being 25-30 years old, thin, 5'7" or 5'8", short, with light brown hair, wearing glasses, a blue plaid long-sleeved shirt, and blue jeans. She suspected he was not what he claimed to be and requested Jake tell her what she should do if he came back, or what anybody should do if that man or anyone else ever actually removed a child from the museum under such circumstances.

My father reassured Lizzie and Fran that there seemed to be no immediate emergency, and he promised he would think about it and get back to them.

I would have surely somehow flushed the two of them down some grinding giant sinkhole before I ever let things get this far, but not my father. No, he was not fazed. Not even now. He resolved, first, to inquire of the police about truant officers and under whose authority they operate. He called them and was told they operate under authority of the school system. Jake gave the officer Lizzie's description of the man claiming to be a truant officer, just in case. He then spoke with Dr.

Bonaventura who informed Jake he was, beyond being Superintendent of Schools, the sole truant officer of the Town of Camperdene. As such, he said, he did not go out and track down truant children. Anyone representing himself, or herself, as being a Camperdene truant officer would be an imposter. Jake asked if the best course, should this ever occur again, would be to detain the individual and call the police, and Dr. Bonaventura said yes.

When it came about that Lizzie Cunningham applied for the job of Administrative Assistant at the museum, Dr. Bonaventura quietly slipped Jake a copy of The State Ethics Commission publication, "A Practical Guide to the Conflict of Interest Law for Municipal Employees." This document made it plain that Jake would be in violation of conflict of interest laws were he involved in the selection process through which the position would be filled. The State Ethics Commission noted that "Public employees must avoid conduct which creates a reasonable impression that they will act with bias. The law states that if a reasonable person having knowledge of the relevant circumstances would conclude that a public official or employee could be improperly influenced, the public official can dispel this impression of favoritism by disclosing all the facts which would lead to such a conclusion."

Any disclosure Jake might make regarding members of the Board of The New Museum of the Year 1912 Trustees and their assorted familial or sordid relationships with museum staffers could cause even the brave to cry. Any "reasonable person" could see Jake's dread of further trustee harassment exercised an influence over him which would lead to his "favoring," in his fear of further reprisals, the appointment of a particular Town and museum employee who had applied for the post. Accordingly, Jake made his disclosure. He could not recommend for or against the particular museum staffer who had applied for promotion to the position. For him to do so obviously would have been, one way or the other, a violation of the conflict-of-interest laws.

It now remained for an elected official, a museum trustee, to disclose, per The Practical Guide to the Conflict of Interest Law for Municipal Employees (page 20), "a personal relationship with someone appearing before his or her Board. An elected official's public disclosure must be made in writing and filed with the city or town clerk. In addition, an elected official would be well advised to make a verbal disclosure for inclusion in meeting minutes if such an 'appearance' of a conflict arises in a public meeting. These disclosures must be made prior to any official participation or action.

"Once this public disclosure has been made, the official may participate in the matter notwithstanding the 'appearance of a conflict.' When officials do act on matters affecting individuals with whom they have a private relationship, they must act objectively and be careful not to use their official position to secure any unwarranted privilege or benefit for that person. Use of an official position to secure an unwarranted privilege for people is always prohibited, regardless of whether the disclosure process is followed." It was up to the Board of Curators to consider what action would be taken in the matter of filling the vacant position.

The meeting came and went and, after it, Jake went to his office and typed up a letter to the Commissioner of the State Ethics Commission, Boston, Massachusetts:

"Dear Commissioner, Yesterday evening, at a meeting of the Board of The New Museum of the Year 1912 Trustees, I informed the Board that under the terms of the State Ethics Commission's 'Practical Guide to the Conflict of Interest Law for Municipal Employees,' I could neither recommend for, nor against, the promotion of a museum staffer 'favored' by an elected official, a museum trustee. 'To do so,' I informed the Board, 'would give the appearance of my succumbing to a trustee bribe and trustee influence well known among museum staff if not widely known by the public.' I herewith formally file a complaint concerning the undisclosed conflict of interest, asking that an investigation be conducted regarding Trustee/Staff relationships, the attempted bribery of a municipal employee by an elected official, and other related ethical dilemmas, and corruptions, that have too long plagued Camperdene."

On April 1st, Jake reported to the Town Accountant that, "at their last meeting, the Board of Museum Trustees voted to table the filling of the M.A.P.E. Secretary to the Trustees/Director's Administrative Assistant post."

On April 12th, Jake wrote to Town Council Carson, "You will know that no one is more pleased than me to learn that Mr. Wallace Barrow, yesterday appointed Chairman of the Board of The New Museum of the Year 1912 Trustees, has publicly pledged 'harmony.' This brings to mind the front page story of the Camperdene Daily Journal a few years ago, when it was reported, 'Bowing to the fact that in-fighting has tarnished their image, the Board of Museum trustees last night unanimously elected Wallace Barrow as Chairman. The trustees unanimously selected Jacob Wright new museum curator. "It was time to set some good professional standards," said Dr. Michael Bonaventura. "As soon as I was made Chairman," Barrow said, "you could feel the spirit of unity." '"

Jake wrote to the head of M.A.P.E., "I received your note of May 20, regarding this latest M.A.P.E. grievance filed for Ms Cunningham. As you were yourself present at the pertinent Museum Trustees' meeting, you know that the matter of the filling of the vacant M.A.P.E. post, which had been formally tabled at a previous meeting, remained tabled. I could make no recommendation to the Board regarding the filling of the post. I believe the grievance, by virtue of my being formally unable to settle it, must now go to the next level, perhaps to be resolved by the Board of The New Museum of the Year 1912 Trustees, who will next meet on Wednesday, June 12, at 7:00 p.m."

Jake wrote to Town Counsel Carson in June, "The Board of The New Museum of the Year 1912 Trustees gave me the mandate to proceed with the interviewing of candidates from the pool of applicants who applied for the vacant MAPE post, Secretary to Trustees / Director's Administrative Assistant. But I find myself in a situation wherein I feel I cannot comply, for reasons which I will explain. First, let me ask if you will provide me with a copy of your recent letter to the Chairman of the Board of The New Museum of the Year 1912 Trustees, Wallace

Barrow, written in response to his inquiry regarding the above named vacant post. It has been said that there is 'only one' real candidate for the position, namely, that applicant who is currently a Camperdene Association of Paraprofessional Employees – an employee of the museum. As I am familiar with that individual's record, personnel file, and job performance, there is no way that I could recommend this individual to this position. Not to recommend this individual could lead to accusations of anti-union animus, or animus toward this individual's known alliance with the leading member of one faction of the longstanding "feuding" two factions of the Board of The New Museum of the Year 1912 Trustees. While I honestly have no animus of any kind toward any staffer for any connection with, or participation in, any union, still it could be reasonably maintained that I feel animus toward the staffer for that staffer's widely reputed intimate connection with the current chairman of the Board. That trustee has himself made admission to me of his intimacy, and alliance, with this staffer. For me to comply with the wishes of the Board of Curators, to recommend to them a candidate from the pool of applicants for the above named post seems, to me, to be an impossibility. Clearly, I would be entering into a conflict of interest situation should I recommend the currently employed MAPE staffer, just as I would be were I not to recommend that staffer. Consider further: you are aware (at least you know that I have told you) one museum trustee has offered bribes to me relative to my showing favoritism to, and advancing, certain museum staffers, and has made threats against me when I have not complied. I need not tell you about certain 'protected' personnel files (overflowing with reprimands). In not recommending the one particular candidate, favored by one particular trustee, I could ultimately be understood to be reacting to the threat made, and accomplished, while a favorable recommendation by me on behalf of that staffer could be understood to be the acceptance, out of fear of further repercussions, of the bribe. I authentically fear further reprisals from that trustee with whom the contesting MAPE applicant is, by his admission, so closely allied.

"With the non-renewal of my contract, I now no longer need fear the promised loss of my job should this staffer, and yet still another staffer, not be advanced. Still I fear further harassment, further abusiveness. It seems to me that my obligation, under the Ethics Commission's 'Practical Guide to the Conflict of Interest Law for Municipal Employees,' is neither to recommend for nor against this particular promotion. I have no idea where this could take the Board in their formidable task of hiring an individual to this post. Please do hand down to me a formal opinion regarding Massachusetts conflict of interest laws in regards to this, a museum curator's removing himself from the process of selecting who shall fill just such a vacancy under the above named circumstances. I say I cannot make a recommendation; perhaps you will determine that I must. Also, regarding the trustees' filling the vacancy, should the currently employed MAPE staffer come under consideration for the filling of the post, would it not be warranted that a public disclosure be forthcoming from the elected official on the Board of Curators with whom the staffer is well known to be intimate and allied? Doesn't such a disclosure have to be made, and the disclosure included in the meeting minutes? The State Ethics Commission advises an elected official publicly "make a verbal disclosure for inclusion in meeting minutes if... an 'appearance' of a conflict arises in a public meeting. These disclosures must be made prior to any official participation or action."

Jake wrote to the Massachusetts State Ethics Commission, "I am enclosing a courtesy copy of a letter written to Camperdene's Town Counsel regarding issues that not only trouble me greatly but have, in fact, affected me most adversely. I wish not only that you be aware of this situation, but that you might act in some way so as to help set aright a very bad situation, which deteriorates steadily. To that letter I am attaching related documents which, hopefully, will give you a context for evaluating this current situation in light of the overall recent history of The New Museum of the Year 1912. Please understand that 'alliances' and 'counter alliances' seem to be at the root of the problem. Even our Town Council has made statements to me that suggest a strong and particular political alliance, which may yet aggravate my attempt to get appropriate legal advice. I am curious to know whether elected officials, namely museum trustees, are exempt from such standards of ethics as Massachusetts municipal employees are held to (as disclosed in the Practical Guide to the Conflict of Interest Law for Municipal Employees) and, if they are not exempt, can somebody do something to see that they are held to such standards?"

It is interesting to me that my father, so far as I remember, never gave me any particular advice. Atticus Finch he was not. I did find, long after the events related here, among his papers, one tidbit of advice that his father had given him, Atticus Finch-like: "In this world, to cope in society, a person has to get the right degree of skin. One must be tender and thin-skinned – but not too thin-skinned. One must to a degree be hard-boiled, thick-skinned enough so that the evil and cunning in the world don't get under one's skin, poisoning and wearing one out. Just-right degrees of thick and thin skin determine your floating or drowning."

Just then his father's son was drowning.

It was almost four in the morning now, and my father still had not left the museum. Overcome with sudden dizziness, rapid heartbeat, and difficulty breathing, Jake grabbed for his phone as he fell to the floor. He attempted to cease trembling, but could not. There was now a piercing pain in his chest, as if a spear had been driven through his heart. His discombobulation was increasing. Jake worried what might happen if he proved unable to get his body back under control. He dialed 911. He tried to speak, but could not. He could not make his body do his bidding. Convulsions came on. Jake lost control of himself. Something awful was going to happen, he knew.

CHAPTER THIRTY-NINE

"Labyrinthical intricacies started immediately to unravel," my father later noted. That same morning, while Jake slept soundly between crisp white hospital bed sheets, Powderkeg Cunningham led his daughter Lizzie furtively to Jake's office, where they got hold of Lizzie's personnel file. Lizzie stood guard while the Captain frantically puzzled over the papers, photocopying some and shredding others.

It was the newest member of the trustee board of the Massachusetts Museums Coalition, Veronica Pillsbury, who caught them red-handed. Oddly, they admitted to their deed at once, and even apologized. But this was not the strangest news that day.

The Camperdene Daily Journal headline that day: "Woman's Body Discovered in 1912 Cement."

Carlena Lagorio's body.

"Staffers at the New Museum of 1912 are disoriented and distraught," Alice Armour Armstrong reported. "Museum curator Jacob Wright, hospitalized in the night after an apparent heart attack, on learning of the past trustee's body's being found embedded four feet deep in concrete by investigators three days ago, had no comment. 'What can you say about such a thing?' queried Wright rhetorically, apparently saddled with neither sadness nor remorse."

"I've been telling the investigators of the probability of this since nearly time immemorial," Captain Richard Cunningham told reporters. "My words fell on deaf ears. *No, no* – they wouldn't listen to The Captain. Oh no, they wouldn't listen to *me*. I told them, *loud and clear*: the bad attitudes and bad acts at this too highly politicized institution through too many years would lead to something like this. I had no political agenda. My purpose was to get through the politics to determine if the law held something useful for resolving some or all of the institution's conflicts, through the legendary convolutions of entrenched local politics. I got booted out of the Association while Wallace went on to become Chairman of the *new* New Museum of the Year 1912 Board of Curators. I knew what he was up to. He thought I was out of the loop, but I wasn't out of the loop. I knew what he was up to. He was the man, the big man," The Captain rambled on. "Chief Honcho and lead member of the one faction of the feuding two factions of the Board. But I feel no venom for the man," The Captain confessed. "No venom. It was a very bad situation. We should not have done what we did. It is not now *venom* that I feel."

A full confession was not soon forthcoming from Wallace Barrow. But it was only a matter of time. Eventually, Barrow cracked, too.

On the Fourth of July, Richard Cunningham and Wallace Barrow were read their rights and arrested, charged with the murder of Carlena Lagorio. The two were led away, looking like two of Rodin's pathetic, burdened, leaden, green Burghers of Calais – sans dignity. In the next few days, witnesses from the construction crew would come forward, identifying both men as having been seen at the site of the New Museum of the Year 1912 building "*in suspicious circumstances*" – unloading an "*undetermined cargo*" into freshly poured concrete. One witness would claim Captain Cunningham had killed the woman, and Barrow had kept her body hidden – in plain sight in the Barrow Funeral Home – until he could keep the body there no more. When the concrete had been poured for the foundation of the new museum building, Barrow and Cunningham had driven to the site in the Barrow Family Hearse and had unloaded the body – in plain daylight.

It certainly must have been very gratifying to my father and to a lot of other people that at last there seemed to be some justice in the world. It appeared that all the appropriate people doomed for imprisonment and death were in fact all making their inevitable way to these. I say, Hallelujah. You can fool some of the people all of the time and all of the people some of the time, but you can't pull the wool over the eyes of Karma.

The two men were brought to trial in Worcester. The preliminary hearing was held July 24th, twenty days after the arrest. Grand Jury proceedings were held on September 11th. The Grand Jury decided there was enough evidence to bring the men to trial, issuing an indictment charging Barrow and Cunningham with premeditated, first-degree murder. Judge Theodore Daniel Wyckes presided over the case. Jury selection ended in mid-August. Cunningham and Barrow entered the courtroom, on the 20th, in chains. There were TV crews and journalists from all the world over, covering "The Commonwealth of Massachusetts Versus Wallace Barrow and Richard Cunningham." The "Wallace and Cunningham Defense Fund Committee" was launched. Police protection was increased, in the course of the trial, about twenty-fold.

Eventually, it came out that Captain Cunningham, after studying at Yale University, had arrived in Camperdene and, at a certain point, had given Carlena Lagorio a wedding ring. The two had spoken of getting married! Cunningham had taken a job as gardener and groundskeeper at the Camperdene Lutheran Church. Carlena and Cunningham had stopped seeing one another. Cunningham had got engaged to a different Camperdene woman, a nurse.

At the time the old Museum of the Year 1912 was ending and the New Museum of the Year 1912 was getting underway, museum heiress Carlena was threatening to adhere to a tiny small-print clause in the will of Simon and Louisa Lagorio stipulating that, in the event of the dissolution of the Museum of 1912, its contents – all of its treasures –would go to the eldest living Lagorio heir – which, of course, was Carlena.

Barrow had had designs on the soon-to-be-empty museum; he wanted it to become an extension of *his* business – his mausoleum, the funeral home. He'd wanted to see it empty. But he'd also wanted to see the treasures of the old museum go to the new museum. Intending to be on the board of the new museum, he did not want to see the treasures fall into Carlena's hands, to be sold away. He felt sure he could manage, in the process of transferring treasures from the old museum to the new one, to make a fortune for himself through mysterious misplacement and outright theft. As for Cunningham, he felt similarly – and he wanted Carlena dead and in hell.

One night, Carlena had gone to dinner with some "old friends." The next thing she knew, she was on the floor of the restaurant, vomiting. She supposed she'd contracted food poisoning during the dinner, but her table companions, who'd shared the meal, were not in any pain. Carlena was tied up in knots, convulsing. Barrow had offered to take her home. Carlena had arrived home safely – barely able to walk. It was difficult to use her hands or feet or hold her head steady. The poison affected her involuntary muscle system. Her body began twitching wildly. She had sustained a lethal dose of arsenic, enough to kill her a few times over. By morning, the heavy metal had worked its way out through her skin – sores on the tops of her hands and on her neck and face. Her body was trying to purge itself of the poison – to no avail.

The two masons, Cunningham and Barrow, helped each other out. Cunningham had poisoned Carlena; Barrow had kept the body in his funeral parlor a few days; then the two had together put her in the freshly poured concrete of the new museum. An autopsy had revealed the poison. Tests showed arsenic had caused severe trauma and the breakdown of blood vessels. On September 6th, the defendants – and the world – learned the verdict of the jury: guilty, as charged.

Though the *principles* the trustees had claimed their institution embodied looked good on the surface, the trustees themselves, over time, had hardened into sordid, sinister, degraded criminals. Here were truly prison-worthy injurers, misrepresenters, falsifiers, scoundrels, conscienceless thieves.

Still, for all that, they would not have been sentenced, punished, and imprisoned had they not also been *murderers*.

Well, at least – at last – they were in prison now.

My father said Captain Powderkeg's family would probably go on pretty much as it had before. The Barrow family, on the other hand, would be thrown into utter turmoil. Candy Barrow would sell the contents of the house at auction, and return to Scandinavia. Her husband's brother, Broderick Barrow, would appear from out of nowhere to grapple with the chaotic Barrow family affairs, and would put the house up for sale – up for grabs.

Before things could get any worse on that front, Town Counsel Carson went before Town Meeting members with a proposal to purchase the defunct and empty funeral home at an offering that could hardly be refused, proposing also that the street between the mansion and the Museum be ripped up, and that the two buildings be renovated and joined, thus creating a new Camperdene Police Department headquarters. (This was put to a vote that same evening. It passed unanimously.)

Town Attorney Carson informed my father, who had recovered fully from what had not been a heart attack, but rather something like apoplexy, a panic attack, was now *his own man*. He was free to fill the vacant post, Secretary to the Board of Curators and Administrative Assistant to the Curator, as he saw fit. Jake needed only to interview at least three of the more than twenty applicants seeking the job. Carson assured Jake it *truly* was his call on this; Carson said he would "quash any other resolve."

On the Fourth of July, the day that Barrow and Cunnningham were arrested, my father wrote to the Captain's wily daughter, Lizzie, "Thank you for applying for the position, Secretary to the Board of The New Museum of the Year 1912 and Administrative Assistant to the Museum Curator, and for advising me that your resume can be found in the museum's personnel files. Your letter of intent came two days after the 'seven (7) calendar days' in which current members of the Camperdene Association of Paraprofessional Employees could apply to be considered for promotion to such a vacancy. While you submitted it in time to qualify for the general deadline for applying, you were not among those considered for interviewing."

Even as witnesses had been giving testimony regarding Captain Cunningham and Wallace Barrow's disposing of Carlena Lagorio's body, my father had selected Judith Parker Brown from West Virginia to fill the vacancy. Recently graduated with a Master's degree from Georgetown University, bringing half a dozen irresistibly formidable letters of reference, Ms Brown had showed up at the interview wearing a violet crushed-velvet blouse with matching slacks and purple sneakers – both shoelaces untied. She had said she'd heard "irresistibly intriguing things" about The New Museum of the Year 1912. "This," she had assured my father, "is where I want to be."

It is recorded, he responded: *Good luck.*

CHAPTER FORTY

This story approaches its conclusion a week before Christmas, when my father took a big chunk of vacation time allotted him even as he left the employ of the museum. Within a year, the buildings of the old Museum of the Year 1912 and the Barrow Funeral Home would make way for the new police station and jail; the New Museum of the Year 1912 would be boarded up and, eventually, after more than a decade of complicated legal wrangling and court battles, be re-opened as a bank.

Jake packed away all his papers in white cardboard banker's boxes and was resolved not to look back. He would start a new job in the first week of the new year as a west coast writer and editor for a San Diego area travel magazine, *Freewheeling*.

On December 22nd, Lucille Jameson, Chairwoman of the American Museums Coalition, sent my father a handsome certificate of appreciation for his "Vivid Demonstration" of "How Museums Change Lives."

On Christmas Eve, Jake pressed through sixteen inches of fresh fallen snow to the museum to stuff his battered briefcase with the final odds and ends of all his stuff. He set his keys down lightly on the massive, bare curator's desk, strolled down the hall, set the alarm, and walked out.

My mother had arranged this surprising big deal thing. We just showed up. On stepping out of the museum, Jake saw her standing there in the snow with Mark and me. "Daddy, Daddy, *Daddy!*" Mark and I cried out. Over the snow we flew. Jake's arms were open. Down on his knees, seriously radiant with gratitude, he gathered us up. He took one child in each arm. In my father's later memories of this, he'd say that he could see dazzling sunlight – but that was impossible. This was at night.

We stayed with friends of Minna's and, the next morning, Christmas morning, she dropped off Mark and me off at our familiar house while she went off to see her friend Orlando or whoever it was she was seeing at the time. I'd wished my father would stand up to my mother and sweep her off her feet and change her mind – and change the world and fix every broken thing. But no – not him, not then. It was not in his power. Her whims were incontrovertible law in our family. He – well, sometimes it seemed like he'd only recently fallen from the sky and hadn't really yet got the hang of things. He accepted her as he accepted everything. He could be so infuriating! He just stood there and he took it. He was so glad she was giving him something he wanted so much, if only for that little while.

My father got a good blazing fire going in the fireplace. Rotund, silver-bearded Nicholas Wentworth showed up in his gold-trimmed purple velvet St. Nick outfit, carrying a dozen donuts and two beautiful books he'd bound himself – *Old Possum's Book of Practical Cats* (signed by the author, Thomas Stearns Eliot) for Mark and *My Father's Dragon* (signed by Ruth Stiles Gannett and Ruth Chrisman Gannett) for me. "If you must make trouble, make it the unexpected kind!" he admonished, handing us our precious gifts. "Or is it the *expected* sort? I can rever november. *Bum cack! Bum cack!*" he clucked hilariously. "We dreed our nagon!" It was clear he was tipsy. He took a seat in the coziest available chair and motioned for Mark and me to come sit with him. He gave us surely his most buoyant, best boozy reading ever of Dylan Thomas' *A Child's Christmas in Wales*.

Then I remember my father put Mark and me to bed and tucked us in, but it wasn't long before I snuck back out and crawled to my secret hiding place behind some book-filled fruit crates in a corner of the living room. The place was now hopping with laughing people. Six or seven people I didn't recognize at all had just showed up and were sharing in the revelry and libations.

"I'm breathing. They can't take that away from me!" my father offered as a toast, raising high a big brandy snifter full of egg nog, nutmeg, and whatever.

"*It's nice, isn't it?*" affirmed an amused chorus of revelers.

"Be as deep in your thinking as Thomas More while as light on your feet as Fred Astaire," merry Nick Wentworth toasted, raising his glass.

"*Thanks to Fred, and More!*" affirmed our chorus of reveling guests.

The assembled drank, recited, affirmed, and laughed a little while longer, then said good night and left – except for Nicholas Wentworth. My father was nodding off but Nick was still tipping them in, then he snoozed and… they'd say his heart just stopped, just like that. I swear, I remember this. He died right there in that chair, him smiling and with the Dylan Thomas book still open, perched precariously on his knee. I remember the irony – the incongruity – of the ambulance's racing up to get him and then racing away. Well, that was that.

Both hurriedly and also in slow motion in the course of the year that followed, my mother and father divorced. There seemed to have been firm ground, but no. It was very painful for me. Mark and I moved with Minna to Berlin, where she married her second husband, our step-father, property-developer body-builder dull Rolf. Seriously, a moron. For years it irked me, the loss – that Mark and I had to grow up like *Hansel and Gretel* in polished lederhosen and neat braids in over-developed Germany and not like wild Jem and Scout in their ragged coveralls in *To Kill a Mockingbird*.

Mark saw Jake occasionally during the years he was studying Rhetoric at the University of California, Irvine (he would later become some sort of rhetorician or other at a Seattle marketing firm), but it would be twenty-plus years before I ever saw my father again. I reconnected with him first via e-mails. He told me that for the past twenty years he'd just been letting his beard grow, him standing on a street corner greeting people as they entered Idyllwild. Very funny, Pops. He was pulling my leg. He'd worked at an art gallery (or two, or three) and had been writing. I was so happy that he was writing *me*, I finally went to see him.

He still seemed somehow very elegant, at least to me, despite his now having dirty fingernails and the long Walt Whitman-style white beard, and wearing sandals all the time. He was living in what looked like a mountain man's hermitage, half bungalow and half log cabin, surrounded by ferns, juniper trees, manzanita, cedar, fir, and pine. Birds were hopping and singing all over the place – chickadees, wrens, nuthatches, and tanagers. On entering the hut, it seemed to expand magically to the size of a high-ceilinged many-chambered tumbling-tome-filled used books store. Books and papers everywhere. He had an old wooden ladder leaning against one wall of high-reaching bookshelves where the ceiling was highest. His dream come true. I was surprised he hadn't yet fallen off that ladder and killed himself. You talk about dangerous. My father lighted the place at night with candles. He had a fireplace and plenty wood and paper. I was amazed he hadn't burned the place down.

In his kitchen he had a clean sink, a clean tiny white fridge, a clean stove, a shiny black frying pan on the stove, plastic picnic cutlery, ceramic turquoise dinnerware for two, a dozen wine glasses, and nine glass fishbowls full of rocks from assorted places in the world he'd visited. In the living room was a copy I'd made as a child of a drawing by the Frenchman Antoine de Saint-Exupéry which I'd given him (of what many took to be a picture of a hat but was a picture of a boa constrictor digesting an elephant), framed nicely, over his dark brown almost black oak roll-top desk. On the desk was a single red rose in a tiny white ceramic vase there amid the gobs and gobs of his white and ivory papers. Pulled up to the desk was an antique dark oak almost black chair on casters. This was one of only two chairs in the house. He had a cramped guest room that looked like every other room in his house, filled with the same old familiar stuff. Books, books, books. Seriously. He had hundreds of books – thousands. A lot of good they did him.

He did have one last trick up his sleeve. Mark and I were of one mind that, when he did alas shuffle off this mortal coil, we would slip everything of his into a big secret dumpster and look away, look away. But we actually had no heart for that. And, among his things, we would find two amazing treasures, both earmarked for us – a first edition, first printing, of Ernest Hemingway's *A Moveable Feast* (New York: Scribner's, 1964), signed by the author's granddaughter, Mariel Hemingway, the actress, and a first edition, first printing, of Robinson Jeffers' *Flagons and Apples* (Los Angeles: Grafton Publishing Company, 1912), signed by the author. So now Mark and I both saw our father had not lived in vain. We were so glad he had left us both a little *something*.

So here he was living like Johnny the Walker of the White Mountains, or English Jack of Crawford Notch. English Jack had famously survived on trout and beer. Over Jake's fireplace hung Jack's poetry:

> *I left England then for good and all,*
> *And do not think I ever shall go back;*
> *I've waited long for death to sound my call,*
> *But I'm still here. – Your humble servant Jack*

English Jack had died in Crawford Notch, New Hampshire in the year (drum roll, please) 1912.

A further thing in Jake's Idyllwild house that was not lost on me but stood out and caught my eye and really moved me was that beat up old red attaché case or valise that had belonged to my grandparents, it having in it James Simpson's *The Spiritual Interpretation of Nature* (London and New York: Hodder & Stoughton, 1912) and all their favorite newspaper clippings and magazines all about the American Indians, North African camel drivers, Aztecs and Mayans, Jews and Gypsies, the Chinese, Ibn Battuta, Giordano Bruno, Baruch Spinoza, Saint Francis of Assisi, and on and on, the favorite articles my father's young family had always kept with them, travel where they would. There it was – Jake still had it – with all the yellowed almost ancient articles all still intact. My father had written in cream or ivory white on the inside top left corner of the ebony wood lid, "Rosebud." I think that must have been a secret term of endearment he had for me, meaning that he intended I should have the valise one day. Seriously, that brought tears to my eyes. I knew that day was coming soon. For all Jake's laughter,

I could see his underlying agony. I didn't ask him about it, but I wish now that I had. Because I never saw the briefcase again. And it would not be long before I would never be seeing him again, either (except, as my mother insisted, in the underworld in the afterlife among infinite pomegranates, maybe).

We would cast his ashes to the winds upon the waters at Laguna Beach (where still stands a statue or two of the Laguna Greeter). "Here flies Jacob Friedman Wright." Given the news that my father was dying, my mother stayed in Germany. My brother flew down to Palm Springs at once. Our mad old man, now having pancreatic cancer, in pain ("but happy") in that musty scholar hermit's lodge in the California mountains, unlike English Jack vowing never again to go back to England, deliriously said he was going to go back to Massachusetts to revisit some of the old romping, idiotic ghosts of Camperdene. I advised him to forget about it. I said he should never let anything in the world make him go back to Wild Island. He got my meaning, and so agreed he'd let go of all that. But – well, he both did and he didn't. Because of me, of course. Because now it was me who was writing all this down. Seriously.

I was combing through all his miscellaneous papers and old news clippings and was asking him a lot of questions. I told my father I had started writing this that you're reading now, which I promised him I'd really actually sit down and write. He initially suggested a French title, *Le Passant* ("He Who Passes Through"), then *The Camperdene Greeter* (Ha ha! Right. I can just see them now, putting up a statue or two of him). My original working title was, sensibly enough, *The Museum of the Year 1912*. Mark had suggested I call it *The Wright Stuff*. Our father loved that! I famously promised him I'd write that book and then put all this aside and again get on with my own life. *Amen.*

Oh, and he said he hoped that in the end, when he went back to his own planet (when his body finally *ceased to persist*, as the doctors would report it), he too, like his friend old Nick, could slip away in his sleep with a smile on his face.

Which is exactly what happened, more or less.

———

Edwards Brothers Malloy
Oxnard, CA USA
March 22, 2016